HOMETOWN BOY

AUDREY MCCLELLAND

To my Nana and Grandma, who always had a good romance novel in their hands, this one's for you.

1

Samantha McKay had no intention of staying in Barrington for too long. Even referring to Barrington as home now seemed a little strange to her. Rhode Island hadn't been home in over ten years. The second she'd graduated from high school, she was gone. She had big plans. But once she'd left all those years ago, not everything had gone exactly to plan. But, then, what plans ever really do?

That's the thing about life. Everything is a mystery until it happens.

Visiting Rhode Island had been something she'd limited to short weekend trips a few times a year, but not this time. Her closest sister, Sarah, was getting married. There was no way she could avoid her sister's wedding, and she didn't want to. She just wished she wasn't so stressed. Unfortunately, there was no way out of this one.

She looked out the tiny window of the private jet and saw the land and ocean and clouds beneath her. Those beautiful images calmed Samantha. Her stomach was in knots. At its core, Rhode Island was one of the most beautiful places she had ever known, but her dreams had been too big for that little place. She'd always known that if she wanted to accomplish big things, it had to be done somewhere else, somewhere big, somewhere like New York City. That place had always called her name. New York City was the place she had dreamt about. It had been and still was, the only place she'd ever wanted to live.

Sam smiled to herself when she remembered her mom saying, a million times throughout the years, *"I'll never forget Sam saying in 5th grade that someday she'd have a big office overlooking Times Square."*

Her mom had been right. She did have that office. And she was proud of it.

She also had a huge two-bedroom apartment overlooking Central Park. A beach house in the Hamptons. And a "satellite" office (as she liked to call it) in Palm Beach. She might not get to her beach house often enough, but that was OK. Life had been good to her, but she'd worked hard every single second of every single day to get where she was. It hadn't been easy. She had definitely paid her dues. Big dreams required big commitments.

Usually, Sam would spend the flight doing a million work-related things, but this time she was content to sit back and think about her family and the past ten years.

Samantha was the CEO and founder of her own fashion line, appropriately named "Samantha K," after herself. Throughout her life, people had always said her last name so quickly that it just sounded like the letter K, so she went with it years ago as part of the name of her company. Her "little" company had grown to be one of the most successful global online retailers in the world, not only carrying its own label, but also those of up-and-coming designers.

Fashion had always been in Sam's blood. Even as a little

girl, she would cut and sew and glue and tweak and add lace and glitter to anything and everything she could. If her mom came home with a new pair of jeans for her, she would alter them somehow, just to make them her own. She loved putting her own special fashionable stamp on everything she wore.

That fashion passion never left her in middle school or high school, and it led her directly to Parsons School of Design in NYC after high school. She was finally where she'd always wanted to be, and when she graduated from Parsons she knew that New York City was the only place for her.

The fashion capital of the world had been her home for the past decade, and during that time she had been lucky enough to work under incredibly talented women who had helped her get to where she needed to be. She knew that luck had definitely played a part--being in the right places at the right times--but she also knew that her talent and drive, and dedication to her craft, had carried her the rest of the way.

Right out of college, she remembered telling her first boss that she "would pick up pins on the floor." And that's what it had taken, and that's what she did, always with a smile, knowing that she was exactly where she wanted to be and if picking up pins was the first step, so be it. There was never a job that was too good for her, and that attitude was rare in the fashion industry. Learning everything she could from designers and cutters and seamstresses, she honed her skills, designing and sketching every free second she had.

That same boss became her mentor and her very first investor. She helped bring Samantha K to life. Sam's vision had been to create a fashion brand for the everyday woman, giving her access to fashion and style at reasonable prices (although her Mom still thought the prices were still too high). She had done what she had set out to do and she was proud of herself. In all the years of working to get to where she wanted, her focus never wavered. It was all about business all of the time, so much so that she hadn't really let herself take in her own success. This was something her family and friends were always encouraging her to do, but she always claimed she needed to make time for it (as crazy as that sounds). Sam had built an incredible team of people around her in NYC, a family of sorts, and as much as she relied on them, she knew they relied on her and the continued success of her business. That, more than anything, was the reason Sam allowed her work to take up so much of her time.

Consequently, Sam didn't have time for extended family visits, or visits with anyone else for that matter. She'd come back to Rhode Island for two or three days. "In and out visits" was how her father put it, which made her feel bad, but it was the truth. It wasn't that she didn't like seeing them, that wasn't it at all. There was more to it than that. It just wasn't the same for her as it had been when she was a kid. She loved her Mom and Dad more than anything, and felt great pride in being able to help them financially over the years. Her parents had been teachers their entire lives, so when she decided to go out on her own and start her own business, they were worried. They preferred the safe route. They preferred a steady paycheck with regular advancement. They believed in her and knew that she was talented, but they were worried about her. New York City was a long way from Rhode Island. Fortunately, she'd proven to them, over and over, that going off on her own had been the best thing in the world.

She had so much to be thankful for, not the least of

which was her family. Four girls all within four years. People couldn't believe that it was possible, but Ann McKay had birthed four babies in four and a half years.

Being the oldest of the four girls had its advantages and disadvantages and Samantha had always been the trail-blazer of the McKay sisters. She was the first to do every-thing - first one off to school, first one to date, first one to get a license, first one to go off on her own. All the firsts started with Sam. A year apart in school, the McKay sisters were as thick as thieves.

Samantha, Sarah, Sasha and Susan.

They all possessed the double threat that some girls hate - brains and beauty. Each a carbon copy of the others; blonde hair, green eyes, and a dimple on their right cheeks. They were beauties. They'd been mistaken as quadruplets enough times over the years to prove that they definitely looked alike. Growing up, they weren't always the best of friends, but their sister bond was undeniable.

It was Sarah's wedding that was bringing Samantha back home to Barrington. Sarah had asked all three of her sisters to stand up for her at the wedding and they were all super excited. Samantha wouldn't have missed her sister's wedding for the world, but being back in Barrington wasn't always easy. Barrington invariably brought up things she tried to keep closed off—things she did not want to re-live or think about ever again.

She was upset that her guy, Phillip, wasn't flying with her to Rhode Island. She had booked a private plane from New York City, thinking they'd at least be able to travel together, but Phillip's plans had changed just this morning and he would fly out later in the week. They'd both been so busy with work lately--her new collection and Philip about to close a huge deal--that she felt they needed a little alone time before the craziness of the wedding. Even though they both understood and respected each other's crazy, hectic work lives, she was still a girl at heart, a closeted hopeless romantic who certainly wouldn't have minded being doted on by her boyfriend on a getaway weekend.

Phillip wasn't overly expressive with his feelings, and she was OK with that. He wasn't always the best at communicating his feelings or making grand romantic gestures, but he was a good man and she knew if they were eventually going to get married, he'd be a solid partner for life. He'd take good care of her, and really--what more could she ask for in a man? He did love her, he just didn't write it in the sky. Anyway, how many men actually do that? Those crazy over-the-top romances eventually fizzle out and she knew it was important to have stability and friendship with a partner. She wanted someone she could actually grow old with and still have a pleasant conversation across the dining room table when they were eighty.

"Excuse me, Ms. McKay? Sorry to disturb you, but we're going to land in about ten minutes." Samantha was surprised to hear that they were almost at their destination, and she couldn't believe the time had passed by so quickly.

She sat upright in her seat and stopped looking out the window. She was afraid if she kept looking at the beauty of Rhode Island beneath her, she'd start to feel nostalgic. She took out her phone and realized she'd forgotten to call her father to give him her arrival time. With private planes, you had the ability to know exactly when you'd be landing, and not have to worry about a crowd of people all trying to be first off. She had wanted to call a private car service to pick her up, but her father wouldn't hear of it. Her parents also wouldn't hear of her staying at a hotel, which slightly killed her. She liked her own space when she traveled, but she knew her parents were extra excited about her coming home for an extended visit--an entire week—and she didn't want to crush their feelings. The plan was that she would stay with her parents until Phillip arrived and then they'd move to a hotel.

She hadn't yet booked a return commercial flight back to New York. She figured she'd do that once she was here and got her schedule firmed up. Her assistant, Ashley, told her to let her know the second she knew and she would take care of it. Taking a week off before the wedding hadn't been her original plan, but Sarah had called her a few weeks ago in floods of tears, begging her to come early because she was crazy stressed. Apparently, planning a wedding with her parents, her in-laws-to-be and her wedding planner hadn't been as easy as Sarah had thought. Too many cooks in the kitchen or in this case, too many people wanting to "help". Sam didn't exactly know what she could do to help, but Sarah let her know that since she had missed her bachelorette party, she owed Sarah a solid week at home to help her run around and tie up any loose ends.

Samantha could never say no to her sisters, especially Sarah. They were just about Irish twins, born exactly 12 months and 3 days apart. Her three sisters had always been her anchor in life, her saving grace, and her built-in friends. She could not imagine life without them. One of the things she appreciated about them was that they weren't impressed with her money, but Sam loved to shower them with gifts whenever she felt like it - and they didn't seem to mind. Samantha had designed Sarah's wedding dress herself and it had been a labor of love. It was one of her wedding gifts to Sarah. She couldn't wait to see Sarah in the dress at the final fitting this week.

Sam's parents had already met Phillip in New York City a

few months prior, but her sisters would be meeting Phillip for the first time this week, so she was extra nervous and excited to get their reactions. Samantha knew that Phillip would be a little too serious and conservative for them, and she also knew her sisters would tell her exactly what they thought, but she also knew they'd be happy for her, too.

As the plane touched down at the private airport in Providence, Samantha took a deep breath. She would be here for a full week, the first time she'd been here for an extended stay in years. She could do it. She *would* do it. She'd have her sisters. She'd have her parents. And, in a few days, she'd have Phillip. It would all work out just fine.

She took another deep breath as the plane slowly came to a stop at the hangar. Sam looked out the window and saw her father waving at her with his big smile. She let out a giggle and suddenly felt relaxed. Of course, David McKay had found his way to the airport and onto the tarmac without even a call from her to let him know her arrival time. Rhode Island is so small that she was sure everyone at the airport knew her Dad and why he was there. It wasn't every day that a private jet arrived and he'd probably been there for ages telling everyone about the wedding and Sam's visit. It wouldn't matter to him that she was thirty years old. His precious girl was home.

2

———

S am walked into her bedroom and it looked exactly
the way it had in high school. It was as if time had
stood still. Posters of the Jonas Brothers were still
hanging on the walls. Her knickknacks and trophies and
yearbooks were on the same shelves. Her old TV was still
positioned on her dresser, along with at least 100 old CDs.
Her pink light-up phone even remained attached to the wall
next to her bed. Everything was exactly the same.

Samantha sat down on her bed and looked around. It
was like a time warp. Nothing had changed. Nothing in this
room anyway, but so much had changed for her. She slowly
fell backwards onto the super-soft bedspread, letting her
blonde hair cascade all around her. She had begged her
mom to buy this Laura Ashley bedspread with the floral
print. Begged her. It had been pricier than her mom had
wanted to pay, so Sam started babysitting on the side to save
for it. When she finally had enough money, her Mom had
surprised her and said to keep that money and use it for
something else. Ann McKay had taken on some extra
tutoring jobs at school to buy it for her, a gift for her oldest

daughter. Sam had cried in appreciation when her Mom told her what she had done to be able to afford the bedspread and, from that moment on, it had always been one of her prized possessions.

"Looks like someone's getting pretty cozy in here," a soft, familiar voice rang out from the open door.

Sam tilted up her head to lock eyes with the owner of the voice and a gigantic smile spread across her face, "MOM!"

Ann McKay walked over and plopped herself right down next to her daughter. With an embrace that only a mom can give, she engulfed Sam into her arms and gave her a hug that spoke a million "I love yous."

"I've missed, my girl," Ann whispered into Sam's hair. "Even at thirty years old, I still miss my girl every single day."

"I know, Mom. I miss you, too," Sam said with a smile. "It feels like ages since I saw you and Dad in New York just three months ago."

"Three months is a long time when you get to be my age!"

"You sound just like Dad did in the car!" Sam laughed. "You both make it sound like I never see you."

"Listen, it's not the same as seeing you here at home. In New York, you are always running around like crazy. Dad and I usually feel like we're in the way when we visit. Don't get me wrong, we love to come and stay with you, but it's different when you're here at home. Not so much hustle and bustle."

Sam sat looking at the beautiful vision in front of her. Her mother was truly stunning. As Ann McKay aged, it was as if she was aging backwards. She resembled all four of her daughters, but her hair was more of a dark blonde with a bit of grey beginning to show at the crown. She had a few wrinkles, but they only made her look more beautiful. How is that even possible? Time certainly had been good to her and Sam hoped that time would be kind to her, too, someday. She truly was blessed with amazing parents; she couldn't deny that. They may make her crazy from time to time and made her feel a little bit guilty about not spending more time with them, but they supported her unquestioningly. They knew she worked very hard, and even when her parents came to visit her, they always wanted to help out at the office. Sam continuously explained to them that she had staff for everything, but they didn't want to hear it. They figured there must be something they could do to help, so inevitably, Sam would send them on an errand or ask them to sort out fabric samples, just so they had something to do.

"Well, you've got me for a whole week, Mom!"

"Of course, you come home when we're all out of our minds crazy busy with this wedding," Ann laughed. "Your sister has given me more grey hair over the last few weeks than I thought possible. Don't tell her I said that, but it's true. She's thinking, non-stop, about every little thing that could go wrong, rather than every little thing that will go right. It's driving me mad."

"What do you mean? I know she mentioned she'd been stressed, but she didn't mention anything specific."

Ann looked at Sam and rolled her eyes; "A few months ago, she decided that she wanted to make this wedding more homegrown. The problem is-every week there's something new and she thinks she can do it on her own. I'm about to lose my mind and lots of money."

Sam started to laugh, "Homegrown, huh? I didn't know about any of this. Is it a budget thing for her? Is she worried about the cost? I can help out if that's the problem. I don't mind at all."

"That's sweet of you, Honey, but don't you dare. It's not a money thing. We've got it under control. I think she needs to stay off Instagram and Pinterest. And I think she just wants to add all of these little touches on her own. I wouldn't be so stressed about it if the wedding wasn't one week away. As much as I'm happy that she wants to put her own distinct mark on her wedding, I don't think now's the time to change everything."

"How's Chris holding up with all of the wedding plans?" Sam asked.

"Oh, you know Chris. Cool as a cucumber. Anything Sarah wants, Sarah gets." Ann reached down and grabbed Sam's hand in hers. "I hope you all find partners like Chris."

"Well, you sure did. Dad is *so* like Chris." Sam smiled at her mom. "He adores you and does whatever you want, which is adorable, even after all of these years."

Sam got up and looked over to her bedroom window, which directly faced the street. Her eyes remained focused there for several seconds as she couldn't shake the familiar feeling that came over her even after all these years. A tug at her heart. The impulse to go look outside. Ann knew exactly what her daughter was thinking, although no words were exchanged. When Sam finally looked back at her, Ann thought it best to change the subject.

"So. Phillip. We're finally going to get to meet him this weekend."

"You met him once before, remember? That night on the sidewalk, right outside my apartment building."

"Yes, but it was so quick, I'd hardly call that a meeting. He was rushing off to a dinner meeting and we were just arriving for the weekend. It was a quick hello and good-bye at best. Not to mention he was on the phone the entire time, so we didn't actually get to talk."

Sam smiled, remembering how annoyed her parents had been that night, but trying not to show it. She could even sense an underlying tone with her Mom now. "I know, I'm sorry it worked out that way, and I know he felt badly about it, but that's why I'm happy he's coming. And he is, too. I really want you all to get to know one another better. He's a wonderful man and we've become much more serious. I'm dying for the girls to meet him. God only knows what they'll think of him, but I'm anxious to find out."

"As long as he makes you happy, that's all I care about. You're my hopeless romantic, the only one of the four of you, and I don't know anyone who deserves a happily ever after more than you."

Sam smiled and hugged her mom. "That was a long time ago, but thanks, Mom."

Ann got up from Sam's bed and walked over to inspect the six suitcases that were sitting in the middle of the room. "Got enough stuff?" she smiled.

"You mean, is there anything in there for me, right?" Samantha joked back.

"That obvious?"

"MOM! You're too much! Yes, of course, I brought home a bunch of stuff for you and the girls. I think you're going to love my new collection. It's the one I was working on last year at this time. I brought home samples of everything for you."

"It pays to have a famous fashion designer as a daughter! I don't have to buy any new clothes! Can't wait to play dress-up with you later!"

Samantha smiled and felt a surge of happiness course through her. This is why she loved what she did. She helped women feel beautiful. She loved watching her clothing transform a woman into a confident badass. Her mom had worked so hard to make a beautiful life for her and her sisters, and she loved being able to give her something back. Even if it was just clothing, it felt good. She loved seeing her mom all "dolled up" as she called it. She wasn't doing anything that was truly changing the world, but she was making women feel better about themselves through fashion. This had to be worth something.

"Sam, why don't you get your things sorted and then get ready? Dad and I are taking you girls out to the Lobster Claw for dinner tonight. Your sisters are coming over right after work, and they should be here around 5:30. Once everyone's here, we'll head out."

"Sounds good, Mom. I'll be ready."

"And Sam," Ann turned and looked at her daughter before leaving the room, "I'm glad you came home early. It means a lot."

Sam smiled back, "Me, too, Mom."

Ann left the room and shut the door behind her. Sam still couldn't believe she was back home, lying on her old bed. Everything had remained the same in this one tiny room, yet so much had changed for her. Her old life, here in Rhode Island, was so different from her current life. She couldn't walk down the street in NYC without being stopped at least once by somebody or someone snapping her photo to post online. As much as it was good to be here in Barrington, it did feel a bit awkward. She knew she didn't fit back here the same way she used to. Life was so funny. She had planned and plotted and worked her tail off to leave this town, yet here she was, still feeling that familiar pull in her heart.

Sam stood up and looked over to the window again. She

used to spend hours every day looking out that window, a window that had been the door to her heart so many years ago. But now? It was even hard to look at it. She knew she needed to leave the past in the past; she needed to put everything behind her, once and for all. If she didn't do this, she wouldn't be able to move on-at least not in the way she wanted. But, at this moment, it felt like cinder blocks were strapped to her feet. She needed to push past the over-whelming feelings of fear and regret and anger, and just walk over and look out the damn window. She needed to do it now without anyone seeing her, or anyone judging her. That window needed to be conquered.

And maybe when that happened, Colin Dasher would be conquered, as well.

3

He knew she was back in town. He didn't need anyone to tell him, although he knew his family and friends were more than interested in knowing his reaction to the news. It was as if, even after all these years, the electric current between them was still active. Colin didn't like the fact that his mind and his body were reacting this way; the need to see her, the need to talk to her. But he knew enough to stay away. He knew enough to keep his distance. He knew enough to know that time doesn't always heal. He knew it, and she knew it. She had made it perfectly clear to him to stay away. He'd known she was serious, and he'd actually listened.

Samantha McKay. He hadn't spoken those two words aloud to anyone in years. He'd kept up with her success and read about her anytime she hit the papers or made the news. It was impossible to disregard the story of a small-town girl turned superstar.

It didn't help that his childhood home was directly across the street from the McKay house. It was tough to ignore her when, at least once a week, during dinner with your mom and dad, her name would come up. She had been able to escape him over the last ten years, but he had never been able to escape her.

HE STILL KEPT in fairly close contact with her family, which was only natural, but he wasn't sure that Sam knew about it. He had always loved Mr. And Mrs. McKay and her three sisters. He and his brother had grown up with the McKay sisters, like siblings, throughout their childhood. Living directly across the street from each other, they always had built-in playdates. They played outside together; running through the sprinklers in the summer and tobogganing down the street in winter. Always up to something. Always causing some sort of havoc in the neighborhood. All of them - the McKay sisters and the Dasher twins, Colin and Cole, had been inseparable.

A noise from the corner of the auto shop startled Colin. He jerked his head around to see his twin standing there.

"Hey? You about done with that car yet?" Cole asked.

"Just about. I've got one more part to tweak and then it will be as good as new."

Colin could sense Cole had more to say. They were twins. He knew his brother inside and out.

"You hear who flew in today on a private plane for her sister's wedding?" Cole asked.

"Ahhhh... there it is," Colin whispered to himself.

Colin didn't want to let anyone know, including his brother, that he knew all about it, but he did. Small town. People talk. The second Sam's plane was booked, Gary Landing down at the airport called Colin to let him know. "Hey, Bro, guess who's coming in on a private jet?" He didn't know why people still thought he would care. He knew she'd be coming in for her sister's wedding. It was her sister, for God's sake. What else would she be doing? Did he know she would be flying in on a private plane? No. But when you have that kind of money, you can do whatever you want with it. She could burn it, for all he cared.

Playing dumb, Colin turned his back from his brother, pretending to look for something on the shelf, "No - who? What are you talking about?"

"YEAH, right - don't try to tell me you don't know," Cole laughed. "Can you believe she can afford a private plane? That's crazy. Imagine if you two had stayed together? You'd be living the high life right now, my friend!"

"Yeah. Imagine that," Colin shot back.

Rubbing the back of his head and looking a bit uneasy, Cole said, "Listen, I know you guys didn't part on the best of terms, but maybe this time you should try to talk to her while she's here. Take Mom's advice once and for all. You can't let more time pass without telling her."

"Yeah, well, thanks for the advice, but she doesn't need to know anything," Colin answered in a tone that told Cole he'd better back off. "And I told Mom to stay out of it. As you well know, we've been over for years. It doesn't matter now."

Cole pressed on, knowing he should probably cut his losses, but at this point, he didn't give a shit. "I'm not saying to get back together with her. I'm just telling you that you should at least talk to her, and make some sort of peace."

"What? So that you and everyone else can feel better about everything?" Colin was steamed now, and Cole knew there was a lot of hurt in that anger. "And what good would that do anyway?" Colin asked.

"I don't know. I think she has a right to know your side of

the story. That's all. You guys have history. I know you've moved on, and she's moved on, but you still have a past and you're going to see her this week whether you want to or not. She's practically family."

Colin didn't know what to say to his brother. Deep down, he knew Cole was right and maybe he should try to talk to Sam while she was here. He couldn't avoid her forever, although he'd been doing a good job of that for the last decade. And, to be fair, she was pretty good at avoidance herself.

Colin looked at his brother and shrugged his shoulders, "Look, I'll think about it."

"I KNOW you're bullshitting me, but I'll take it," Cole laughed and put his hand up for a high five.

"Give it a rest," Colin laughed back. "Let's wrap this up so we can call it a night. I'm covered in grease, and I want to get home and shower."

Running the town's auto body shop wasn't the most glamorous job in the world, but it was a busy business with steady pay, and he was able to work with his dad and brother every day during the summer and during weekends all year round. During the school, year Colin worked at Barrington High School as a guidance counselor. He loved working with kids, but also enjoyed the family business side of his life, too. Living in a small town like Barrington, it was nice to have a family business. Everyone knows everyone in small towns and that helps make small businesses that much more important. Jumping into the family business had never been Colin's dream job. He had been one of those kids in high school who had never known what he wanted to do with his life until long after high school. But ten years ago, he'd known his dad had always dreamed of having his sons working with him, so it was an easy decision to turn a part-time job in high school into a full-time job. The last ten years had been good to him, and he was thankful and grateful to his father and brother for giving him their blessing to go after a bigger dream, yet still be able to part of their dream too.

College was something Colin had never had on his radar, always assuming it was not for him. He never had the desire to go when he was in high school, probably something to do with not having been a good student. School had never come easy for him. He struggled throughout his time in elementary school and middle school, but his entire four years of high school had been utter hell. College wasn't for him. He'd graduated high school - just barely - feeling embarrassed and stupid. He didn't need nor want history to repeat itself in college. Fortunately for him, he had been an incredible athlete, and sometimes teachers had looked the other way, or tried hard to help him out, but grades were grades and there was no way to disguise his terrible marks. College was never in the plans for him.

While working on a customer's vintage car eight years prior, he had struck up a friendship with the owner, Ed. Ed was an older guy who had traveled all over the world and was now back in Barrington. He would stop in and chat with Colin for hours while he worked on the car. They talked about everything, something Colin appreciated. They talked about travel and politics, restaurants and cars, and everything in-between. As their friendship grew, Ed asked Colin about his life, his hopes, and his dreams. When the topic of college came up, Ed told him it was never too late. At first, Colin had laughed and thought he was crazy, but when he told Colin that he hadn't gone to college until later in life,

Colin thought about it differently. He helped Colin realize that not every path in life is the same for everybody; sometimes it took time to realize who you were and what you wanted to do.

For the first time in his life, Colin felt like giving college a second chance. He had always regretted not going. Ed encouraged him to look into classes at Rhode Island College or the University of Rhode Island, and to set his sights on earning a bachelor's degree. Colin looked into it and quickly realized that this was something he wanted. The more he thought about it, the more he realized there was something in life he wanted to do, something he knew he'd be good at. He wanted to help kids, so the thought of becoming a guidance counselor intrigued and excited him. The older he got, the more he realized he wasn't stupid, not at all. He had needed someone to connect with him, to show him what else was out there besides the traditional college route straight out of high school. He wanted to help guide and mentor kids who were just like him. He wanted to be there to help kids find their way after high school, especially if college wasn't the answer. Colin knew counseling teens would be the perfect way to fulfill his passion, a passion sparked by Ed and his vintage car. Colin couldn't thank him enough. He had started classes that fall after talking with Ed. It was challenging to balance work with a heavy school course load, but he got through it. He knew what he wanted and felt fueled to keep going. The athletic mindset in him kicked into high gear, but this time the focus was on good grades. Ed had changed Colin's life.

Cole interrupted Colin's thoughts, "Listen - I'm heading over to Mom and Dad's tonight to help them move in a new refrigerator. Any interest? Or are you steering clear since she's home?"

Colin looked at his brother. It was crazy sometimes to look at someone who looks just like you, "I'm not afraid to see her."

"I know you're not afraid. I was just asking. Mom's making pot roast, which I know is your favorite."

"I'm going to bow out tonight," Colin said. "I've got a date with Jessica."

"Hey, how come I didn't know about this? This must be your 3rd or 4th date with the beautiful Jessica Lane."

"Leave it to you to be excited about me dating!" Colin shot back. "And eyes off of this one!"

"I'm happy for you. That's all. You haven't dated someone in awhile. Jessica is a great girl, very up your alley. And I know she's liked you for a long time, so I'm glad to see you two finally connecting."

"Yeah, we're having fun and if you're counting, this is date number five."

Cole tossed a rag at his brother, "Right on!"

Colin grabbed the rag and started rubbing his face. He looked up at Cole and became serious for a second, "But hey, if you see Sam tonight, tell her I said hi."

"It's been so long since you've seen her that maybe she'll think I'm you," Cole smiled, adding, "You want me to break the ice for you, don't you?"

"Yeah, maybe."

But he was 100% sure Sam would never mistake the two of them, even after all this time. Even though they were identical twins, she'd always known who was who. Like she always used to tell him, "We're soul mates, Colin. I'll always know which one you are."

4

Sam was a basket case at the idea of seeing Colin. It was crazy because she wasn't nervous about being around anyone. Not celebrities. Not NY socialites. Not the wealthiest people in the world. She'd dressed many impressive people, but none of them made her nervous like Colin Dasher. She knew that at some point before the wedding, she'd cross paths with him. Whether at their parents' houses, the local coffee shop or just walking down Main Street, they were bound to bump into each other. It was almost impossible for them not to. It's what small-town living is all about. She just wanted it to happen sooner rather than later so that she could just move on.

"I can't tell you how great it is to look around this table and see my four beautiful girls all together. Makes a father very happy," David McKay said, tearing up, "Cheers to my McKay Girls!"

The McKay girls erupted in a symphony of "awes", followed by a collective, "CHEERS!" Being home with her family was such an amazing feeling, and Sam felt badly that she had let it go so long without a visit. She now realized that she had missed her family so much, and it felt so good to be here at the Lobster Claw with them.

Sam's youngest sisters, Sasha and Susan, were still single. They co-owned a floral business in town and they were super excited to be helping with the floral arrangements for the wedding. Both sisters were dying to find "the one" themselves and were on every dating app possible to try to meet that special someone.

"So, where exactly is Chris tonight?" Sam whispered to Sarah as they sipped their wine, trying to tune out their younger sisters who were talking - quite exuberantly - about their latest dating adventures.

"I wanted tonight to be just the six of us. The last hurrah! Chris understood, and I think he was looking forward to a night off of wedding talk," Sarah answered.

"Everything good, Sarah? Weddings can be hard on a relationship, strange as that sounds. You're happy, aren't you?" Sam asked her sister.

Sarah smiled and reached out to squeeze Sam's arm. "Yes, I'm really, *really* happy. Chris is the best thing that has ever happened to me."

"I always knew that, but I'm so happy to hear you say it. You make a great couple. So, tell me, what does he think about your homegrown wedding idea?"

Sarah rolled her eyes, "You've been talking to Mom, huh?"

Sam took a sip of wine and nodded her head, "You got me."

"In defense, I like the idea of creating what I can for our wedding. I'm off school right now on my summer break, so I have extra time during the day to do the work. I just wanted to have some personal touches—things that really express who Chris and I are as a couple. Is that so bad?"

"Hey, it's your wedding! I think if I ever do it, I'm going to elope to the Bahamas! Short and sweet and super simple," laughed Sam.

"Oh, please, Sam! That's such BS. You've been planning your wedding in your head since before you could walk! You want the fairy tale, let's face it. And there's nothing wrong with that."

Sam grabbed her wine glass and shook her head, "I don't know, Sarah. The older I get, the more I'm realizing that the fairy tale is exactly that, a fairy tale. Sometimes just getting close to it is actually better than not having it. Just too much pressure."

Sarah couldn't believe what she was hearing. "I'm shocked to hear you talk like that. Of all of us, you are the happily-ever-after romantic. The one who believed that love that will last a lifetime. I actually think that might be a direct quote from you."

Both sisters started laughing so hard that their eyes began to water, which caused the whole table to stop and stare at them.

"What you are two laughing about over there?" Sasha asked.

Everyone's eyes were on Sam and Sarah. It was like old times when the six of them would gather around their dining room table for dinner each night. It was never quiet. It was always loud, dramatic and full of life. It was so nice to have this warm feeling again. Sam had forgotten about times like this when she wasn't at home. For her, dinner was often spent in the back of her town car, eating take-out on the way back to her apartment. She'd be working on her phone while inhaling a quick salad or sandwich. That was it. No talking. No laughing. Just planning and plotting the next day.

"Sam said that when she gets married, she wants to elope. Can you believe that?" Sarah asked, still incredulous.

All the sisters laughed in unison. "Never in a million years would you elope," Susan chimed in. "Don't you have a wedding binder that you made, still upstairs in your bedroom? You made it and then put Colin's head and your head on all the magazine cut-outs!"

"OMG! That's right, you did!" Sasha laughed. "I remember Mom was so upset that you cut up all of your prom pictures to make that wedding binder. Where is that? We need to find that tonight!"

"Ha! Ha!" Sam chimed in. "Yes, I did do that, back when I was young and naive. And if I find that binder before you two, I'm burning it." Sam laughed, but she was deadly serious.

Sam took a deep breath. She'd love not to be thinking about this right now. She had forgotten about that wedding binder, something she'd worked on back in the day when she thought she knew how her life would go. It was before everything. Before she moved. Before her success. Before her fame. It was funny to think that it wasn't even that long ago. All she'd wanted was something simple, something every girl wants - love, a beautiful wedding, a man to come home to and love her endlessly, and maybe a few kids along the way. She'd had it all planned out, but that's not how it had turned out, and she had come to terms with that. She was better for it. She was stronger now. She would never let anyone break her heart like that again.

The waiter and the busboy arrived to clear the table and take the dessert orders. The two of them were brothers who lived down the street from the McKay's. Ann McKay had taught both of them and she was asking them about their time at college.

Everyone was in such a good mood and Sam took a moment to relish the simple, uncomplicated situation. It made her feel happy and sad at the same time.

"So, tell us about Phillip," Sam's dad said. "When are we going to meet him?"

All of a sudden, all eyes were on her.

"Well, Dad, like I told Mom earlier, you've met him already."

"I know, but that doesn't count because it was too quick," answered Dad.

Sam rolled her eyes and laughed, "And that's exactly what Mom said, too." Sam picked up her glass of wine and took a sip. "Phillip is a great guy, and you'll get to meet him this week. He's handsome. He's athletic. He loves to travel. He's in finance, so his hours are just as hectic and crazy as mine. He's from New York," she paused and looked around the table. "I mean, I'm not sure what else to tell you. He's very supportive of me, which is great because you know that not many men understand my crazy work schedule. I don't know, we just sort of click. It works. I'm excited for you guys to meet him."

Everyone just stared at Sam. Nobody knew what to say. She basically had just given them a high-level resume of Phillip.

Susan was the first to break the silence, "And he's super rich. Let's not forget that tiny little fact!"

"Amen, girl!" Sasha laughed and clinked Susan's wine glass.

"Susan and Sasha!" Sam laughed, "Come on, that doesn't matter to me."

"We all know it doesn't, but come on, you're dating a McKnight. A freaking McKnight! That's like NYC royalty, isn't it?" Susan asked.

Sam didn't know what to say. Yes, Phillip was a McKnight, but in defense of herself, she didn't know that when they first got together, not that it would have mattered anyway. She didn't need a man to rely on financially.

Sasha broke the ice, "Are you guys serious?"

Sam looked around the table at her family, "Yes, we're serious. We've been together for just about a year and pretty serious for the last couple of months now. Honestly - he's a great guy and you are going to love him. You would never know he has the family history he does. He's not pretentious or anything like that. He's a hard worker and he's a really nice guy."

Sam was wishing this conversation was not centered around her love life. She didn't want to be grilled about Phillip.

"How did the two of you meet, Honey?" her mom asked. It was obvious her mom was trying to keep the conversation light because she could tell Sam was becoming uncomfortable.

"Actually, he was working on a licensing deal for me. We were spending a lot of time together at the office and then one night he asked me to dinner. Pretty simple. I hardly have time to do anything, so it was nice meeting someone who understood my lifestyle."

"Wow. Sounds riveting!" Sasha laughed with an eye roll, only something a "little" sister could get away with saying.

"So he's a McKnight from the big McKnight Publishing Company, right?" her father asked.

Sam nodded. They were not going to make this easy for her. "Yes, that's his family's company. He's the only one of the three sons who didn't go into publishing. He took a job on Wall Street right out of college. Actually, we realized that while he was at Columbia, I was at Parsons. We only lived one block from each other. We'd probably bumped into one another a million times, but had never met."

Everyone tried to look excited for her but, in truth, they seemed a little surprised. None of it sounded very romantic for the defacto romantic in the family. Picking up the vibes, Ann said, "Well, Honey, we're all excited to meet Phillip when he gets here for the wedding!"

"So," Susan asked, "when *is* he arriving in Barrington?"

"The plan is for him to fly in on Thursday night. He's really looking forward to getting to know each of you."

Sam looked around the table and saw that all eyes were still on her. She didn't want them to look at her like that; she knew what they were thinking without even having to ask. They were still wrapping their heads around the fact that she didn't believe in fairy tale love anymore. But they'd just have to get used to this new side of her. That was all there was to it. Sam wanted to break the ice, not wanting this perfect evening to go sour because of her.

"Listen, I have something for all of you," Sam said. I know this week is going to be a little crazy with the last minute wedding plans, but I want you all to know that I love each one of you so much. And I miss you all so much. This dinner has been so lovely, and I am going to do a much better job in the future of getting out here more often. I promise. Anyway, I brought along a little gift for each of you."

At that moment, the waiter arrived with dessert. While that was being arranged, Sam got up, opened her tan leather tote bag and placed a small, iconic Tiffany blue box in front of everyone at the table.

"Oh, gosh, this looks better than dessert," Sarah exclaimed.

Inside the boxes for her mom and sisters were stunning

pairs of 2-carat Tiffany Solitaire Diamond Earrings. They were round, brilliant diamonds in platinum and just perfect for the wedding. For her father, she gave him a Tiffany 1837 Makers 27mm Square Watch. Nobody knew what to say at first. Everyone just stared at their gifts with their eyes wide open. Sam had always been generous, but this was beyond generous, and so unexpected.

"Oh, Sam," her mother spoke first. "This is too much, Honey."

"No, Mom, it's not. You guys are the most important people in the world to me, and I wanted to give you something to show that. If it's OK with Sarah, I was hoping we could all wear these at the wedding and share that special McKay bond with each other on that very special day."

Everyone was speechless and they just nodded their heads. Tears streamed down the cheeks of her sisters. Sam was incredibly touched. Her sisters never asked her for a thing, and she was so happy that they all seemed to love their gifts.

"I didn't mean to make everyone cry!" Sam smiled, trying to hold back tears herself. "I just wanted you to know how much I love each of you."

"We love you, too, Sam. More than you know and we couldn't be more proud of you!" And with that, Sam's Dad got up and came around to give her a bear hug. Everyone in the restaurant was staring at this point, but Sam was used to that, especially here at home. Most people in New York knew who she was, but when she was back home in Barrington, she was big time famous. Sam knew that a loss of privacy was part of the package as one succeeded in a job like hers. Thankfully, people here respected her privacy with her family.

"Let's head back to our house and have coffee and

liqueurs," Ann said. "If we stay here much longer, I think we'll make the front page of the Barrington Times!"

"I think we will anyway," Sasha laughed. "If that happens, they'd better have a good picture of me and mention that I'm single."

With that, everyone started to laugh and pack up. It had been a good night. Sam needed this. She hoped everyone would love her gifts. She knew they were extravagant, but she'd never had an excuse to do anything like that for her family. It made her feel good to shower them with a little luxury. But she knew she hadn't sold them on Phillip. It had been ten years since she'd introduced anyone to her family. This was a big deal for her and for them. She just wanted them to like Phillip for Phillip, and not think about the fact that he was a McKnight. He was definitely not a small-town boy, but he would make everyone feel comfortable. He actually hated to be identified as one of the McKnight boys, which made Sam like him even more. He wanted to make it on his own, and she respected him for that.

Just thinking about Phillip made her smile. She was excited to have him here and to be able to introduce him properly to her family. They would finally get a chance to see firsthand just how great he really was, and how good they were together. Walking out of the restaurant behind her sisters, Sam felt happy and relaxed. For the past few hours she hadn't given Colin a thought or been worried about running into him, and it felt good, really good.

Then, just as she was thinking that very thought, Sam heard two words from behind her that sent goosebumps up and down her arms.

"Hi, Sam."

5

Sam knew who it was without even turning around. She knew that voice almost better than anyone's. It was him. It was Colin. He was directly behind her, and if she were a smart girl, she would just keep walking and pretend that she hadn't heard him. But she also knew that was just a little bit childish.

Sam's family had been walking in front of her as they left the restaurant. They knew if Sam exited first, she'd be stopped every two feet by someone wanting to say hello, or ask for a photo. Colin had appeared out of nowhere from behind, so none of her sisters were there for backup. They were all walking ahead, not even realizing she had stopped.

Sam was on her own.

She stopped and turned around, nervous about what she would see. Childish as it was, she secretly hoped and prayed that time hadn't been good to Colin Dasher. She hoped to see a bald head or someone with lots of deep wrinkles and extra weight packed onto his frame. She'd never admit it, even to herself, but she'd thought about him over the years, wondering what he looked like now. She hadn't dared ask her parents or her sisters about him. She didn't want them to think she cared about him anymore. She wanted them to believe that he never even crossed her mind.

As Sam locked eyes with Colin, her body quivered and she thought she might faint. It took all of her control to remain calm and act as if this encounter was the most normal thing in the world.

Colin looked exactly the same as he had ten years ago, maybe even better. Sure he looked a little older, but in a masculine way, not in a "what the hell happened to you" way. He looked good, really, really good. His dark brown hair was cropped short, just how she liked it. She remembered a time in high school when she would cut it for him. His crystal blue eyes were still the most crystal blue eyes she'd ever seen. They'd always been that way, baby blue eyes that saw right through to her heart. His physique was incredible, muscular and powerful. He was obviously still in shape. And he smelled so good. She couldn't identify the cologne, but it was incredible.

Two simple words were a long time in coming. "Hi, Colin," she said with a smile that she was sure looked forced and uncomfortable.

In a quiet, controlled voice he said, "I saw you earlier with your family having dinner, but I didn't want to disturb you guys. I just...just wanted to say hello."

Sam could tell that Colin was just as nervous as she was, which made her feel a lot better. She had wanted this moment to come just so it could be over and done with, but no way was she going to let him know that she was shaking like a leaf.

Sam looked over her shoulder towards the door where

her family had disappeared, "Oh, yeah. We were just out celebrating Sarah."

"Yeah, I figured. Big wedding coming up!"

Sam nodded her head and took a deep breath. She was trying her best to steady her voice and appear confident, as if meeting like this was no big deal at all. "How have you been?" she asked. "I knew we'd eventually run into each other at some point."

"Yeah, I know," Colin said. "That's why I thought I'd just say hello now. Rip the Band-Aid off. I know it's been awhile."

Sam nodded. "Yeah, better to just get it over with, right?"

Colin took a breath and relaxed a little bit more. "Yeah, something like that," he answered.

They stood there, staring at each other, not knowing what to say next or even where to look. If one didn't know their history, or who they were, it would seem that these two were on the most awkward first date of all time.

After a few seconds, Sam broke the silence. "Listen, I don't want to keep them," she said motioning towards her family, who seem to have disappeared. "It was nice to see you. I'm sure I'll see you again this week. I want to make sure I see your parents while I'm home, too. It's been forever since I've seen them."

"They'd love that. Mom keeps tabs on everything you do," Colin said. "So, I guess I'll see you this weekend at the wedding, then."

Sam froze. Her eyes squinted in confusion as those words left Colin's mouth. Wedding? He was invited to the wedding? Why would Sarah do that to her? Why would she think that it would be okay to invite Colin to the wedding? She knew their history and knew how uncomfortable it would be to have him there.

Trying her best to collect her composure while not looking like a raging lunatic, Sam smiled at Colin and responded, "Yup, I'll see you there."

And then, out of nowhere, came a voice that let her off the hook, "Colin! Our food is here!"

Colin turned around and waved to a pretty brunette sitting at a table by herself, motioning for him to come back over.

"Looks like your dinner is ready, so I'll let you go," Sam said.

Colin knew it was now or never. "Listen, Sam - if you have any free time this week, I'd love a few minutes with you."

"Oh?" Sam said rather abruptly.

"I'd just like to talk to you."

Sam couldn't believe the next words that came out of her mouth, but they did. "About what?" she asked. This man. This man in front of her had been everything to her ten years ago. This was the man for whom she would have given up everything. This was the man she wanted to marry, the man she wanted to have kids with, the man she wanted to grow old with. Suddenly, she felt overwhelmed, just by looking into his eyes. How, after all these years, did he still have that magnetic power over her?

"I just want to talk, that's all. Can you find some time before you leave?" Colin answered, ignoring her tone.

Sam stood there, staring into Colin's eyes. She counted to ten in her head, a business technique she'd learned years ago when negotiating with people. Make them wait and wonder. It allowed you to calm yourself and concentrate on something else for a few seconds.

"Yeah, I'm sure I can find some time. I'll be here all week.

My boyfriend comes into town in a couple of days, so let's do it before then, OK?" Sam said.

Then, just like that, she turned and walked away to look for her family who seemed to have abandoned her, at the same time feeling like she had the upper hand after leaving Colin standing alone in the restaurant.

Feeling like he had just been hit with a ton of bricks, Colin watched her sweep out of the restaurant.

6

S econds after Sam walked out of the door of the Lobster Claw, she caught up with Sarah on the sidewalk and said, "You invited him to your wedding? Are you freaking kidding me?"

Sarah was completely blindsided by Sam's attitude after they had just had such an incredible family dinner together. Never one to back down, she gave it right back to her sister, "*You've* got to be kidding *me*. Are you serious right now?"

"Yes! I'm still shaking!" Sam said, breathing heavily. "I just saw Colin in the restaurant on the way out and he told me he was coming to the wedding."

"Was I not supposed to invite him?" Sarah asked, looking over at her parents and sisters who were obviously confused by Sam's anger.

Sam couldn't even look at her sister. She walked over to her parents' car and got into the back seat, which was awkward considering Sarah was supposed to be getting in next to her.

As if no time had skipped a beat since high school,

Sarah walked to the car and slammed the door as she scooted next to Sam, "So, wait...I wasn't supposed to invite someone I've known my entire life and, let me add, a friend of Chris's, too - all because *you* don't want to see him? Come on, be serious!"

Sam looked out the window, trying to ignore her sister. Their parents were in the car and trying to stay out of what was going on. Thankfully, they only lived a few minutes away, so Mr. McKay started the car and got on with the drive.

"Sam? Are you seriously going to ignore me the whole way home? Are you freaking thirteen years old?" Sarah asked.

Sam turned to look at Sarah. She didn't want to fight with her, but she'd felt blindsided when Colin mentioned the wedding. She felt he had one-upped her. "You're my sister. You know how I feel about him. That's all I'm going to say."

Sarah let out a frustrating grunt. "You broke up ten years ago. I don't understand why you even care about this. You never talk about him. You have a boyfriend. And, apparently, according to Chris, Colin has a girlfriend. So, seriously - why are we having this fight?"

"I just wish you would have told me you had invited him," Sam answered.

"Sam, my guest list has been online for over two months. It's not my fault you're too busy to look at it. Not to mention, you know I would never do anything intentionally to hurt you. I just can't imagine why you would think I *wouldn't* invite Colin. He's a good family friend of ours."

The car came to a stop in the McKay driveway. Ann and David gave each other a knowing look, got out of the car announcing they were going for a walk, and if anyone wanted a drink to please help themselves.

Sam looked over at the white house across the street. She knew the Dasher house inside and out. She knew every nook and cranny. She turned to Sarah and said, "I just would have appreciated a heads up, that's all. I was completely thrown by seeing Colin tonight at the restaurant."

"Look, I'm sorry you didn't know, Sam. I really didn't think it was that big of a deal. You know that Mr. and Mrs. Dasher are like parents to me. How could I not invite Colin and Cole? They're like brothers to me. I see them all the time around town."

Sam looked at her sister, knowing she was right. She got out of the car and headed into the house. She knew she was overreacting, and it would be terrible to end the evening like this. She would apologize to her mom and dad when they got back. She didn't know why Colin still got under her skin. It was ridiculous. Sam could hear Sarah a few feet behind her.

"I'm sorry, Sarah, I didn't mean to fly off the handle at you," said Sam. "I feel badly about this and hope I haven't totally ruined the evening."

Sarah let out a laugh and put her arm around Sam, "Sheez, it was like the old Sam came out to play. You went a little psycho for a moment."

Sam shook her head and laughed back at Sarah. "I did, didn't I? I'm so sorry," she apologized.

"Listen, I know that you and Colin have history," Sarah said. "I also know that there's probably a lot I don't know, but I do know that life has moved on for the two of you. Colin has remained one of my friends because he was a friend before everything happened. Of course, it was awkward at first, but as time went by, I realized that you were happy and living your best life in New York, and he was doing the same back here."

Sam smiled at her sister, "I know. You're right."

Sarah looked at Sam straight in the eyes, "Are you just saying that, or do you really believe it?"

Sam nodded, "I do. I know. I never wanted anyone to take sides."

Sarah laughed, "Yes, you did!" And then she put her arm around Sam and pulled her tight. "Listen, I'm telling you this as your sister. It couldn't have been easy for him watching you literally sky-rocket into the world of fashion. After high school, Colin went to work at Dasher Auto. He went to work every day while you scaled the heights of fame and fortune. And you know what? He was happy for you. He really was. You know that here in Barrington, everyone is in everyone else's business, but Colin has never said anything disrespectful about you. He's done nothing but support you."

"I've never really thought about it like that before," answered Sam.

"I'm just saying, try to be a little sensitive about what he's gone through here, and see it from his point of view."

Suddenly, Sam began to boil again, she could feel her face getting red, "Sensitive? Sarah, he's the one who left! NOT ME!"

Sarah rolled her eyes and shot back in frustration, "Oh, my God, Sam. It was ten years ago."

Sam walked through the front door and went to the kitchen. She grabbed a stool and plopped herself down at the counter. Sasha and Susan must have arrived and heard the commotion because all she could hear now were three sets of footsteps walking toward the kitchen.

Her three sisters came into the kitchen and surrounded her. She could feel them stroking her hair and rubbing her back, "Sam, what's going on?" Susan asked quietly.

She was mentally fried from the night. She lifted her head and her sisters could tell that she'd been crying. Sarah couldn't remember the last time she'd seen Sam cry, not like this. Sam didn't break. She was a powerhouse. She commanded every room she was in, a force to be reckoned with. She was breaking and her sisters didn't know how to handle *this* Sam.

Her sisters could have and should have been jealous of Sam, but it was just the opposite. In fact, they all looked up to Sam and loved her. Even with all the success and fame and money, they were never jealous of her. She worked hard to get where she was, and they all loved that about her. She was a go-getter. But this Sam, sitting in front of them right now, was someone they didn't recognize.

"Sam. Please tell us what's going on. We're not used to seeing you like this," Sarah said, grabbing the tissues.

Sam wiped her tears and smiled at Sarah. "Oh, I don't know. I'm sorry. I don't even know what to say. It's still really tough coming home."

"Because of Colin?" Sasha asked.

Sam nodded her head. "Yeah. I wasn't sure how it would be to see him again. I wanted to stay away for as long as I could. I just wanted to avoid having to face him."

"But you know that's impossible. At some point you were going to see him."

"Eventually, yes. But I guess I wanted it to be on my own terms."

Sarah looked at her big sister. She knew Sam's heart had

been broken by Colin, but she also knew that Colin's heart had been broken, too. Neither of them knew just how much the other was hurting. Sarah hadn't fully realized that the pain of the break-up had stayed with Sam all this time. She wished Sam had said something to her before, but the topic of Colin had been well off-limits. They both had moved on with their lives, but obviously there was unfinished business. Things needed to be said, but would they have the strength to tell each other their own truths.

Sam grabbed a handful of tissues. "He broke my heart and that was it. I guess I've never been able to pick up all the pieces. I didn't realize that until tonight, 'til I saw him."

"Are in you still love him? Or are you still mad at him? And why haven't you said anything to us?" asked Sarah.

Sam laughed, "No! That's not it. Just seeing him tonight brought back a flood of feelings. Not all bad, but I didn't know what to say or do. I probably sounded like a bumbling fool to him. I don't even remember what I said, I was just trying to play it cool."

"I'm sure you did just fine," Sarah answered back, looking at her other two sisters. They were staying a little too quiet and Sarah needed help.

"I know. But seeing him, out of the blue, it was just-- "

"He looks good though, doesn't he?" Sasha interrupted, always the one with guys on her mind.

The sisters all looked at her and then started laughing in unison. Their laughter was contagious as they looked at each other, becoming louder and deeper. Sam chimed in, "Why the hell couldn't he have aged horribly?"

"Please! The Dasher boys have always been hot. And popular! Wait till you see Cole!" Sasha chimed in.

Susan added, "It's true, everyone asks about the two of them all the time. No detail too small. Colin started dating this girl, Jessica, and Cole is still Barrington's ultimate ladies man-- not much has changed there since high school."

"I just can't believe you haven't seen Colin since you guys broke up," Susan said. "Honestly. Ten years. How is that even possible?"

"She never comes home for more than a day, that's how it's possible," Sasha practically shouted. "I had a feeling that was why you hardly ever come home anymore. You kept saying it was because you were so busy and everything. But, come on, I knew it was because of Colin. You two just always had this crazy chemistry."

"Listen, I wasn't hiding from him. I have come home. I just haven't wanted to spend a lot of time here because I didn't want to run into him, and the chances of that are pretty good, especially since his parents still live across the street. Plus, there are too many memories here that remind me of him. Not only have I known him my whole life, but we were together all through high school. I swear, every memory I have involves you three crazies, and him and Cole."

"Didn't you guys 'go out' in middle school, too?" Sarah giggled.

Sam stopped to think for a minute and then nodded her head. "Yes, actually both 7th and 8th grades. So, see? Can you imagine how tough it is to come back and see things that remind you of the past everywhere you turn?"

"Remember the summer he changed? Like he lost all his baby weight and just sort of became this super good looking guy?" Susan laughed. "OMG. I remember thinking to myself, 'If only Cole did this, I'd be first in line to ask him out!'"

"Yes!" Sasha laughed. "He went from geek to hottie in a summer!"

Sam closed her eyes and smiled, "He used to get made fun of by some boys in our grade, so he decided to start working out. It was the summer before 8th grade. I told him I didn't care what he looked like, but he was sick of the taunting. He killed himself that summer to get into shape and it worked. He also made the varsity football team as a freshman after that summer."

"Oh, my God, that's right!" Sasha smiled. "You two looked like Barbie and Ken walking around. You this blonde fashionista and he this athletic stud. You were quite the couple."

Sam looked down at her hands and took a breath. "Yes, we were, and now you see why it's so hard for me to come home. I have so many memories with him and of him. It wasn't easy for me after he left. Coming home wasn't an option for me anymore. Or, at least that's how I felt. I just tossed myself into work. I wanted to make him pay some-way, somehow, and I just thought being ultra successful was the only way to stick it to him."

"Well, you won," Sasha chimed in.

"Did it work?" Susan asked.

Sam took a moment and looked at each one of her sisters. "I've never actually said that out loud before. I guess it did work for me in terms of driving me to succeed, but saying it out loud makes me sound so freaking petty."

"Well, forget him. We're so glad you did because we get to reap these awesome benefits," Sasha joked as she pulled back her hair and showed off her new diamond earrings. "Thank God one of us is super driven because I sure as hell ain't!"

That got them all laughing again. They all sat at the counter, looking at each other and wiping away the tears of laughter. Sisters. This was something Sam missed. She should have turned to her sisters ten years ago. She should have let them know how she was feeling and trusted them to help her. She needed to know that she didn't always have to be the strong one, especially not when it came to her heart.

7

Colin couldn't get Sam out of his head. Crap. She'd been right there in the restaurant. He should have just let her walk on by and out the door. Why had he chosen that moment to say hello? She looked so freaking good. And she looked so freaking happy with her family. Shit. He hadn't seen her in ten years, and he was pretty sure that she still hated him. He hoped she hadn't noticed him looking at her from across the dining room at the restaurant. It was hard not to look. She was beautiful, more beautiful than he could've imagined. He'd googled her from time to time to keep up with her life and to see what she was up to, but nothing could have prepared him for the real thing.

It had all started with a comment from Jessica, "Don't look now, Colin, but isn't that the fashion designer Samantha McKay? She must be in town for her sister's wedding. That's her, isn't it?"

Colin turned his head in time to see Sam walking toward the table where her family was sitting. As she made her way across the restaurant, he watched as table after table of diners stopped her to say hello. Yup, that was Sam McKay.

He and Jessica had just ordered dinner, and for a nanosecond, he wanted to cancel everything and just leave. Instead, he sat there, looking directly toward her table, trying to pretend that her presence wasn't affecting him. He even tried his best to downplay her to Jessica, but Jessica wouldn't stop talking about her. It nearly killed Colin to sit there and listen to her go on and on. Thankfully, it had been so long ago that she knew nothing about their past.

"She's dating Phillip McKnight! Can you believe that? He's actually going to be at the wedding, too. I can't believe I will be there with you!"

Colin just smiled and nodded his head.

Phillip McKnight. So that was the guy—the boyfriend.

And, just like that, Jessica took out her phone to show him photos, and within five minutes she had a full bio on Phillip. He'd never heard of him, but he knew the McKnight name for sure. Thank God he wasn't on social media.

The guy had to be beyond loaded. He was good-looking, smart, and successful—the holy trinity. And the guy had Sam. What could Colin say? Philip McKnight had it all. His mom must've known all about Phillip, but she had never mentioned him. His mom had been really good throughout the years about keeping talk about Sam to a minimum. His mom loved Sam, loved her like a daughter. She was as proud of Sam as she was of Colin and Cole. When Sam and Colin broke up, it actually devastated Poppy Dasher. She cried. She actually sat and cried when Colin told her that they'd broken up. She didn't ask what happened. She didn't pry. She'd never really had known exactly what had happened, but she knew enough that it was tough for Colin to hear about Sam. It sort of became an unspoken rule at the Dasher house; don't talk about Sam in front of Colin.

Colin had to admit that it had definitely been awkward

talking to Sam. Not that he expected anything different. She looked so beautiful and it was tough not to be tongue-tied. It took all of his confidence to keep his cool and pretend not to be mesmerized by her. She'd always had that effect on him. Even in middle school, he remembered sitting in class and just staring at her across the room, confused as to why this girl actually liked him. He was a semi-pudgy, awkward middle school kid who was in love with the blonde beauty from across the street. When he finally got up the courage to ask her out in 7th grade, and she said yes, he thought she was just joking around with him.

But he realized rather quickly that she felt for him exactly what he felt for her.

They'd grown up together, and falling in love with her just seemed natural to him. They'd always been best friends, biking to school together and playing outside with each other. The McKay girls and the Dasher boys. They did everything together as kids. Somewhere along the way his feelings for Samantha McKay became something more than just friends. And, thankfully, the same happened to her.

When 7th grade ended, on that first weekend of the summer, both families went to the beach together. Living in Rhode Island, there's a beach wherever you turn. They loved their town beach because it was easy to get to and there were always people there to hang out with. Colin remembered getting to the beach and seeing Sam in her brand new bikini. She was so excited to wear it and show it off for him. He also remembered that there had been some other guys from their grade there, too. They were all going into 8th grade together, in one big group. He saw some of them looking at Sam in her bathing suit and obviously thinking the same thing he was thinking--how good she looked.

Then those same guys started making fun of him in his bathing suit. It nearly killed him. They were yelling over to Sam, "Why are you dating pudge boy?" Pudge boy. Even remembering it now made his blood boil, still remembering the names of the kids. He'd never really been an athlete as a kid. He'd play youth baseball and flag football, but that was about it. Nothing else. He'd never worked out nor had an exercise plan beyond P.E. in school. He wasn't overweight by any means, but he didn't have muscle tone or muscle mass. It was just as his mother said, baby weight.

After those boys did their best to humiliate Colin, screaming 'Pudge Boy', Sam grabbed his hand and said, "I don't care what you look like, you're the most handsome boy to me." And that was it. His heart, in that moment, was completely owned by her. She loved him for him, not because of the way he looked. It was at that moment that Colin wanted to give her the best version of himself, on every level, and show those bastards what a real athlete looked like. He went crazy that summer, working out and getting himself into shape for 8th grade, doing daily work-outs and conditioning. When 8th grade rolled around and he went to school that first day with Cole, he couldn't get over the stares from the girls. He had changed his entire appearance and it had given him so much confidence. That confidence and ego boost never left him and he continued to push himself throughout high school and still, to this day, he worked out regularly. He knew he was a good-looking guy. Lots of people told him that he resembled Josh Duhamel, although he really couldn't see it himself, but when enough people tell you that, you just go with it.

He had done it all for Sam. As crazy as it sounds, he just wanted to look good for her. Fuck those kids that made fun of him. He became a better athlete than all of them. They ended up kissing his ass on the high school football field. And Sam was the reason behind it all.

And then there she was tonight, looking better than ever. It brought him back to high school when he would see her across the room or gymnasium or football field and his heart would beat fast. One thing about the two of them was that they had always had great chemistry. They had never been able to keep their hands off each other. Ever. They had made out in secret just about everywhere they could. They just loved being together. Even just out and about walking around town, or driving in the car together, they would hold hands. They had waited until the end of their senior year to have sex, but did pretty much everything else that could be done before that. Seeing her tonight, he felt things all over his body that he shouldn't be feeling for her. Even now his groin was beginning to throb just thinking back to the way things used to be with her. He had felt this immense need tonight to just grab her and kiss her, but he knew he couldn't. He knew he would never be able to do that again.

Colin's phone started to ring, which snapped him out of his trance. It was Cole, calling at 11pm at night. Nothing like a late night call from his brother who was probably calling to brag about a new girl he'd just met. The guy was a chick magnet. Mrs. Dasher was hoping one of them would settle down sooner rather than later and all bets were on Colin being the first. Cole was with a new girl each week and Colin was beginning to think his brother might never get serious. He was a good-looking guy with an over-the-top fun personality to match. He was a girl's fantasy come true, but a nightmare when it came to commitment.

"What's up, Cole? Find the girl of your dreams tonight?" Colin asked.

"Very funny. Tonight was my night off, remember? But I

like the way you're thinking," Cole replied. "I wasn't sure if you'd pick up. You still with Jessica?"

"I just dropped her off. I'm on my way home."

"So, listen to this. I went to Mom and Dad's to help with that new fridge tonight."

"Oh, that's right. I forgot about that. How'd it go?"

"Fine, but that's not why I'm calling. I was in the kitchen when I heard Mr. McKay outside talking to Mom and Dad in the driveway around 9:30. They were just chatting about the wedding and Mom and Dad were volunteering to help any way they could."

"OK. Yeah. And?"

"Jeez, buddy. Let me finish. So then I hear Mr. McKay saying he was glad to have all his girls home, but he'd forgotten how crazy it was. Apparently, they were all in the kitchen with Sam who was crying and Mr. McKay was just kind of venting about how he thought all the drama with four girls would have ended after high school."

"Well, why was she crying?"

"I don't know. I couldn't really hear everything, but it was--you know--two couples venting about their kids." Cole laughed. "But still, I thought it was weird that she was crying."

Colin hadn't planned to say anything about having seen Sam at the restaurant, but figured "what the hell," Cole would find out anyway, "I saw her tonight, Cole."

There was silence on the other end.

"What do you mean you saw her tonight? Weren't you out with Jessica?"

"Yes, but I saw her at the Lobster Claw with her family. As she was walking out I went over to say hello."

"You did? I'm shocked you had the balls," Cole said bluntly. "Good for you. And what happened? Oh, shit. Are you the reason she's crying?" Cole asked, not knowing if he should make a joke or not.

"No! Jesus. Come on. I'm not the reason she's crying. At least, I don't think so. It was awkward, but yeah, we talked. It was super quick, we talked for a few minutes and I took your advice and asked her if we could meet up while she's home and have a talk."

"Holy shit. You actually said that to her? What'd she say?"

"I could tell I caught her off guard and, to be honest, I was caught off guard, too. I wasn't sure what I was going to say, but it just sort of just came out. She was cool about it and said she would have some time before her boyfriend arrived this coming week. Then she turned around and walked away. I don't know if it will actually happen, but I don't want her to hate me forever. And I do agree with you. I think I should clear the air."

"Well, Mr. Dasher - I'm proud of you. I honestly really didn't think you'd have the balls to do it. You proved me wrong."

"Let's hope I have bigger balls to follow through. I know she never comes home, so this is probably my one and only opportunity."

"You could always go to New York," Cole said.

"Yeah – well, I tried that, remember, and it didn't work out too well for me, so I'll just see what happens here. We've both moved on and I think it's the perfect time to hash it out once and for all."

"How did Jessica take it? Must've been weird seeing you talking to THE Samantha K," Cole asked hesitantly.

"She was shocked to realize that I knew Sam. I'm actually kind of shocked that nobody's filled her in on our past, knowing how people around town love a good bit of gossip.

I told her we were old friends and that we had dated in high school, but I didn't give her any additional details beyond that. Jess was cool with it. I think she loved the fact that I'd be able to introduce her to Sam and Phillip at the wedding. So I'm kind of leaving it at that, if you know what I mean."

"So tell me, how'd she look?" Cole asked.

Colin took a deep breath. "Fucking amazing," he said with a sigh. "Just like she did when I left her."

Then before Cole could say another word, Colin hung up.

8

Samantha woke up feeling refreshed. It was weird waking up in her childhood bedroom, but it also made her smile. Her own apartment was big and modern with no real color, just lots of whites, creams, and greys. White couches. White bed. White kitchen. Grey and cream rugs and textiles. The only pops of color were the fresh flowers she had delivered every Sunday and Wednesday. Seeing all the pink around her. A pink pop star girl wannabe made her laugh. When did she change? She was a fashion designer, for Pete's sake. Her apartment should be full of color. Maybe this little excursion home would be a personal inspiration trip, too.

Sam bit her lip and felt a tug at her heart to take a peek under her bed. She knew what was there. She didn't have to think about it not being there. Nobody would've touched it. She had left it at home when she first went to New York. It was so special to her that she actually thought that someday she would pass it down to her own daughter. She had those warm, fuzzy feelings thinking about how her own children would love to know their parent's love story. She had chronicled the entire thing. It was all there, right from the very beginning. But she was not sure about looking at it right now. She knew what was inside. There were no surprises there, just memories.

Curiosity got the best of her. Her hair cascaded over the side of the bed as she looked underneath. There it was, just as she remembered. It was the hot pink hatbox that she had bought at a street fair in NYC when she was in high school. She had gone there with her mom, Mrs. Dasher, and Colin to look at Parsons School of Design. It had been the ONLY school she wanted to attend with F.I.T. a close second. After she toured Parsons, fell in love with the school, and they all went out to explore New York together.

As they walked around New York, they stumbled upon a street fair that spanned 10-12 blocks on Fifth Avenue. Colin and Sam were holding hands and looking at all the cool treasures. The moment Sam saw the round hot pink hatbox, she knew she had to have it. She didn't know what it was about the box, but she knew she needed it. Colin saw the sparkle in her eyes and insisted on buying it for her, which she had appreciated.

"You know what I want to put in it?" Sam said excitedly.

"What's that?" Colin had asked.

"Everything about us. All of our notes, photos, journals and my diary. I want to keep it all in here and pass it down to our kids someday. I want them to know our story."

She remembered Colin smiling and saying, "Well, then, now I definitely need to buy it."

And he had done just that and when they arrived home from that trip, everything that she had saved from their relationship went right inside the box. It had been a love time capsule of sorts. Every note. Every photo. Every ticket stub. Receipts from date nights. Everything was inside. The best was that it was the hottest pink box Sam had ever seen, and she had loved it.

Sam snapped herself out of the memory and just stared at the box under her bed. She knew her mom wouldn't have moved it, or even touched it. Her mom knew how much it meant to her. As Sam reached down to try and grab it, she somehow lost her balance and fell off the bed, head first.

"What the heck was that?" she heard her mom yell from downstairs and then the familiar sound of pounding feet on the stairs.

Seeing stars for a moment, Sam yelled back, "I just fell off my bed, Mom!" She felt a little silly and thought maybe it was the universe's way of telling her to leave the box alone. Kind of like the universe saying to her, "Don't open the damn box. There's nothing inside that will make you feel better."

Within seconds, Ann McKay was inside Sam's bedroom. Sam should've known her mom would come to see what had happened. Once a mom, always a mom.

"Oh, Honey! Are you OK? That sounded horrible from downstairs!"

Sam slowly sat up and looked up at her mom, feeling like a ten-year-old kid again. She smiled and nodded her head. "Yes, Mom. I'm fine. It just surprised me. I had forgotten how high my bed is."

"What the heck were you doing? Some sort of special New York yoga?" Ann giggled. They just loved to jab at her with New York stuff.

"No. I was just trying to look for something under my bed. I thought I had my hand on it, but I lost my balance and fell right off. Honestly, I'm fine."

Ann looked at the ground next to Sam and smiled. She

knew what Sam was looking for, and must have wondered if it was still there.

"Oh. The infamous pink box," Ann said and then sat down on the floor next to Sam.

Sam shrugged her shoulders and looked up at her mom.

"I just wanted to take a look. It's been so long, I was just wondering if it was still there." Sam looked at the box. And there, it was in the same spot. "You never moved it, huh?"

"It wasn't mine to move, Sweetie. I knew it was important to you."

"I actually don't even know why I care about this box. I should've just tossed it away years ago when I tossed everything else out." Sam answered.

"You didn't do that because it's your history, and someday you're going to be able to share that lesson with your own daughter."

Sam smiled and put her head on her mom's shoulder. "I always thought it was going to be *our* daughter who would get that pink box. Not someone else's."

Ann smiled and patted her daughter's knee. "I know you did, Honey. But remember, life doesn't always go the way we plan. Things happen. People change. Circumstances happen. You don't have control over everything. Think of it this way, I never thought my baby girl would live in NYC and become hugely famous!" Ann laughed, trying to make the situation a little lighter for Sam.

"I know, it's just... well... being back here, being back in this room, it brings back a lot of memories for me."

"I know it does, and I know that's why it's tough for you to come home."

"Believe me, it's not because of you and Dad."

"Oh, Sweetie. We know. Colin was your first love. When

you two broke up, it was tough for everyone. You know how much we love Colin. He was part of our family, part of you."

"Yeah, that's true."

"And, just so you know, we still love Colin," Ann said. "It took a little time to adjust to him not being with you anymore, but he's such a good guy and we will always love him. But you're my daughter, and my heart and my soul will always want to take care of you."

Sam wiped a stray tear from her eye. She needed this pep talk with her mom. This should've been done years ago. She thought shutting herself off from everyone had been the best thing to do, and now she couldn't believe just how wrong she had been. She had needed this outlet.

"And you know what?" Ann said, reaching for the pink box, "Someday your daughter will get this box from you, and even though it's maybe not how you intended the box to be used, she'll get the chance to see her mom as a different person. A young woman in love. And who knows, maybe this box will help your daughter get through a tough breakup someday."

"You think so?"

"I do." Ann took Sam's hand. "Now, tell me this, without getting mad or annoyed at me — are you going to talk with him?"

Her sisters, those traitors. They had told their mom everything. She should've known they would have spilled the beans. You can't keep many secrets among the McKay women. Everything is open season, she knew that about them.

"I don't know, Mom. What good will talking do? Besides last night, the last time we spoke was ten years ago and things didn't exactly end well. At the end of the day, he left me and that was it. He never came back. He told me not to call him. He never even tried to reach out. Nothing."

"My question is, why does it still bother you so much after all of these years?"

Sam closed her eyes and let out a small, frustrated grunt, "I don't know!" she blurted. "It only bothers me when I'm back home, being reminded of everything. I just don't get how he was able to just come back home and go on with life as usual. I guess that's what bothers me the most. It's like it didn't even bother him."

"Oh, Sweetie," Ann smiled and looked at her beautiful daughter. "I don't know the answer to that question. I do know that you two have a lot of history together and it might do you good to clear the air so you can move on in a good way. Maybe that's what he needs, too. Let's face it, you're not an easy ex-girlfriend to have."

Sam laughed, "Oh, please! He was with a pretty cute girl last night. I don't think Colin has had any trouble in the girl department over the years."

"Probably not, but you know what I mean," Ann smiled. "I swear his mom has never said anything to me. It's kind of an unspoken thing between us. We don't talk about the two of you. But I do know that, throughout the years, he's asked about you. And when he's asked me, I can tell he really wants to know."

Ann got up and reached down to help Sam stand up. Ann missed Sam more than she was willing to admit and worried about her constantly. She knew Sam had created quite the life for herself, but she was concerned that Sam wasn't actually *living* her life. Fame and fortune hadn't really changed Sam, which she was grateful for. She just wished Sam came home more often and that when they visited her, she would make more time for them. Ann loved having her home right now, seeing her actually live in the moment. No assistants. No crazy work calls. No meetings. No late nights. She was just home with her family, being the old Sam McKay. She hadn't had this Sam home in ten years.

As Ann got to Sam's bedroom door, she turned around and looked at her beautiful grown daughter standing in her little girl bedroom. Sam was placing the pink box on her bed, looking apprehensive about opening it up.

"My motherly advice? Meet up with Colin before Phillip comes. Turn the page once and for all, and start fresh. When you let that piece of your life go, the one in front of you will open right up, and I think that's what you want."

With that, Ann closed the door, leaving Sam standing in the middle of her bedroom more confused than ever about what to do, and how she felt.

9

Colin wasn't sure how to contact Sam. He didn't have her personal phone number and he didn't want to ask his parents to get it, nor did he want to bother Mr. and Mrs. McKay about it. He didn't want to ask her sisters, either. He actually didn't want to get anyone involved, because he didn't feel like listening to unsolicited advice, or worse, the judgment.

The only thing he could come up with this morning was to go to his parent's house on the pretext of getting something out of his old bedroom and wait until he saw her come outside. This was a rather strange thing to be doing at thirty years of age, he thought. He remembered doing stuff like this when they were in middle school and high school. He would sit in his bedroom and just watch the McKay house, waiting for a glimpse of Sam. The second he would see her come outside, he'd rush down the stairs, head outside, and pretend that their timing just miraculously synced.

Not having a better plan, Colin went to his parent's house bright and early, hoping he'd get his chance to see Sam.

"While you're here, could you go through a few boxes your mom has put together?" Colin's father asked. "She's been collecting things around the house that are yours and Cole's and she's put the boxes in your old bedroom. Take anything you want," his father said.

Colin's old bedroom window faced the McKay house, just as Sam's faced his house. Both of their bedroom windows were directly across the street from each other. When they were in high school, they would stay up late at night and talk on the phone while watching each other in their bedrooms. He used to look forward to going to bed every night, knowing Sam was across the street.

As Colin walked into his old bedroom and looked out over at the McKay house, he saw that the shades in Sam's bedroom were drawn. Tell tale sign she was still sleeping.

She had never been an early riser. He remembered that about her back in high school. She would always oversleep or miss her alarm. It became a habit for him to call her in the morning, just to make sure she was up.

Colin looked around his childhood bedroom and realized his mom must have taken down the photos of Sam. He hadn't taken them down, so she must've taken it upon herself. As much as he hadn't really opened up to his parents about what had happened, he thought it was thoughtful of his mom to help him out. He must've been in that room a hundred times over the past ten years, but this was the first time he realized the photos were gone.

Just then, out of the corner of his eye, Colin saw movement outside. He walked to the window to see Sam stretching her legs against her father's car. There she was and in that very moment, she took his breath away. His heart started to beat faster. She looked like she'd just returned from a morning run. There went his theory about her being a late sleeper. A lot does change in ten years. As nervous as he suddenly felt about going outside to talk to her, he knew it was now or never. If he put this off, he might lose his nerve and never get the chance, especially with her boyfriend coming into town this week.

Colin ran down the stairs and bumped directly into his mother as he took the corner to head to the front door of their house.

"Oh, geez! Sorry, Mom!"

"Where are you going so fast?" Poppy said, surprised to see him.

"Just getting something outside," Colin said quickly as he raced out the door. "I'll be back in a minute."

Sam was about to walk into her parent's house when Colin rushed out his front door. As much as his stomach was in knots, he knew he had to do it. "Hey, Sam!" he called.

Sam stopped quickly and turned around. She had beads of sweat on her face and her hair was soaking wet. She wasn't wearing a trace of makeup. Colin was always amazed at how beautiful she looked without it. It had always been that way in high school, too. She was effortlessly beautiful, and he had always wondered if she actually knew what kind of natural beauty she possessed.

Sam looked as nervous as he felt as he walked over to her, but he could tell that she was trying to keep it cool with a smile.

"Hey, Colin," Sam said, still a bit out of breath from her run. "I thought there was an extra car in the Dasher driveway as I was looping back down the street."

"Yeah, I came over early to grab something."

Sam thought that sounded funny. This early? And as much as Sam didn't want to admit it, Colin looked quite good for 7am.

"I'm actually surprised to see you up. I figured you'd be sleeping in every morning while you are here," Colin teased with a smile.

"Those days are long gone for me. I've been up working since 5am. I'm trying not to work like a crazy lady here, so I'm doing what I can in the morning. I felt like I needed to get out and get my blood pumping. I forgot how beautiful it is here in the morning. This town sure is peaceful."

Colin smiled and put his hands in his pockets. He knew he just needed to get down to business. The longer he waited, the more awkward it would be. "Listen," he said. "I know I mentioned seeing if you had any time to meet up and talk before you left town. I don't know what your plans are tonight, but if you're free, do you have time to grab dinner?"

Sam looked at Colin. He wanted to talk. Her heart was beating out of her chest and she was hoping he couldn't hear it. It was beating a mile a minute and she was pretty sure it wasn't just because of her run. Sam thought back to what her mom had said to her, that she would never be able to move on with her love life until she truly ended this one from the past. She was still holding on, and she needed to let the hurt go. As tough as it would be to talk with Colin, she knew she needed to do it.

Sam nodded her head, "Yes, I'm free later today after my sister's dress fitting. I should be done around 5pm, so maybe sometime after that?"

Colin felt like he had just won the lottery. He nodded and smiled. "Yes, that works for me. We usually close up the shop early on Wednesday nights in the summer, so I'll be done around that time, too."

"So, 5pm." Sam didn't want to sound rude, but she knew it needed to be said. "If it's OK with you, I don't want to go anywhere in town. I know how this town is, and I just don't want to be on full display for everyone."

Colin smiled and joked, "You think people in town will talk if they see us together? Really?" He smiled.

"Yeah, why would I even think that, right?" Sam joked back with a smile.

For a moment, it was normal between them and they could both sense that old comfortable feeling.

"How about this, why don't you come over to my place? Anywhere we go around here we're bound to run into someone. This way it's definitely private."

"And you don't think people will talk if they see me going to your house?" Sam asked with a sly smile.

Colin shrugged his shoulders, looking almost amused at the fact Sam was worried about being seen with him in public. "If you can think of a better plan, I'm game," Colin answered.

As much as he looked the same after all these years, Colin had this quiet confidence about him now that Sam didn't remember from all those years ago. "Fine," Sam shot back. "Your place, then. I'll have Sarah drop me off after the fitting. I'm sure she knows where you live."

"OK, great. See you just after 5 and, Sam, let me assure you there isn't any paparazzi following you around, not here in Barrington anyway," Colin laughed as he turned and started walking back to his house.

She stood speechless for a moment. Did Colin Dasher just make fun of her? "I'll have you know, Colin Dasher, that some people like to take my photo and post it online," Sam shot back at him.

"Well, in that case, I'll make sure I shower and look my best. You know, just in case," he laughed as he walked back to his parent's house. "I'll grab burgers from the Creamery.

They actually have a burger called 'SAM' after you, just the way you used to order it."

Sam stood silent and confused, trying to take in what had just happened. Here she was trying to avoid Colin Dasher at all costs, and now she was meeting him tonight at his house to talk and have burgers. She was nervous already.

As she walked through the door to her house, she saw her parents scrambling to get back into the kitchen.

"I know you saw us talking," she yelled to them as she walked upstairs to take a shower.

Colin had the same experience when he walked back into his house, his mother dashing upstairs, trying to avoid being caught.

"It's OK, Mom. I know you saw me," Colin said loudly enough for her to hear.

"Saw you what?" Poppy called down.

"Oh, come on, I know you saw me talking to Sam out front. I'm pretty sure Mr. and Mrs. McKay were watching us, too. It's like being in high school all over again."

Poppy walked downstairs with a basket of laundry, "OK, fine. I did see you. Your dad just told me to mind my own business, but I should've known that's why you came home this morning. Did you come to talk to her?" She looked concerned.

Colin took a seat at their kitchen table while Poppy poured him a cup of fresh coffee. He didn't know what to tell his mother. He knew that she loved Sam, and he also knew that something had changed for Poppy Dasher after they broke up. A piece of her heart had been broken, too, and she'd never let that go.

"Yes, I wanted to see if she'd meet up with me to talk," Colin said as he grabbed the cup of coffee from his mom. "I didn't have her phone number, and I didn't feel like asking anyone for it, so I figured I'd come here and hopefully see her."

"The old 'stalk the house until she comes out' trick?" Poppy giggled.

"Something like that, yes," Colin laughed.

"I know that it's been years since you two have had the chance to talk. I think it will be good for you, but I want you to be careful."

"Mom, there's nothing to be careful about. I'm not in love with Sam. I just want to talk and finally end things in a good way."

"Are you going to tell her?" Poppy asked quietly while looking directly at her son. Colin always figured Cole had told their mom about what he'd done back when Sam was still working hard at Parson. Hearing her ask this question confirmed what he had always suspected. He could see in her eyes that she was worried what his answer would be, but he knew his mom well enough to know that she would not interfere.

Colin took a sip of coffee and slowly put his cup down, looking directly at his mom, "I don't know yet. If it feels right, I will." He took his cup and put it in the sink, turning to his mom, saying, "I'd better get to work before the boss fires me."

10

Sarah's final wedding dress fitting could not have gone more wrong. Sarah showed up an hour late, thinking Sam had said 4pm, not 3pm. Sasha and Susan showed up late because they had been slammed at work and their assistant had called in sick. Ann McKay was annoyed because three people had canceled their RSVPs that morning, and now they'd have to change the seating plan. And, to top it all off, Sarah was in a fight with Chris.

The last thing any of them needed was added stress on the Wednesday before the Saturday wedding.

Sam was the only one who was remarkably calm and cool. She had amazing people in New York to look after things at work, and thankfully there hadn't been any fires to put out. She always had her cellphone close by, so anyone could get in touch with her, but it was almost like they knew to let her be. Her team wanted her to enjoy this week with her family. She never took time off; this was very uncharacteristic of her. When she went back to work next week, she was going to do something special for her staff. You're only as good as the people who work with you, and she knew that. They were the pillars that kept her and her company on solid ground.

While she waited for everyone to arrive, Sam walked around the small bridal shop looking at the dresses. Since she had personally designed Sarah's dress, there hadn't been a need to go dress shopping. Sarah had come to New York a few times over the last few months so that Sam and her team could craft and create her dream dress. Sarah had known exactly what she'd wanted and Sam made that vision a reality. Sam didn't usually do wedding gowns. This was a new one for her, and for her sister, she would do anything

Once the dress had been made, it was shipped back to their local bridal shop in Barrington. This was a place Sam knew inside and out. In high school, she would come here to watch Fatima, the owner and master seamstress, work her magic. Fatima had been an inspiration to Sam, showing her up close how well designed clothing could truly change a woman's outlook on herself. Sam learned that fit was everything, and a well-constructed dress could flatter any woman. Fatima dressed women on their most special of days, their wedding day, and she never took that for granted.

Sam had learned so much from Fatima and she was excited and grateful to have Fatima there to do the final fitting for Sarah. She knew Fatima would make it extra special and perfect. As Sam walked around the bridal shop, looking and touching and holding up various dresses, Fatima smiled.

In her Lebanese accent, Fatima said, "Even though you're a big shot now, you're still my little Sam, still in love with all the pretty dresses."

"Fatima, you always choose the best bridal gowns, bridesmaid and prom dresses for your shop. You have an eye for trends. Every dress in here is stunning. They're magnificent, Fatima! How many of these did you make by hand? I know you always have a few that are yours," Sam said.

Fatima looked around, "All the prom dresses on the rack over there, I made by hand."

Sam turned to see five dresses, in various beautiful colors, hanging on a rack. They were exquisite. There was beading work on two of them, full sequins on another, and a gorgeous satin fabric on the last two. "Your work is so precise. I wish I had someone like you on my staff in New York."

Fatima smiled, "You know I could never leave this town!"

Sam laughed, "I know, I know! But the second you want to, you've got a job!"

"Oh, my sweet girl, I always thought I'd pass this shop onto you someday. Isn't that funny? You soared much higher than a tiny town bridal shop, my girl."

Sam smiled and looked at Fatima. She had to be at least 65 by now. She worked long, hard days, always on her feet. This shop was her body, heart and soul. She had two sons who were older than Sam, but they had left right after graduation to go to university and, like her, only came back for visits once in awhile. Her husband had passed away years ago. It made Sam sad to think that she really had no family here in town. The town was her family, and that was a beautiful thing, but she had nobody to go home to every night.

Sam was so touched by what Fatima had just said about her that she walked over and hugged her. "I didn't know that, Fatima. You never told me that."

"I figured if you ever came back here after college, this would be your place. You were so eager to get to New York and make your mark. I wasn't sure if you'd stay or not, but you made us all proud when you stayed and went after your dreams. Talent like yours can't be bottled up. It needs room to blossom and grow," Fatima said.

"You know, I used to dream about owning this shop when I was a little girl. This was before I really knew you. Mom would bring all of us girls down to Main Street and we'd always walk by your shop. I would beg mom to let me look in the windows."

"Oh, I remember that, the four of you little blonde babies walking with your mother. She was an angel herself."

"And you would come to the door with lollipops for us," Sam smiled.

"You remember that, eh?" Fatima smiled. "I used to keep a bag behind the counter for you girls. When I would see you walking with your mom, I'd grab four of them and walk outside. You always used to ask me who made the fairy princess dresses!"

Sam smiled at the memory. Cinderella had always been her favorite fairy tale and this shop always embodied that happily ever after to Sam. She would see happy people in here, and how they would leave with tears in their eyes, happy to have their dream dress realized. Even as a kid she'd wanted to give people that same feeling and it was part of the reason she'd chosen fashion design as a career.

Sam walked over to a beautiful strapless wedding dress with more tulle underneath than she'd ever seen. This was a real princess wedding dress. She smiled as she touched it and looked over at Fatima, "This one is my favorite."

"Your sisters are still not here, why don't you try it on?" Fatima smiled back.

"Oh, my God, no! That would be silly! It could be bad luck."

"Why would it be silly? Do you know how many dresses I've tried on throughout the years here? Plenty! You mean to tell me as a fashion designer you've never tried on a wedding gown?" asked Fatima with surprise on her face.

Sam shook her head, "I have to say, Fatima, the opportunity has never presented itself to me. Don't forget that Sarah's wedding gown is the first one I've really ever designed."

"Well, now is your chance! Your sisters and mom are all running late, so lets you and me have some fun! Go toss that dress on and let's take a look," Fatima insisted.

Sam hesitated for a moment. She'd never tried on a wedding gown. Seen them a million times? Yes. Helped women choose the perfect one? Yes. Designed one for her little sister? Yes. But she'd never once tried one on, and now she was actually excited about the chance to do it.

"OK, but nobody in my family hears about this, all right? I would never live this down!"

Fatima clasped her hands together and smiled, "Your secret is safe with me. OK, go try it on!"

As Sam stepped into the dress, she suddenly felt like a new woman. She pulled the dress up over her breasts and called Fatima in to zip her up. It was breathtaking. She almost didn't recognize herself in the mirror. This dress was her style. Strapless to show off her shoulders and breasts, but fanned out with the massive tulle skirt underneath to make her feel like a true modern day princess.

"Oh, Sam. You're beautiful. Come out here so we can look at you in the larger full-length mirror," Fatima insisted.

Without missing a beat, just too wrapped up in the magic of the wedding dress, Sam walked out of the dressing room to the center of the bridal shop. She glided over to the full-length mirror and saw herself staring back at her. She was a vision. This was her dream come true, to be in this dress walking toward the man of her dreams. Tears started to swell up in Sam's eyes as she looked back at herself.

"SAM!"

Suddenly, Sam snapped out of her reverie to see Sarah and her mother standing in the shop staring at her.

"Oh, my God, Sam. You look incredible," Sarah said, staring in awe at her sister.

"Oh, Honey, you're a vision. It's perfect on you," Ann McKay whispered with a tear in her eye.

Sam didn't know what to say. She just stood silent, looking at both of them with tears streaming down her face.

Fatima saw the emotion on Sam's face and her heart broke a little for this girl she had loved for so long. "I made her try this one on," Fatima explained. "She's been eyeing it since she walked into the shop today and I knew we had a little time to play dress up. Right, Sam?" Fatima covered for Sam beautifully.

Sam regained her composure and turned back to look at herself in the mirror again. She wiped her tears away and smiled. "And look at me! It's making me cry!"

"How could it not? It looks beautiful on you, Sweetie," her mom said.

"OK, well, enough playing dress up!" Sam walked toward the dressing room area saying, "Enough about me, it's Sarah's turn. We have your dress hanging in the fitting room for your final fitting, ready to assess. With any luck, even though today's gone a little crazy with other stuff, the dress will fit you like a glove."

And with that, the moment was broken.

Sasha and Susan bounded into the bridal shop at that moment, almost on cue, just in time to see Sam and Sarah walking into the dressing room area, Sam in a wedding dress. They both stopped, fell silent, and looked directly at their mother.

"What did we miss, Mom?" Sasha asked.

"Oh, nothing. Maybe everything. Your sister was trying on a wedding dress since we were all so late arriving today. I think we caught her off guard, but she's OK. I kind of like seeing her throwing a little caution to the wind and doing something impulsive!" Ann McKay answered.

Sasha and Susan had no idea what they'd missed. Fortunately, they were so focused on the cute new guy at the local coffee shop, they didn't put much effort into thinking about Sam in a wedding dress. After all, who really cared about Sam trying on some wedding dresses? It was fun to do and they'd done it a number of times at Fatima's shop. Fatima was used to them by now.

But Jessica had been passing the shop and glimpsed in at the very moment to see Samantha McKay in a gorgeous wedding gown. She stood outside with eyes wider than the sun. She thought Sam McKay was just dating Philip McKnight. She didn't know Sam was engaged. Maybe when you become big and famous, you keep stuff like that to yourself to avoid a million questions from people. She couldn't believe her good fortune to stumble upon this as she was walking down Main Street.

Samantha McKay was buying a wedding dress from Fatima. Right here in town. How incredible was that? She needed to share this info, and quickly.

11

"So, she's coming over your house tonight?" Cole asked, sounding almost shocked. "To talk?"

"Yeah," Colin said, tossing Cole a rag.

"And whose idea was this?"

"Jesus, Dude, I took your advice and asked her to talk. Why the hard time all of a sudden?" Colin asked, sounding pissed off.

"I just didn't think you'd actually ask her. Usually, you ignore whatever I say when it comes to women. But, tell me - why the hell are you getting together at your house?"

"She was worried about being seen with me in town, and having people talk and maybe jump to conclusions."

Cole rolled his eyes, "I guess this is what happens when you become famous."

Stephen Dasher worked quietly next to his sons, taking in their conversation. Over the years he had heard a lot, but he found the best thing was to keep quiet. Besides, he was no expert in matters of the heart. He had opinions, of course, but only his wife Poppy knew what they were. She was good at giving the boys advice, so he always left that side of things to her. One thing he did know for sure was to stay out of anything that had to do with Sam McKay. That was a line in the sand he didn't dare cross because he knew it would just upset Colin.

"Believe me, I actually agree with her," Colin continued. "The last thing I need is this getting back to Jessica, or people in town making a bigger deal out of this than it is."

"Are you going to tell Jessica about it?"

"What do you think, you dork? Jessica and I have just started dating, and I don't want to upset her. Anyway, this really doesn't have anything to do with her. It will be a short meeting, Sam and I will clear the air, and that will be it. End of story."

Cole looked at his brother. For all his talk, he could tell Colin was nervous, but trying his best not to show his feelings. He knew his brother still carried a flame for Sam. Hell, most likely Sam still had feelings for Colin, but they were both too stubborn to admit it.

"What are you going to actually talk about? Are you going to tell her?" Cole asked.

Colin let out a shrug, "Fuck, man, I don't know. I just don't know. Honestly? I just want her to know that I'm proud of her and that I don't want her to hate me anymore."

"You really think she hates you?"

"Yeah, I do. I really think she hates me," Colin laughed, but it wasn't funny. "Even the way she looked at me, I could tell there's still a lot of hurt there. I don't want her to feel like she can't come home because I'm here - and I know that's why she stays away. I don't know if she'd actually admit that, but I'm pretty sure it's the reason."

"Dad, what do you think?" Cole asked, looking over at their father.

"What do I think?" Stephen Dasher looked over at Cole.

"I think Colin needs to do what Colin needs to do, and I think *you* need to get back to work." He looked over at Colin and winked at him.

Cole rolled his eyes at his father but continued to give Colin advice. "Make sure you keep it short and sweet. When you two get going on things, you don't know when to stop."

"Kinda like you," Stephen said to Cole.

"Look, you guys. I know, all right? I just want to say my piece and get it done," Colin said, returning to the oil change.

Two seconds later Cole looked over at Colin.

"What time is she coming over?" he asked.

"Oh, for Pete's sake, Cole. Give it a rest. She'll be over around 5, so I really need your help right now. Stop talking and help me close up early tonight. I want to get home and take a shower before she arrives. I don't want to be covered in oil and grease."

"Most ladies find that sexy," Cole laughed.

Unable to ignore Cole, Colin said, "That works for you, Bro, not me. Girls flock to you like a bee to honey. I don't know how you do it, even after a full day shift."

"We're identical twins, you just have to put yourself out there like I do," said the man of experience.

"Or, maybe I just choose *not* to put myself out there like you," answered Colin.

They both started laughing. Colin loved working full time in their auto shop all summer long with his brother and dad. As much as Cole loved to bust his balls, he wouldn't trade being with him like this for anything.

As they both got back to work, Colin was reminded, again, about how his life had unfolded over the past ten years. He'd never really had big dreams growing up, apart from doing work he enjoyed, making a living, and getting married. When everyone else in high school was talking about college and their 4-year plans and what they wanted to do someday, he didn't have a clue. Knowing that Sam's big dream was in NYC, in essence, that would be his dream, too. He would finalize his plans once Sam was settled. That had never seemed pathetic to him. But, at the same time, he knew his options in New York would be limited.

When he moved to NYC to be near Sam after graduation, he saw it as a great adventure for himself and figured he'd give it a shot. He got a job, almost immediately, waiting tables. He knew it would be temporary, but it was a start. He lined up an apartment share with two other guys before he left Barrington. It all seemed to fall into place for him in NYC, just as it had for Sam.

He just hadn't banked on hating New York City as much as he did. Everything about it turned him off. The hustle. The noise. The crowds of people. The cost of living. The lack of friends and family. Sam was his only silver lining. Thinking back now, it seemed crazy that he didn't have a solid plan in place for his future. Everyone in NYC seemed to have some sort of plan. Some sort of idea about their future or they were working toward something. He had never felt more lost or deflated or out of options in his life. He had been the big fish in a small pond in Barrington, in NYC he was a little minnow.

Later on, as the Dasher boys were closing the shop, Cole came back to their earlier conversation, "Colin, just promise me one thing about tonight."

"What's that?"

"Don't go too deep into the past. If you really just want to make this talk about moving forward, and not having her feel weird about coming home, then keep it simple. Tell her

how you feel, and that you've always been her biggest cheer-
leader. Keep it like that. It will be better for the two of you."

"Jesus, when did you get soft?" Colin asked, walking
toward the office area.

"I would say the same thing," their Dad chimed in.

"There's not much more I can do to fuck things up with
her. I just want a clean slate, that's it."

"I know. But just keep it simple. Maybe it's not worth
telling her about coming back to see her in New York.
What's that going to change now?"

Colin stared at his brother. Only Cole and his parents
knew the real reason he went back all those years ago. He
had sworn them to secrecy - to never tell a soul - and they
had never breathed a word. What he'd never fully realized
was just how crushed they were for him when he'd come
back to Barrington almost immediately. Cole especially.
What they never knew was just how devastated he had
been. Thinking back on that time gave Colin a horrible
feeling in his stomach.

As different as they were, they always had each other's
backs. Not just because they were twins, but because they
were best friends. When Colin came back from NYC, he
knew Cole was worried about him for a long time. He
seemed to have lost his sense of humor and nothing interested him. It took years for him to come out of the "Sam
funk" as Cole called it. Cole decided back then that his job
as Colin's brother was to keep his spirits up and not mention
Sam's name. Cole figured Colin needed to start dating again,
and since neither one of them had issues attracting girls, he
couldn't see what the problem was. Even in high school,
with Colin and Sam as tight as ever, Cole would make it his
business to let Colin know about all the girls crushing
on him.

Cole was the complete opposite of Colin in high school. He never had a girlfriend. He'd never had the slightest intention of having a girlfriend. He loved the attention he got from the girls and he loved being as free as a bird. He eventually would - of course - like to settle down, but he'd never found that one girl who changed everything for him. He wasn't actively looking either. He knew he had time. There wasn't any rush. The only one putting a timetable on anything was his mother. She was longing for a daughter-in-law and wishing for grandchildren.

Colin came out of the office with his work backpack over his shoulder, ready to go. He appeared a little stressed, but ready to get home and freshen up before Sam arrived. He'd had women at his house dozens of times before, but this time he really wanted to make sure it looked perfect, nothing out of place. He'd worked hard on making his house a true home. He'd even hired an interior designer to decorate his place. He didn't want it to look like a bachelor pad, so he had chosen a clean, classic look. He loved living by the water and he loved a nautical feel. He'd saved money and had invested fairly well throughout the years, buying a couple of rental properties. He wasn't a millionaire, not like Sam, not by any stretch, but he'd done well, well enough to not worry, and well enough to buy the things he liked and wanted.

"OK, I'm heading out."

"Good luck. Call me later."

"I will and, as much as you're a pain in the ass, thanks for the pep talk," Colin smiled.

"Not that I need to tell you this, but keep your hands off her, too," Cole smirked. "Nothing good will come from the two of you touching."

"Words I never thought I'd hear come out of your

mouth," Colin laughed out loud at this piece of advice, "What do you think I'm going to do? Jump her?"

"You two have this chemistry, man. I know it and you know it. Just keep yourself on track and do not – for any reason whatsoever - touch her."

"Duly noted – I will not touch her!" Colin teased back as he left the building.

Do not touch her! Like he actually needed to be told this by his brother. He wasn't stupid. He was dating Jessica and Sam was dating Phillip McKnight. All he wanted was for the two of them to have a friendly conversation, and to have a chance to say that he was sorry about the past.

12

"You're sure you want to do this?" Sarah asked Sam as she pulled up in front of Colin's house.

Sam didn't answer right away. She couldn't get over Colin's house. It was absolutely adorable, a subtle, yet beautiful cape-style New England house. She wasn't sure what she had expected, but this wasn't it. This was the perfect family home. Beautiful front yard with a brick path leading to the front door, flowers lining the path. White picket fence surrounding the perimeter. Freshly cut grass. The house was painted grey, with black shutters and a white door. It screamed New England family home, not the bachelor pad she had imagined.

"I'm fine, honestly. It sure is cute, though, huh?" asked Sam.

"Colin's house?" Sarah asked.

Sam nodded her head as she asked the question.

"Yeah, he's done a great job transforming it into this. You should've seen it before. It was a disaster."

"I love the color. It looks just like my beach house in the Hamptons," Sam said.

"Oh, please. Your beach house is three times the size of this place!"

"I meant the paint color, it looks identical to the new color I picked last summer."

"Too bad you never get to go and enjoy it," Sarah jokingly jabbed at Sam. "Look, just call or text me when you need me to pick you up, OK?"

"Yes, I will. Please keep your phone on you. This shouldn't take too long. He was going to get burgers from the Creamery, but I honestly don't think this will last that long."

"So what do you think? About an hour?"

"If that," Sam said. "I'll call you when we're done."

"No problem, I'm just heading back to mom and dad's. I'm ten minutes away. And remember, you've both moved on, so make sure you leave on good terms this time."

Saying goodbye, Sam stepped out of the car and walked up the path to the front door. Suddenly, Sam's stomach started to do flips. Was it nerves or butterflies? She couldn't tell. This was going to be the first time in ten years that they would be alone together. Whenever they were alone in the past, they practically tore each other's clothes off. They had become pros at making it quick before getting caught by their parents. She needed to push those memories out of her head. This would definitely not be one of those times, and she had to stop herself from going there. She was scared, yet ready at the same time.

Colin must've seen her pull up because the door opened and there he was, standing in the doorway. He had just showered, she could tell by his wet hair and he smelled like Ivory soap, always his favorite. Funny how some things never changed. He was tan from the summer sun and wearing a white crewneck tee along with a pair of navy blue mesh shorts. He was casual, as if he was about to sit down on the couch and watch television, or head outside to do a little grilling. Either way, he looked very Colin, handsome and not aware of just how handsome he truly was, even as casual as this.

"Are you going to have your sister sit in the driveway the entire time? Or do you have her on speed dial to pick you up in 10 minutes?" Colin joked.

He knew her well. "Ha ha, very funny. I told her I'd call her when I needed a ride," Sam answered.

"Any paparazzi follow you here?" he joked, pretending he was looking out at the street.

Sam laughed, "I knew I shouldn't have said anything! You're just like my sisters with the little funny jabs."

"I'm sorry... I needed to say something," he responded warmly. "Thanks for coming. Come on in." And with that, Colin stepped aside as Sam entered his home. It was beautiful, a complete open floor concept. Big navy blue couches against white walls in the living room area. A gray dining room set that popped against the white walls in the dining room. And a gorgeous white and gray kitchen with a marble island.

Just having Sam here in his space seemed surreal to Colin. She was dressed so familiarly in a white tank top with jeans that had holes at their knees, along with a pair of pink high strappy heels. She looked summer ready and summer beautiful. Her hair was neatly tied back in a ponytail with wisps hanging down, framing her face. She was beautiful.

"Your house is beautiful, Colin," Sam said as looked to her left and then to her right. "You did a great job decorating this place. It's so cozy looking."

"Thanks, I actually hired someone to do it, so I can't take all the credit. I knew I wanted it to be more on the nautical side, but she helped me pull everything together."

"It really is beautiful, Colin," Sam said, looking around. "I love your couches. They look like you could sink right in and stay for days," Sam smiled.

"And you've nailed my weekends at home in a nutshell!" Colin smiled back. "Hey - can I get you a drink? I've got beer, wine, water, soda..."

She wasn't sure she should be drinking, but holding a glass of something would be a good distraction and some wine would certainly calm her nerves. "Thanks. Sure, I'll take a glass of wine," Sam said.

"Still a Pinot Grigio drinker?"

Sam smiled and turned towards him, "That hasn't changed, I'm surprised you remembered!"

"Of course I remember that. Red wine used to give you a migraine, and you've always hated Chardonnay. Am I right?"

"Seriously, even after all these years, I still cannot get into Chardonnay."

Colin walked into the kitchen area and pulled a bottle of Pinot Grigio out of the fridge. Sam wondered if Colin had bought the wine purposely, knowing she was coming over. As quickly as she thought it, she dismissed the thought. He probably stocked all kinds of wine.

While Colin poured the wine, Sam walked around his living room and took note of the pictures on the walls and the books on the table. There weren't any photos of any girls, but there were photos of him and Cole and their parents. He had kept everything rather minimal, not a lot of stuff out and about. As she walked past his dining room area, she noticed a few books stacked on the chair, and realized they were textbooks.

"What are these, Colin?"

Colin looked up and saw that she was pointing to his books. "Oh, just some textbooks from school."

"School?" Sam asked, surprised.

"Yeah, I guess word hasn't spread to New York. I'm a guidance counselor at the high school."

Sam looked shocked. She thought someone would have said something to her. Apparently not. "At the high school? What about the auto body shop?"

"Yup, I work at the high school. There's actually a bunch of teachers still there from when we attended. I've been there for three years now. I work all summer at the auto body shop and usually on weekends throughout the school year when they're busy. It may have taken me a little longer, but finally figured out what I wanted to be," Colin smiled.

It took a second for Sam to process everything Colin was saying. She hadn't known he went back to college and was working at the high school. Nobody had told her any of this. Sam turned and looked at the books again. She was happy for him; glad that he had found something he wanted to do. She'd always wondered if working with his dad and brother fulfilled him. He'd never expressed any desire to want to do that, so when she heard that's where he was working after he moved back to Barrington, it definitely made her scratch her head. That decision of his had confused her all those years ago when he had broken up with her. She had had a tough time understanding how he'd leave New York and her, too, to work at a job he had no passion for. It had been easier for her to ignore those thoughts rather than face them, head on, or God forbid, talk to anyone about them.

Handing Sam her wine, Colin took a deep breath, "Listen, I'm glad you came. As uncomfortable as it might be for each of us, I feel like there's unfinished business between us and I just wanted to get it squared away before Sarah's wedding."

Sam looked at Colin as he took a bottle of beer out of the fridge. Some things just didn't change. He had never, ever been a wine drinker.

"I know. I agree. As much as I wasn't sure if I should come, I'm glad you asked me. I know there are things to say."

Colin smiled, looking a little relieved, "OK, so we're actually on the same page on this one."

Sam smiled back, "Yes. We're on the same page."

"Before we get started," Colin said, swallowing hard from nerves, "I do want to tell you this. Regardless of what you think of me, I need you to know that I'm proud of you. What you've built and what you've done is just incredible. I always believed in you and it's pretty cool to see that your dream has come true."

Sam knew he meant it. "Thank you, Colin, that means a lot to me."

She took a sip of wine from her glass, not quite sure what to say. Her hand was shaking and she hoped Colin didn't notice. Whether he did or not, she knew Colin wouldn't be rude to her, and she actually knew he wouldn't hurt a fly. As built as he was, and as big as he was in stature, to the core he had the kindest heart of anyone she knew. Or, at least, he did. She couldn't imagine that changing, even after ten years. He'd always been kind and considerate.

"Listen, I've just gotta say it," Colin continued, "It kills me to think that you might not come home to see your parents and your sisters because of me."

Sam's eyes started to close a bit and she started to feel her blood rise a little, "Who told you that?" she asked.

Colin sensed her agitation and answered back quickly,

"Nobody did, but you never come home, and I do wonder if it's because of me. I feel like I ruined this town for you by coming back here after New York."

"Really?" Sam asked.

Colin looked straight at Sam and nodded his head, "I never intended for that to happen, if that is the case," he said.

"You think that you're the reason I don't come home?"

Colin knew already he'd approached this the wrong way. Sam was getting upset and this was not the way he wanted this conversation to go. He'd waited all these years to talk to her, and he didn't want it to be dead in the water before they even got started.

"I didn't say that, Sam. I'm just saying that I don't want what happened to us to affect your coming home," he explained.

"And what exactly happened to us? The way I remember it, you just decided one day that New York wasn't the place for you, and you left. You didn't even give me a chance to respond. You just up and left one day, out of nowhere."

Colin stood staring at this woman that he had loved so deeply.

"I don't feel like I just up and left one day, Sam," Colin explained. "I was miserable in New York. I honestly always thought you knew that, deep down inside. I was afraid to tell you how much I hated it because you were so happy."

"I was happy in New York with you there. I wasn't happy with you gone. You were my saving grace in New York," Sam said quietly to him. "You were my anchor there, and I thought we had planned to build a life together. I just didn't understand how you were good one day and then gone the next."

"Listen, I never meant to hurt you, Sam," Colin said,

looking directly at her. "You were the most important person in my life. I was worried if I told you how miserable I was, you'd want to leave with me."

Sam looked at Colin with a sense of hurt in her voice, "But you didn't give me the choice, Colin. You never let me decide what would be best for me. You decided for the two of us. It's the one thing I feel you never understood."

Colin looked down at his bottle of beer sitting on the counter. He didn't want it to go this way. He didn't want there to be animosity between them.

"And I am sorry, Sam. I really am. I was young and stupid and I thought leaving was the best thing I could do for you. I was this dumb kid waiting tables while you were this fashion star on the rise. I felt like a dead weight for you there. It wasn't easy for me to make that choice for the two of us."

"You weren't dead weight, Colin. You just didn't know what you wanted to do with your life. You were street smart, and such a good people person. You still are. I knew you'd eventually figure it out or...I thought you would."

"It wasn't easy watching you with all of your college friends working hard and advancing yourselves while I was serving eggs and bacon at a greasy diner in midtown. I had no idea what I wanted to do with my life, but you guys all did. And, honestly, I just felt like I was weighing you down. But I admit it was a lot harder than I thought it would be."

Sam had always wondered if it had been tough for him to watch her in college. He'd never alluded to the fact, or that he was jealous or anything like that, but she'd always wondered if he felt diminished by not being in college with them, working a job in a restaurant instead.

"It wasn't easy coming back to Barrington with my tail between my legs. You know how people talk here, and worse was coming back without you. It crushed my ego," Colin added.

Sam looked over her wine glass at Colin, and she could tell he was serious. She could hear the emotion in his voice, and she knew he was telling the truth. Yet, she still couldn't ignore the feeling of being upset, even after all these years. She couldn't push past the fact that he chose this life over one with her.

"Well, it was tough on me, too," Sam answered. "I was crushed after you left. My heart was broken. I'm sure my ego was just as bruised as yours was." Sam closed her eyes for a minute, not wanting to remember it, but knowing it would always be there. "I remember begging you that one night on the phone to come back, and you just said that it was over and that I needed to move on. And that's what you were doing, so I needed to do the same. Do you remember that?" Sam asked.

Colin felt sick just thinking about that night. He couldn't even look her in the eyes. "Yeah, I remember."

"You wouldn't even let me get a word in. You just ended it. That was it. I was positive you were seeing someone else, or had cheated on me. That's how it sounded. I actually think I cried myself to sleep for the next month after that. It took me forever to pick up the pieces and move on. I never knew if I had done something, or if you had cheated while you were in NYC. You just left. Here today, gone tomorrow, after all that time together. No explanation. That was so not like you."

He remembered that night all too clearly. He'd just arrived back home in Barrington and Sam had tracked him down at his parents' house. He was in his bedroom looking across the street to her empty dark room. He felt sick as a dog regretting everything that he'd done, but knowing it was for the best. He couldn't go back. She was going places and he was stuck in the here and now, not knowing where the hell to turn. Sam had called and was sobbing on the phone, begging him to come back and give them another chance. She even said that she'd drop her internship just to make sure they'd have the chance to spend more time together. That was the last thing he wanted her to do. That was exactly what he was afraid of - her sacrificing her dream for him. The way he saw it, he didn't have a dream to sacrifice, not back then, anyway.

"For what it's worth, I was just as broken being back here," Colin looked directly at Sam, "And you know I never cheated on you, right?"

Sam nodded her head in silence.

"I missed you every single day. I thought by leaving, I was helping. I know it sounds stupid now, but it's the truth," Colin explained. "I hope you believe me, Sam."

Sam let out a breath and a small smile started to form from her lips, "I do believe you, Colin."

"I can't take away the past and I can't take away the hurt from all those years ago," Colin said as he came around his kitchen counter standing closer to Sam. "I just wanted to talk to you because I wanted to tell you how sorry I am about what happened between us. I was young. I was naive. I was lost. I didn't know that what I was doing would cause so much hurt."

Colin stood right in front of Sam, inches away from her face. Their eyes locked. Sam felt years of anger and resentment start to slip away. He was sorry. He had been hurt, too. He had suffered, just like her, but in a different way. He regretted what he had done and was telling her now, ten years later.

"I just wanted to say I'm sorry," he said. "I've been

waiting to tell you this for years. I'm sorry for not choosing us all those years ago. I really did think I was doing the best thing for you."

Sam's eyes started to tear up. She couldn't help it. This was the man she had wanted to spend the rest of her life with. This was the man she would've done anything for. This was the man who - when he left her - made her question everything there was about love and fairy tales and happily ever afters. Colin reached up and wiped Sam's tear away from her cheek. He hated to see her cry; he'd always hated to see her cry. As soon as he touched her face, Colin could hear Cole's words vibrating through his head, "Do not touch her!" He had already messed up that rule and now all he wanted to do was move towards her, right there, and kiss her. He wanted all of her, to consume her, and just breathe in every atom of her being.

He shouldn't be feeling what he was feeling in his heart and body right now. His body was telling him to take her right now in his kitchen. But he had a girlfriend, and she had a boyfriend. He couldn't kiss her the way he wanted to. He shouldn't even have touched her, but it came so natural to him. He pulled his hand away from her cheek and looked into her eyes, "I hope you can forgive me, Sam."

Sam took a deep breath and closed her eyes. As she exhaled, her eyes opened and a smile came across her face. "Thank you, Colin. And, in all honesty..." Sam took a moment to continue, "the truth is I haven't been able to come home because of you. My God, everything here reminds me of you, of us, and how it was, and how it used to be. It's funny, even though I've defined myself as Samantha McKay around the globe, when I'm back home in town I'm still just part of the old 'Sam and Colin' routine with everything and everyone, especially my family. I didn't want to hear about it, talk about it or deal with it, so I avoided it. I know that hasn't been fair to my parents or my sisters, either."

"It sure wasn't easy for any of our family members when we broke up. My God, I don't think my mom talked to me for a month!"

"Good!" Sam shot back. "I always loved your mom—I still do. But yeah, especially living across the street from each other," Sam added. "I just never felt comfortable coming home."

"All I ever wanted was for your dreams to come true," he said, inching a little closer to Sam.

A knock sounded at Colin's front door, breaking the moment for them. His face went pale for a second. Who would that be? He didn't have plans and Cole would never drop by tonight.

"Is that Sarah?" he asked.

Sam shook her head, "I don't think so, I told her I'd text her."

Colin walked over to the door and saw a familiar brunette standing there, waiting for him to answer the door. JESSICA. What was she doing here? They didn't have any plans tonight.

"Oh, man. It's Jessica."

Sam felt an odd twinge in her chest, the twinge of jealousy. But why would she be jealous of Jessica? It's not like she and Colin had any intention of getting back together. She had Phillip and he had Jessica. Not to mention, Phillip was due to arrive tomorrow or Friday morning, depending upon his work schedule. Was Colin supposed to stay single and miserable for the rest of his life? Taking one look at him, it was shocking that he wasn't already married with a bunch of kids. Just thinking about Colin being married made Sam's stomach turn for a second.

Colin was still looking at Sam, about to say something about Jessica. Sam looked at Colin and smiled while grabbing her pocketbook off the counter, "Go get the door. It's fine. I'll text Sarah and ask her to come get me."

"Wait, Sam," Colin said grabbing her arm. At that moment, an electric current ran up Sam's arm. It was like a shock. It was Colin's touch on her arm again. Gentle. Sweet. Comforting. She knew that touch and had missed that touch. That touch used to caress her hair, back, breast, arm, leg, every part of her. "Are you sure? Honestly - I can ask Jess to come back later. I'll let her know we were in the middle of something."

He knew now he wouldn't have the chance, or the balls, to tell Sam his whole truth, and with Jessica here, he probably wouldn't have another opportunity.

"Yeah, right, I'm sure that would go over well," Sam laughed.

"I know, but I want to make sure we're good."

"We're good, Colin. I'm glad we talked, and I'm glad we got everything out." She felt a little bit out of control being near him. She had never not trusted herself around anyone but, right now, she needed to leave. Pronto.

"Are you sure?" he asked.

No! She wasn't sure. She missed Colin. Being here, with him, felt right, felt good. She had loved Colin all those years ago because he had been her best friend. Losing that was the toughest part of all. She had experienced everything with him. First kiss. First dance. First love making. He was her first, but also the truest friend she had ever had. As difficult as it was to stand there and know and accept the truths of fate and life, she knew she needed to leave. There was nothing else for the two of them to say.

"Absolutely. Don't be silly, it's fine. Jessica's here and I don't want to ruin an evening for you guys. Besides, I promised I'd help Sarah with some last-minute wedding stuff, and Phillip will be arriving tomorrow night, so I've really got to get going," Sam explained.

"Will I get to meet Phillip?" Colin asked with a smile as he walked Sam to the door, about to say goodbye to her and hello to Jessica.

"I guess you will, at the wedding." Sam looked back up at Colin, "He and I haven't really talked about my past relationships, so let's just keep it our secret that we used to date. OK?"

Colin looked at her with a questioning look, "You've never told him about me?"

"It really hasn't come up and, let's face it, it really doesn't matter now. We've both moved on." It actually hurt Sam to say those words. "But I'm glad we got the chance to talk tonight."

"And, for the record," Colin whispered before he opened the door. "Jess is a big fan, so heads up, OK?"

Colin opened the door and there was Jessica, about to knock again. When she saw Sam standing next to Colin, her jaw literally dropped open. She tried her best to recover from the immediate embarrassment of looking completely star-struck, which wasn't easy since her face was beet red.

Sensing how embarrassed Jessica was, Colin greeted her, "Hey, Jess - come on in. You didn't get a chance to meet Sam the other night at the Lobster Claw."

"No," Jessica said. Trying to catch her breath and remember how to talk, she was able to get out the words, "It's nice to meet you." Jessica extended her hand to Sam.

Fortunately, Sam being the class act that she was knew that Jessica was trying her best to stay cool. She sometimes got this reaction from fans. It was something she'd never really became used to because she really never focused on the fame part of her success. She just wanted to make great clothes for women. That was it.

Sam said, naturally, "I'm a hugger, I hope you don't mind," and then went in to give Jessica a big hug.

"Oh, OK," Jessica said looking like a kid at Christmas. "Yes, me, too."

"I hope I didn't hold up your plans. I was just heading out," Sam said.

Jessica looked up at Colin, and he knew she was hoping he would get Sam to stay a little longer, but there was no way on earth he was going to do that. It was already weird enough to have her here, never mind having Jessica turn up.

Lying through his teeth, Colin said to Jessica, "I tried to get her to stay a little longer to chat with you, but she's got to go meet up with Sarah." Colin was pissed that she would just show up unannounced, he didn't think they were at that point in their relationship where random stop overs were cool. Apparently, he wasn't on the same page as Jessica yet. He knew she didn't mean any harm, but a text or a call would've been nice.

Easily picking up on Colin's situation, Sam added, "Yes, I wish I could stay, but Sarah has a to do list a mile long, so I've got to get myself back."

"Well, it was good to meet, even just this quickly. I'm a big fan and I buy as much of your stuff as I can!" Jessica gushed. "You're my favorite designer by far!"

"Aw, thank you so much. That's so sweet. Next time I come home, I'll bring something for you!"

Jessica lit up. "Really? You would do that for me?"

"Of course! Any friend of Colin's is a friend of mine," Sam smiled. "My sister should be pulling up any second, so I'll head outside. It was nice to meet you, Jessica."

"Thanks for coming over, Sam," Colin said, "I'll see you at the wedding. Tell your sister and Chris that if they need anything, I'm here for them."

"Thanks, Colin, I will." She just stared back at him, not wanting to leave, but knowing she had to. She didn't want to look away. She knew what she felt. It was hard leaving, but feeling good about the fact that they had broken the ice. But with Jessica arriving, she knew she shouldn't be feeling this way. She had Phillip, and she was in love with Phillip. It wasn't like Colin felt anything towards her anymore.

After what felt like a lifetime, but was only a couple of seconds, Sam turned and walked down Colin's driveway to the street to wait for Sarah. She didn't dare look back at the house. She had moved on a long time ago and these feelings meant nothing. She didn't love Colin anymore. She would always 'love' him, but not the way she did all those years ago. He had moved on. She had moved on. It was the way it was supposed to be. She had always worried about the hurt and the pain of being around Colin again, but this had been the first step to deal with that. It hadn't been as bad as she thought it would be.

Almost on cue, Sarah arrived to pick her up.

"You're never going to guess who's here," was the first thing Sarah said to her when she got into the car.

"Who?" Sam asked, trying to collect herself so Sarah wouldn't see she was a bit rattled.

"Phillip."

13

"I can't believe I just met Samantha McKay!" Jessica gushed as soon as she walked into Colin's house. "I didn't expect her to be so nice."

Colin walked back into the kitchen, still semi-annoyed that Jessica just showed up unannounced, but knew in any other circumstance he'd be happy she had. Jessica was gorgeous, there was no doubt about it. She had caught Colin's eyes a few months back and he had been having a great time with her. But right now he was in his own world, not even thinking about entertaining Jess for the night. It didn't seem to matter much because Jessica followed behind texting away on her phone and talking fast and furious to him about Fatima's Dress Shop and Sam being there, not even looking up. He wasn't following along with what she was saying. He was just thinking about being glad his meet-up with Sam had happened.

As much as Jessica was fun to be around, and he enjoyed her company, she was *always* on her phone. Actually, it was starting to drive him crazy. They couldn't go anywhere without her documenting it on social media. Hell, they couldn't go anywhere without her texting her friends to fill them in on every single detail. She was probably filling her friends in right now with her encounter with Sam, and most likely posting on social media, too. This immediately snapped Colin out of his Sam trance.

"Hey, Jess, whatever you do... please don't post anything about meeting Sam, or her being here."

Jessica looked up with a confused face, "I can't say that I just met her?"

"I'd prefer you don't. Her sisters keep everything quiet on social media about her being home, and I don't want her to be pissed that you shared something."

That did it for Jessica. She wouldn't want to piss Sam off. "Oh, that sucks," Jessica said looking rather bummed. "How do you know her so well again? You grew up across the street from her?"

"Yeah, right across the street. Our families pretty much grew up together. Our parents still live across the street from each other."

"Let me just delete this Facebook post," she said, looking back at her phone and beginning to type again.

She was able to type faster on her cellphone than anyone he'd ever seen before. She was a master at it, a true pro. She put high schoolers to shame. She could literally talk and text at the same time without missing a beat. It was crazy.

Colin wasn't sure how, or even if, he should talk to Jess about the history between him and Samantha. Did he have to tell Jessica the truth about everything? He had downplayed his history with Sam with every ex-girlfriend up to this point. He just never felt like getting into it with them. But since Jessica was making such a big deal about meeting Sam, and had probably already informed the masses, he knew it would be better coming from him than anyone else.

"Actually, I dated Sam in high school," Colin tried to mention as nonchalantly as possible. It obviously didn't work too well because Jessica shot her head up from her phone in a nanosecond, her eyes as big as saucers.

"Wait a second. Did you used to *date* her? You and Samantha? I didn't know that."

Colin opened his fridge to take out a beer, trying his best to avoid eye contact with Jessica, afraid if he locked eyes with her she'd know that Sam meant more to him than he'd ever let on.

"Um, yeah. It was a long time ago. But, yeah - we went out or dated or whatever they call it, back in high school."

Jessica didn't seem too fazed by the information Colin was sharing because instead of being super jealous, it made her more inquisitive about Samantha. She walked to his kitchen island and took a seat on one of the stools. The same stool that Sam had been standing next to when she was in his kitchen.

"So, wait, what was she like back then?"

"What do you mean?" he asked, feeling annoyed, which was something he rarely felt.

"Well, did you ever think she'd turn into a famous fashion designer?" Jessica asked with stars in her eyes. "Was she always sketching and creating fun outfits? I bet she always had amazing style."

Jesus, Colin thought. She's a little star struck, and she seems weirdly excited about having the opportunity to get the inside track on Samantha.

"Did I ever think she would become famous?" He thought about Jessica's question, and looked for a way to put an end to the topic. He answered, "Yeah. I think I always knew that she'd turn out to be somebody successful. I think we all did."

Jessica smiled and said excitedly, "I just can't believe you two dated! Do people around town know this? How did I not know this about you?"

"Listen Jessica, it was a long time ago and it is part of my past. No big deal. I really don't talk about it much, or think about it much. It's just part of my story and it doesn't affect my life right now, you know? But, please, don't post anything online. She's a private person, and I sure don't want anything to come back to me either."

Jessica continued talking. Deep in his own thoughts about Sam, and trying to shake himself from his daydream, he took a sip from his beer and looked up as Jessica said, "I just can't believe I'm dating one of Samantha McKay's exboyfriends! This is crazy!"

"Well, I don't necessarily think it's anything that will get you ahead in life," Colin joked. "She's moved onto bigger and better and richer men! Anyway, can we talk about something else? I grabbed burgers tonight and have an extra one if you want to stay for a bite."

Completely ignoring Colin, Jessica blurted out, "OMG! That's right! I should have asked her about her wedding!"

"Her wedding?" Colin wasn't sure he'd heard right. "You mean her sister's wedding?"

"No, her wedding," Jessica lit up, almost as if the information she possessed had some sort of magical powers. "I saw her in Fatima's trying on wedding dresses today! She was there with her mom and her sister. She's getting married to that guy Phillip! She looked absolutely gorgeous! Oh! I'm so bummed I didn't ask her about it, or even just congratulate her!"

Colin stood quietly, trying to look as if the wind hadn't

just been knocked out of him. Christ, what else could happen this evening? He felt dizzy. Sam was getting married? When did this happen? She'd hardly mentioned anything about Phillip tonight, never mind that she was engaged. Did his mom know and just not tell him? He was trying to process everything without looking like an idiot in front of Jessica. What the fuck? Sam was marrying the millionaire from New York? It became clear in that moment that he had truly lost her. He'd always known he had, but this just confirmed it. He needed to admit to himself that he'd been holding out hope that she had delayed getting married for the same reason he had.

Without even realizing Colin had gotten very quiet, Jessica stood up from her stool and grabbed her phone again. "Crap, I can't post anything about the wedding, right? She'd probably kill me. I haven't seen anything about it online. Well, I guess it really doesn't matter anyway. I'll have plenty of time to congratulate her at Sarah's wedding and get some juicy details."

Colin looked at Jessica with a blank stare in his eyes. He knew he needed to say something, or Jessica might pick up on the fact that he'd been completely blind-sided by that information, information that had left him feeling like he would to pass out. He knew that they had both moved on, but this was definite confirmation that she had.

"Yeah, we can congratulate her then," Colin said.

14

S am stared at Sarah, shocked, "Phillip is here?"

"Yup. He's at mom and dad's. He literally just showed up. He didn't tell you he was coming?" Sarah asked.

Sam shook her head, "No. I didn't have any texts or calls from him today. That's so unlike him."

"I wasn't sure what to do, so I just told him you were visiting a friend. He was fine with that, I mean, he didn't ask any questions," Sarah continued. "You didn't tell me just how cute he is in person! He's got a total NYC vibe, showed up in a suit. He's much more attractive than his pictures online. And taller, much taller than I expected," Sarah gushed.

Sam was completely confused by this news. It was only Wednesday. He wasn't due until tomorrow night or even Friday morning. Phillip never came early to anything, and he had never surprised her like this before. He was a stickler for schedules and his work.

"You OK?" Sarah asked. "You look a little distracted. I thought you would be excited."

"No. It's OK," Sam said, trying to collect herself. "I'm just surprised Phillip is here already." Sam looked straight ahead at the road as Sarah drove, trying to piece together her feelings about the visit with Colin and the fact that Phillip was here in Barrington. All of this information was messing with her mind.

Sensing that something was wrong, Sarah immediately felt badly about mentioning Phillip so abruptly. She wasn't sure what to say next, but knew she needed to ask about Colin. Sam had been nervous to see him, and she also knew Colin well enough to know he had probably been just as nervous himself. "I'm sorry I dumped that on you so quickly. How did things go with Colin? Were you able to hash everything out?"

"I don't know if we necessarily hashed everything out in that short amount of time. His girlfriend showed up, but we had a good talk."

What else could she say? Her mind was swirling with everything from her conversation with Colin, and now she was trying to piece that together with the fact that Phillip had arrived.

"Can I ask you something?" Sam asked Sarah.

"Sure, what?"

"When Colin came back from New York, did he ever reach out to you, or talk to Mom or Dad?"

"Oh, it was a long time ago, but I don't think I remember him talking to Mom or Dad. I do know that when he came back he looked miserable and he kept a low profile. He avoided me for awhile, and Sasha and Susan. I don't remember seeing him much. I didn't talk much about Colin to you because I knew you were hurting but, believe me, he seemed barely like his old self. He was a shell of a human being for a long time."

"Tonight, he told me he left New York *for* me. He told me he was miserable there. He was worried that if he told me the truth, I would have left with him and given everything up," Sam said.

Realizing that her sister, sitting perfectly still and not looking at her, was in a crisis, Sarah pulled into the Barrington Police Cove parking lot that overlooked Narragansett Bay. Once parked, she looked at her sister, seeing her eyes well up with tears.

"Oh, Sam, don't cry," Sarah said.

"I can't help it. Funny thing is, I never cry. Ever. But when it comes to Colin Dasher, I'm a mess. It's always been this way with him."

Sarah grabbed Sam's hand, took a breath and asked, "Would you have?"

"Would I have what?" asked Sam.

"Would you have left? If he'd told you he was miserable in New York, would you have given up your classes and internship and dreams and come back to Barrington?"

Sam sat in silence for a good 30 seconds. Her mind was blank. There's no way today she could know the true answer to this question. Her life had turned out amazing. She was at the top of her game. She was doing exactly what she set out to do and had exceeded all of her wildest dreams. She'd always wanted to be as big as Donna Karan and Tory Burch and now she was. It was a dream come true.

"I don't know, Sarah, I really don't know. I was never given the choice to make."

"Does it make it any easier for you to know that he never meant to hurt you?" asked Sarah quietly.

"Yes, it does, in a way. I know now that he actually thought he was doing something good for me. He was worried that if he stayed, I would know how miserable he really was and that it would've affected me."

"I think he was right, Sam. Listen, I know you better than anyone, and I'm telling you right now, it would have affected you. You loved Colin, you are kind and good, and I think if you had realized the depth of his feelings, you would have done something. You would've left."

"I just wish he had told me!" Sam blurted out. "We could at least have talked about it. We could have done the distance thing. There were options. Life could have, and would have, been different right now."

"You can't really know that, Sam. He might have stayed just to make you happy and that would have eaten you up alive."

"I know, Sarah, but I never had the opportunity to work out something for the two of us. Do you see what I mean? He took every option off the table."

"And, because of what happened, you worked your ass off. You poured that hurt and anger into a passion for success. It kicked you into high gear, and you know that!"

She couldn't fool her sister. Sam nodded her head, knowing her sister was right. The second Colin told her he was leaving New York, with no explanation at all, just that he was leaving and that it was over, something inside of her shifted. She remembered saying to herself, "I'll make him pay." She *wanted* Colin to be ridden with guilt and hurt for the rest of his life. She wanted him to feel the pain that she felt the moment he left. She wanted his heart to break into a million pieces. She wanted him to pay, and the only way she could get that kind of redemption was to become successful, so that wherever he went, he'd be reminded of what he had given up.

Sam had just never known that Colin had actually felt

all those feelings. He had watched her succeed and he came back here to build his own life, which he knew would have to be without her.

"So where do you guys go from here?" Sarah asked.

Sam looked out at the water, watching the sailboats in the evening light. "There really isn't anywhere *for* us to go. I'm glad he told me the truth about leaving, and I'm glad that he heard me out, too. I just wish he'd told me this ten years ago, but you can't go back in life, only forward."

"And you know what, Sam? He's built a good life for himself here. He has a beautiful home. He's got a great job at the school. He gets to work with Cole and his dad. Everyone in town loves him. He's a good guy."

"How come nobody said anything about him working at the high school?"

"Why would any of us think to tell you?" Sarah asked.

Sam shrugged her shoulders, "You're right. It just surprised me. Thinking about it, I'm sure he's great with those kids."

"I'm just glad that you actually did go and talk to him. You've held onto so much, for so many years. Just try to let it go now. He loved you. And what you're saying is that he loved you so much that he did what he thought was the best thing for *you*," Sarah said. "That's pretty amazing when you think about it."

Sam sat there nodding as Sarah gave her a little sisterly pep talk.

"I'm not saying it was smart. Men can be so stupid sometimes and need a kick in the ass, but it's not like he grew up with sisters. He's a guy's guy, and you've always known that about him."

"I know," Sam said, thinking about the boy she had

loved. "He's a hometown boy, not a city boy. And I knew it all those years ago."

"Does this change anything for you?" Sarah asked.

"Like what?" asked Sam, knowing what Sarah meant, but not wanting to fully acknowledge it.

"Oh, come on, you can't fool me," Sarah said, reading Sam's mind, "I meant, does it change how you feel about him? Now that you know, does it change anything for you?"

Sam knew the answer to that question without even having to think about it. Her heartfelt it. Her gut felt it. God, even her head felt it, but she knew none of that mattered. They had both moved on. Deep down she'd always known Colin had been her soul mate, but they lost out on that fairy tale ending. A long time ago, she had come to terms with the fact that her happily ever after wouldn't be with him. Seeing him with someone else, she knew it was the same for him, too. As crazy as it sounds, they couldn't deny the attraction and chemistry between them. She had wanted Colin to kiss her so badly when they were standing in his kitchen. Being so close to his face, she thought she would lose herself right there in front of him. His energy near her had always driven her crazy. He had smelled so good and looked so handsome. She had wanted to grab his face in her hands and plant her lips right on top of his. She had wanted to feel close to him again, and she couldn't deny that. But being close to him again was like playing with fire.

Jessica couldn't have come at a more perfect time, and it really had been like the universe saying to them: *It's not supposed to happen. You've both moved on.*

"Well, let me put it this way. I'm just glad that Colin and I have found a way to be open and civil with one another. It will certainly make my being in Barrington a lot easier for both of us and everyone else." Looking at her watch, Sam added, "Maybe we should get going."

As they pulled up to the McKay house, Sam saw Phillip standing outside with her father. Phillip was dressed in a three-piece navy suit with brown leather loafers. He looked like a fish out of water as her father walked him around the yard, pointing to various things in the garden. Phillip had never done any physical labor in his life. If anything needed fixing at his apartment, even a burned out light bulb, he called the building manager. He wasn't someone who could get down and dirty with garden work or home renovations. She smiled, though, as she saw him engaged with her dad. She could tell he was interested in talking with her dad, regardless of what it was about. She appreciated that he was trying his best to get to know him.

Sam and Sarah stepped out of the car as Sam called over to them, "Dad! I hope you're not boring Phillip to death with house talk!"

"Samantha!" Phillip said aloud, obviously excited to see her.

Sarah gave her dad a big hug and then found an excuse to take Phillip in the house so Sam and Phillip could have a moment alone.

Phillip walked over to Sam and gave her a big hug and placed a gentle, yet sweet kiss on her lips. Phillip always smelled so good. It didn't matter the time of day, or where they were, he always smelled good. Funny to say, but he always smelled rich. Not that it mattered, but it was the best way for Sam to describe how he smelled. He just smelled rich.

"What are you doing here early? I wasn't expecting you until tomorrow or Friday."

"I thought I'd surprise you. I know you don't often get

the chance to come home, although I don't know why, it's lovely here," Phillip said. "I've never spent any time in Rhode Island. This town is beautiful and so quaint. I can't believe this is where you grew up. You're such a City girl and this is the polar opposite."

"I can't believe you surprised me. It's so unlike you," answered Sam.

"I hope I didn't mess up any of your plans."

"No, not at all. Everyone was excited to meet you. I'm happy you'll be here for all the wedding festivities."

"Your mom is insisting we stay here," Phillip whispered in her ear. "I'm fine with it if you are. It's like staying in a New England B&B."

Sam smiled up at him. "We don't have to if you don't want to. I know you like your own space."

"I just don't want to insult her. She seems so excited to have you here. I had the chance to have some time with everyone while you were out. Honestly, your family is great. Your mom reminds me a lot of you."

Sam smiled at Phillip's comment. She loved hearing that. "Why don't we stay here tonight and tomorrow, but get a hotel for Friday and Saturday nights. Deal?" suggested Sam.

Phillip smiled at her and kissed her again on her lips. They definitely had chemistry. It wasn't off the charts, the take off your clothes, take me on the kitchen counter, I need you every second kind of chemistry, but it was good chemistry. The kind Sam could have forever with him. She'd had the other kind of chemistry with Colin, but that hadn't worked out.

"OK, so you've already met everyone," Sam said.

"I think so. I've met your parents and your three sisters,"

Phillip smiled. "Is there anyone else? They were the ones here when I arrived."

"That's everyone, yes. Sarah thinks you're cute," Sam smiled up at him as she grabbed his hand and led him into the house.

"Oh, yeah," Phillip smiled back. "Cute is a good thing, right? What else did she say?"

"That's been it so far, but be warned, the interrogation is just beginning from the McKay family. You'd better get ready."

"Everything here been OK so far?" Phillip asked with concern in his voice for Sam. "They said you were meeting up with someone, but everyone seemed a little secretive about it."

Sam smiled at Phillip, "Yes, everything's fine. I just saw an old friend."

Sam's heart ached a little as she voiced her explanation to Phillip, but really, what else was there to say? The past was in the past, and it wasn't worth getting into.

She was with Phillip and Colin was with Jessica.

After all, at the end of the day, Colin really was just an old friend. She just wasn't prepared for how much it hurt to admit that to herself, and say it to Phillip.

15

Sam had met Phillip for the very first time over a year ago. She'd certainly known who he was, not many people in New York didn't. The McKnight name was synonymous with publishing, power and influence. There was no denying that. The family fortune had started with Phillip's great-grandfather over one hundred years ago, right in the heart of New York. He had wanted to publish books and he didn't stop until that dream became a reality. But it was Phillip's grandfather, and later, his own father who had taken McKnight Publishing to become the global influencer it was today. The "little" publishing house now had offices all around the world, and was a multi-million dollar business. Being published by McKnight was a very big deal.

Phillip was in line to take over the company, but he didn't want that life. He wanted something different. He'd studied international business at Wharton and became enamored with the world of finance. He wanted to accumulate his own wealth. He loved analyzing numbers and coming up with different financial strategies. He loved the global nature of his work, and helping businesses make money was fun for him. The family business was not his raison d'être. His father wasn't keen on his decision to walk away from the world of publishing, but he didn't want his son to be unhappy. Thankfully, Phillip had two younger brothers who were happy to take the reigns and work side-by-side with their father. Even at the age of 75, Phillip's father still reported for work every single day. As much as Phillip loved his father, he knew working for his father would have put a huge strain on their relationship. He was happy doing what he wanted to do, building his own company, yet still being part of the McKnight Dynasty.

When Sam had first heard that Phillip McKnight was going to help with a licensing deal for Samantha K, she was confused as to why something like fashion would even be a blip on his radar. Little did she know that Phillip had had his eye on her for some time and saw this as his chance to finally get to know the girl behind the name. He'd been impressed with her keen sense of business and knack for knowing and predicting upcoming trends. Everything he heard about her was confirmed on their first meeting. He knew immediately he wanted Samantha McKay. She was as beautiful as she was smart, and both had attracted him to her immensely.

Sam didn't feel the attraction to Phillip quite as quickly as he had. In New York, being around wealthy, good-looking finance guys was not a big deal. They all thought they were top dogs, and she didn't want to think about dealing with their egos. Her only interest in Phillip was to have him help her cinch the deal for Samantha K, and that was it. But as she got to know Phillip more and more, she started to see a different side of him. He was a master negotiator and never backed down, but he was also kind and empathetic. He was no Wall Street shark. She began to pick up on that from the very beginning. He was nice to her staff and knew all their names. He was considerate about her time. He would always treat everyone in their meetings to coffee, lunch or dinner - depending upon the time of day. It was things like his simple generosity that made Sam really enjoy being around Phillip.

After one late night meeting, as they were rounding up the final negotiation, Phillip asked Sam out for a drink. She was actually surprised by the invitation. She knew Phillip wasn't seeing anyone, nor was he married, but he *was* Phillip McKnight. She kind of thought that he would have been more interested in dating someone from one of the old-school New York families, not a freshly minted, self-made millionaire. Even though Sam was well off and known in the world of fashion, she didn't think they were evenly matched.

Sam had accepted the invitation for a drink, not quite sure what to make of it, but was curious to get to know him a little better. Sam wasn't looking for a steady boyfriend or a husband. She'd sworn off that idea a long before. Over the years, she had had on and off boyfriends and the occasional blind date, but nothing long term, and nothing too serious. She worked so much that it was tough to be serious about anything other than her business. Work had been her number one priority, not finding love.

As she sat across from Phillip on their first date, she found herself drawn to him in a business kind of way. He was so smart and focused on his business life. They shared the same kind of passion for business in general. She also realized that Phillip was handsome in a whole-some, classic kind of way. She hadn't really noticed it before, because it didn't matter much, but he *was* cute. He was a bit over six feet tall, short brown hair, brown eyes and a long, narrow face. He didn't smile a lot, but when he did, it lit up his face. Sam remembered thinking on their first date that he resembled David Schwimmer from his days on "Friends."

"How is a girl like you still single?" Phillip had asked her as they sat in a quiet, up-scale wine bar.

Sam simply smiled and said, "I work too much, and right now I'm focused on my career."

Phillip beamed at her answer and said, "Well, I think I've met my match."

That was kind of it for the two of them. They enjoyed one another and built their relationship on mutual respect and a commitment to succeed. Work came first, they knew that about each other and were comfortable with it. They spent two or three nights together during the week and time together on the weekends. Sam had Phillip pegged as an art gallery opening, symphony-going type of guy, but he preferred staying in, watching a movie or cooking a meal together. He wasn't what Sam had originally thought and that really attracted him to her more and more. They'd been together now for a year, so things were good and moving along steadily. Sam had already met the McKnight family and they all got along beautifully. Mrs. McKnight was a fan of Sam's clothing, so that had been an easy way to bond with his mother when they first met.

SAM WATCHED as Phillip began unpacking a few of his shirts from his suitcase, "How many shirts did you bring? We're only staying a few days," she laughed.

"Oh, you know me, I like options. Although with all this pink in the bedroom, I kind of don't know where to look or turn," Phillip joked.

Sam laughed out loud, "I mean, can you imagine? How crazy is this? Did you see the posters and the CDs?"

"I'm kind of taking it all in as I go," Phillip said, looking around. "It's cute though, it's like seeing you through a whole new lens."

Sam smiled and went over to kiss him.

As she pulled away, Phillip asked, "I never had a chance to ask what you're wearing at the wedding. I wanted to make sure we coordinated."

"Always thinking, aren't you?" Sam said and went over to kiss Phillip again.

"I have to say, I missed you this week," Phillip said and wrapped his arms around her waist and looked down into her eyes.

"You missed me? I don't think you've ever told me that before."

"Really?" Phillip smiled. "What can I say? I guess I can tell when you're not in the City."

Their relationship wasn't the over the top touchy-feel kind, they were very conservative on the PDA front, but their love-life worked. Phillip was up for sex every time they were together, which was fine with Sam because it was nice having a man want her so badly. He wasn't too adventurous in the bedroom, but it was good, and they were both always satisfied. Phillip reached down to kiss Sam and, as he pulled her close, she could feel the bulge in his pants. She looked up at him and smiled, "Really?"

"I told you, I missed you," Phillip said, intensifying his kiss. "The second you got out of the car tonight, I've been thinking about getting you into bed."

Sam smiled. She wasn't used to this kind of Phillip. It was going to bum Phillip out, but Sam didn't feel like having sex, at least not here in her bedroom, at home. Not with her parents right downstairs. She knew they'd have plenty of time at the hotel on Friday. Sam started to push Phillip away a little, "Phillip, my parents are right downstairs. We can't do this right now."

"Maybe we should check into that hotel after all," Phillip whispered into her ear. "I guess it is a little weird having sex in your childhood bedroom, which I can't believe is still set up. You know my parents packed up mine the second I left."

"I know, they've kept everything here the same," Sam said, looking around again. "It's actually crazy to be back here. Even my old sketchbooks are still on the shelves over there. I'm going to bring those back with me and pop them in my office."

"So, how many boys did you sneak up here throughout the years?" Phillip laughed.

Sam had never told Phillip about Colin. He knew she had dated someone when she was younger, and that he'd broken it off and moved back home. But that was it; she'd never gotten into the details.

"Oh, believe me, not many," Sam answered.

"Not many, huh?" Phillip walked to the window and looked out onto the street. "So does that mean 1 to 5, or like more 5 to 10?"

"Honestly, the only guy who was ever here was my old high school boyfriend. He'd sneak in sometimes when my parents were out but, I swear..." Sam laughed, "They always knew."

"So you guys never got caught?"

"Never, which actually makes me wonder if we were just really good at keeping it on the down low, or if we just looked really stupid to my parents because they knew all along," Sam smiled back.

She remembered sneaking Colin into her bedroom and

always feeling this sense of exhilaration about them being alone. They would talk or do homework. They would make out or lay on her bed holding hands. They just loved being together, alone in their own space. Barrington is such a small town that even at the local beach, or out and about in town, they were never really alone.

Sam's bedroom was where they made love the first time, right after graduation. They'd been talking about it for weeks, but they were both nervous about it. Colin didn't want to hurt Sam, and Sam was terrified that her parents would find out. One night, when her parents went out to dinner and her sisters were all out, they knew they had their window of opportunity.

Sam put candles all around her bedroom and tried to make it look as pretty as she could. Colin smiled when he walked into the room and told her it looked beautiful. They were both awkward, but since they were so comfortable with each other, they just did what came naturally, even laughing and giggling. Sam had felt so safe in Colin's arms that night. He had been gentle and sweet and slow and just kind. They had experienced true love that night. Their bodies had fit together like puzzle pieces. They had both discovered and explored each other's bodies in new ways for the very first time. The sex hadn't been off the charts that first time, but it was special and memorable. Every insecurity about love making disappeared. It felt good. It felt right. It felt amazing.

Once they'd broken that barrier of love making, they never stopped. They were ravenous for each other all the time. It was like fire between them. Losing that with Colin had been hard, and she'd never found another man to make her feel the same way. As much as she and Phillip had a great sex life, it wasn't the same as it had been with Colin.

Maybe it was part of being an adult and not feeling as vulnerable as she'd felt as a teenager. She was comfortable with her body now and knew exactly what she liked and what felt good. They didn't explore or experiment with each other; it was very much the same every time. Not that it wasn't good sex, it just was always the same kind of sex.

"Well, maybe tonight when they're sleeping, we can make our own memory in your bedroom," Phillip said.

Sam just smiled, truly not knowing if she could have sex with him there.

As he continued to do a little unpacking, Sam realized he usually had someone to help him with stuff like that, so it was funny watching him do it on his own. She appreciated the fact that he was here, and that he wanted this surprise to be special. Maybe he could tell, over the last few weeks, how apprehensive she'd been about coming home. She'd never told him why, but maybe her trying to be subtle about her feelings about coming home weren't so subtle after all. Phillip really did love her, and this was how he showed her. He might not be shouting it from the rooftops in New York, or declaring "I love you" to her every single day, but that didn't mean he didn't love her. That just wasn't his way. That wasn't him.

Marriage would come along soon enough for them. It was something they'd talked about, and something they both felt was a good next step, but nothing was official yet. Trying her best to erase Colin from her mind, Sam walked over to Phillip as he was about to hang up his last shirt and grabbed his belt from behind and pulled him towards her. He looked down and smiled at the look she was giving him. He knew that look.

"Time for bed already?" he asked.

"I think it is," Sam whispered back seductively. "I just

want to thank you for coming early. You don't know how much I need to have you here."

Phillip grabbed Sam and lifted her onto her bed. She motioned him to flip onto his back and she sat on his thighs, kissing him harder and sexier than ever before. Sam began to undo the buttons on his shirt, but that was taking too long and she just yanked on the fabric, hearing a few buttons hit the floor. Phillip didn't care, he just wanted this *new* sex goddess naked in his arms.

Just as things were heating up, hotter than they'd ever been, Sam heard a knock on her door.

"Sam?" It was her mother.

Sam tried with all of her might to collect her breath. Phillip looked as if he was going to burst. He buried his head against her stomach as she answered back, "Yeah?"

"Sorry to disturb you, Honey, but your cellphone is ringing off the hook downstairs. Want me to bring it up? You left it charging on the counter."

Jesus! How did she forget her phone downstairs? It was usually attached to her hip. It was like an appendage.

Trying to calm down and compose herself she called out, "No, I'll come down and grab it. Thanks." Sam was frustrated. She was thirty years old and surely her mother had half a clue about what she might be up to in her bedroom, at bedtime, with the man in her life.

Phillip looked at Sam, maybe a little surprised at what had happened. At his parent's home, they never, in a million years, would have come up to his room late at night. But he managed to smile at Sam without saying a word.

"I'm so sorry, let me go get my phone. I hope it's not an emergency at work."

"Work" was a magic word to Phillip. He was more than ready to make wild, passionate love to Sam, but work was work, and work was important. "Yes, go see. I'll be up here, waiting for you," and he kissed on her the cheek as she threw on a robe, smoothed down her hair and left the room.

Sam walked down to the kitchen and picked up her cell-phone, realizing she had missed three calls from the same number. It was a local number, but not one she recognized, and certainly not a number she had programmed into her phone. There was no message. Looking at the time on the microwave, she knew it was almost eleven. Why would someone be calling so late? It must be some kind of emergency, so she immediately returned the call.

"Sam?" she heard a very familiar voice on the line immediately after the first ring. It was Colin. Colin had called her 3 three times.

"Colin? Is everything OK?" Sam's stomach started to turn, not quite sure why Colin would have called her three times in the last thirty minutes, especially at this time of the night.

"Well, that depends. I'm at Bluewater Bar in town and your sister is here and, let's just say, I'm not sure she should be driving home. She refuses to get in the car with me, or anyone else, and keeps insisting that I call you. I grabbed your number from her phone."

"Which sister? Sarah?"

"No. Sasha."

"Sasha's there? Is she with anyone?" Sam was confused. "She just left my parent's house a couple of hours ago."

"Seems like she had a blind date, but the guy never showed."

"She didn't say anything to me about a date tonight. Susan probably knows. Did you call her?"

"I've tried her five times. She's not picking up. I didn't want to bother Sarah with the wedding and all. I'm sitting here with Sasha. I wasn't sure what to do. I just didn't want anyone else to really see her like this, so I thought I'd better call someone. Sorry it's so late. I was about to call your dad if you hadn't picked up in a few minutes."

Sam stood biting her lip, wanting to kill Sasha, yet help her at the same time. She knew what she needed to do, she just didn't want to have to do it and see Colin again. Making a quick decision, "Thanks Colin, I'll be there in 10 minutes."

Sam hung up the call and rolled her eyes. Sasha and her stupid blind dates. When was she going to learn to just let things happen when they're supposed to happen. Now Sam needed to get her and take her home. She was thankful Colin had been there to intervene and help.

Sam walked into her bedroom and saw that Phillip was completely passed out in her bed. He had said he was exhausted. Sam tapped his shoulder and he opened his eyes ever so slightly. "What's up? Everything OK?"

"Yeah, my sister Sasha needs a ride home from the town bar. I'm just going to go get her."

Phillip started to get up, but Sam could tell he was beat.

"Phillip, you stay here and sleep. I won't be more than 20 or 30 minutes."

"You sure?" Phillip asked, feeling thankful that she offered to let him stay.

"Of course, I'm fine."

As Sam walked out of the house and got into her car to head to Bluewater, she shook her head thinking about Sasha. She was going to give her a piece of her mind for doing this, especially so close to Sarah's wedding. Not to mention having to come face to face again with Colin, and pretend it was no big deal to see him.

16

S asha was sitting with her head down on the table in a small booth in the back of Bluewater. Colin was next to her, trying to get her to drink some water. She smiled when she saw Colin next to her sister, thankful he'd been here to rescue her.

"Hey," Sam said as she approached the table.

"Hey to you," Colin smiled.

"How's the patient? She OK?" Sam asked, looking directly at her sister.

"I actually think she's sleeping right now, although how anyone could sleep in this position is beyond me," he said with a smile.

"Colin, thanks for doing this. So, what happened?"

"I don't know all the details, just what she's told me. I was here with Jessica grabbing a drink when I saw Sasha at the end of the bar, looking a little tipsy."

Hearing that he had been here with Jessica made sense, though it made her stomach turn a little. Where was Jessica? Was she still here? Was she in the bathroom? Sam didn't want to face her right now.

"Was she alone?" Sam asked.

"Well, that's the thing. I asked her if she was with anyone, and she said she had been stood up by a blind date. It was only about 9:30pm, and she really wasn't too bad at that point. I mean, she couldn't have driven home, but she wasn't falling off the stool. She said she was OK, so I went back to Jess and about an hour later, with a couple more drinks in her, she seemed out of it."

"Oh, man. I wish she would just stay off those dating apps. Thank you for calling me, I appreciate it. I feel bad she ruined the night for you."

"Oh, no worries. Jessica had to get home, but I didn't want to leave Sasha here by herself, so I stayed with her until I was able to get in touch with someone," Colin said.

"Do you mind helping me get her to my car?" Sam asked.

"No problem. She's like a wet noodle right now. Just getting her over here was a bit of a challenge—even for me." Colin laughed. "I think she wanted to kill me when I kept telling her to drink more water. She kept telling me to shut up!"

"Oh, my God. That sounds just like Sasha," Sam said as she helped Colin get her sister on her feet.

Sasha was not helpful as they half carried, half walked her to Sam's car. She kept moaning and asking them where they were going, but they kept her moving, knowing that she needed to get home. Not many people were at Bluewater on a Wednesday night, so that was good. At least there wouldn't be many people talking about it the next day. As soon as Sasha was safely buckled into Sam's car, she immediately fell asleep. They shut the car door and then it was just the two of them standing there in the quiet, dark parking lot.

Sam and Colin's eyes locked and they just stared at each other. The warmth in their eyes, the love in their eyes was, even after all these years, still there. She could see it. He could see it. But neither of them dared acknowledge it.

"Thank you so much," Sam said.

"Anytime. You know I love your sister, even though she can be a pain in the ass."

"Phillip arrived tonight," Sam said suddenly. She didn't know why, she just blurted it out.

Colin stood silent, unprepared to hear that news. He nodded his head and looked down for a few seconds, feeling the blow to his heart. It hurt more than he thought, but he couldn't show her how he was feeling. "Well, I look forward to meeting him."

Sam stared at him, not knowing what to say next. She wished he would say or do something. Scream. Grab her and kiss her. Ridiculous though it may be, she wanted some sort of sign that he still cared, still wanted her, still loved her.

"Colin, I'm sorry I blurted that out. I don't know why," Sam whispered while looking directly into his eyes. She wanted to reach out and hold him tight. She missed his arms around her, the safest and most secure place in the world.

Colin stood still, looking at the woman he had loved the most in this world. All these years apart and he still felt that pull to her, he still felt immense love for her. Their connection and bond hadn't burned out nor faded. He actually wanted her more now than ever. He didn't care about her being in New York, or her fame or money, he just wanted her. All of her.

Standing there, in the dark, he knew it would be a mistake and he knew that he would regret it after he did it, but he didn't care. The look in her eyes made him feel like it was OK. Colin slowly took one step towards Sam, grabbed her in his arms and placed his lips on hers. He wasn't certain what she'd do, but when he felt her arms go around his neck and tighten, pulling him closer, he thought his heart would burst. Her lips parted and before he knew, their tongues were intertwined, their passion for each other as strong and intense as it had ever been.

In the distance, a car alarm rang out, waking them from the deepest and sweetest dream ever. As they pulled away, they locked eyes with each other, just standing there, staring at each other.

"Oh, wow, what just happened?" Sam asked, sounding bewildered and almost drunk, even though there wasn't an ounce of alcohol in her system.

"Sam, I'm so sorry. I don't know. I just got caught up in the moment, being here, alone with you."

In reply, Sam grabbed Colin and thrust her arms around his neck, searching for his lips, and when finding them, started to devour him all over again. Her tongue swirled around his, searching for more with each passing second. They were completely lost in each other, making up for lost time. Kissing felt familiar and right and normal. Were they really doing this right here in an open parking lot behind Bluewater? Anyone could walk out at any time and see them, but they didn't care. They were in each other's worlds for that moment, and that's all that mattered.

This time, a horn honking a few blocks over broke their kiss. They backed away from each other slowly and stared at each other, bewildered as to what just had happened.

"Did we just do that?" Sam asked, touching her lips, then quickly glancing into her car to make sure Sasha was still sleeping in the backseat and not enjoying the view.

"I'm sorry, Sam. I couldn't help it. You look so beautiful and I just got caught in the moment," Colin tried to explain. "But I know one thing-- it sure felt good."

"You still think I'm beautiful?" Sam asked quickly.

"Samantha McCay is asking ME if I think she's still beautiful? Are you kidding me?" Colin laughed.

"Yeah, I guess I'm asking you that," feeling that same vulnerability of being sixteen years old again.

"Sam, I've always thought you were beautiful, you know that. I didn't think it possible, but you're more beautiful now than ever before."

Colin couldn't believe that Sam really asked him if he thought she was beautiful. Here she was, this wildly successful designer with a business that anyone would kill for, with men probably fawning all over her all the time, and she wanted to know if HE thought she was beautiful?

"It's been a long time since someone has really told me that, like *really* told me that, without any other agenda. Even standing here in front of you, without a trace of makeup, my hair in a bun, in a t-shirt and jeans, it feels kind of strange."

"I bet those jeans cost more than my car!" Colin joked.

Sam looked down at her jeans and laughed, "Yeah, probably!"

"So what do we do now?" Colin asked. It was the dreaded question, one that he knew he needed to ask.

"I have no idea," Sam said quietly. "Maybe in some weird way, we just needed to get this out of our systems. We left on such bad terms all those years ago, and I held onto so much hurt and anger for so long. But tonight, after talking to you and hearing you out, I know you never meant to hurt me. I truly, really know that." Sam moved toward Colin and held his hand and placed it on her heart. "You've always had a piece of my heart, Colin. I just didn't want to admit it."

"And now?" Colin asked.

"I mean, what can we do...?" Sam felt her heart pounding in her chest and she turned her head to look away from Colin. "I'm with Phillip, and you're with Jessica. I'm in New York and you're here in Rhode Island. I have commitments and my company to run." Sam's voice started to crack and she knew she was going to start crying. "I'm sorry, Colin, I wish things were different."

Colin looked up at the sky and raked his hands through his hair, "Fuck!" he yelled. "Why is life so freaking complicated sometimes?"

"Don't, Colin," Sam said. "Don't make it harder." This time tears were actually streaming down Sam's cheeks. She didn't care, she just needed Colin to know that, deep down, she would always love him, and she always had.

"And I know now, more than ever, that I'll never be the person you're meant to be with," Colin replied, looking up at the stars, trying hard not to cry.

"What do you mean by that?" Sam asked.

Composing himself and trying to be honest, he said, "Oh, man... because I set up roots here. I moved back. I created a life around my family and friends. I'm the opposite of City. I'm a hometown boy. I'm a jeans and t-shirt, not a 3-piece suit guy. And, quite honestly, I know you deserve that much more than a regular guy like me."

Sam was shocked to hear him say this, and maybe a little bit mad, "You think that it matters to me that you're not a City guy walking around in a 3-piece suit?"

"I just mean that you deserve to be married to someone like Phillip. Someone who can hold a candle to you in your world," he explained.

"I can't believe you're saying this," wiping a tear from her cheek and looking into his eyes. "I would have loved to have had you right by my side. I wouldn't have cared if you were a waiter or a CEO. It wouldn't have mattered because we would've been together."

Colin looked away. In the moonlight, Sam could have sworn she saw Colin's eyes glisten with tears. She'd wanted that kiss as much as he had. To be in his arms again felt like home, felt like coming home to something so comfortable and familiar.

After a few moments, Sam couldn't stand in silence any longer. "Colin, say something... please."

At that very moment, headlights came from around the corner and a car pulled into the parking lot. Sam and Colin quickly distanced themselves from each other, almost like they were afraid to get caught just standing next to each other. Colin recognized the car immediately. It was Cole's white Jeep Cherokee. Cole pulled up next to them and rolled down his window.

"Hey, Sammy!" Cole smiled.

The only person on the planet to call her Sammy was Cole. As much as Sam had hated it back when she was younger, it made her smile now. She needed something to make her smile because her insides were mush and she didn't know what on earth she could do to fix it.

"Hi Cole," Sam said and went over to give him a kiss on the cheek. "It's been awhile."

"Well, maybe for you but, believe it or not, I *follow* the fashion news. I know what's going on, my friend."

Sam smirked, "You watch fashion television?"

"Sure do, ask me anything," Cole joked. And that made Sam laugh out loud at the idea of Cole in a high fashion atelier.

Cole looked over at Colin with a look of annoyance, "Where the hell have you been? I've been calling your phone non-stop. I wasn't sure if you were up for a late night beer. I finally called Bluewater and they said you'd left half an hour ago and didn't know where you had gone. I figured I'd stop by and check it out."

Colin looked over at Cole, "Sorry I missed you, I must've left my phone back at the bar. I was helping Sam get Sasha into the car because she had had a little too much to drink tonight. I called Sam to make sure she got her home."

"What? Sasha on a bender? That's a first. I don't think I've ever actually seen her drunk," Cole said. "Who was she with?"

"No one, actually," Sam said, "she got stood up by someone. I guess she was upset and was drinking to drown her sorrows. I don't think I've ever seen her drunk either, but feast your eyes on my little sister passed out in the backseat of the car." Sam pointed to her car where Sasha was flaked out, but beginning to stir a bit.

"Oh, crap! She's starting to wake up. I'd better get her to our parent's house. I don't have a key to her place. She's going to have quite the hangover tomorrow if I don't get some water and some Advil or Tylenol into her."

"Do you need help getting her home? It took both of us to get her into the car," Colin asked.

"No, I'll be fine, but thank you."

Sam looked at Cole, "It was good seeing you, Cole. You haven't changed one little bit."

"I'm hoping that's a good thing," Cole smiled back at Sam. "As long as I still look the same, that's all I care about!"

"Well, let me put your mind at ease, then. You'll be glad to know that you look exactly like the chick magnet you were back in high school," Sam laughed, knowing Cole would probably be relieved to hear this, adding, "I guess I'll see you Saturday night at the wedding?"

"I'll be there with bells on, looking for all the single chicks!"

"Oh, my God, Cole, you never change. Anyway, I'm glad you are coming. Hope you'll save me a dance," Sam smiled.

"And Colin, I'll see you Saturday night, too. Thanks again for helping Sasha tonight."

"No problem, glad I was here to help."

Then followed an awkward moment when she didn't know what to do, and Colin looked just as confused. He opened the car door for her, and waved good-bye as she pulled out of the lot.

And that was that. This was how they were leaving things tonight. What an emotional roller coaster she'd been on over the past several hours. Sam never thought in a million years that she would've ended up in Colin's arms, kissing him, not just once, but twice. Their passion was still there. She'd felt it from her head to her toes. She felt the zing. She felt those butterflies. She felt it all.

Pulling into her parent's driveway, Sam realized that Sasha was just starting to come around, but she was still very groggy and dizzy. At least she could walk.

"Thank you, Sam," Sasha whispered. "I don't know how to thank you enough for coming to get me."

"Shhh...." Sam whispered to her sister. "I don't want to wake Mom and Dad. I don't have keys to your house, so I brought you back here."

"That's OK, I just need to lay down so I can fall asleep. My head is killing me and I feel like I'm going to throw up."

"I'll help you to the couch," Sam whispered. "Then I'll get you some water and a bowl just in case you get sick."

"Oh, my God, thank you," Sasha said. "I'm telling you, I must've drunk a bucket of Cosmos, because I swear I've been hallucinating tonight."

"What do you mean," Sam asked, concerned for her sister.

"I could have sworn I saw you and Colin making out. How ridiculous is that?" Sasha mumbled as she crashed onto the couch.

17

Colin and Cole sat next to each other at the Bluewater bar, each sipping a bottle of Sam Adams. Even at thirty years of age, they barely looked older than twenty-one. Time had treated them well, and since they were both active and worked out consistently, their bodies looked just as good as their faces. Putting it simply, people were shocked that the Dasher twins were still single.

"I can't believe you kissed her, Dude," Cole exclaimed. "Holy shit, that took balls! That took fucking HORSE balls!"

Colin turned to Cole, "Will you freaking keep it down? There are eyes and ears everywhere in here."

"What were you thinking?" Cole asked, incredulous at the news.

Colin took a sip of his beer. "I don't know. I guess I wasn't thinking."

"Damn right you weren't thinking. In case you've forgotten, she's dating Phillip fucking McKnight." And to stress it even further, Cole slowly said his name again, "Phillip McKnight."

"Actually, I've got news for you. She's *engaged* to Phillip McKnight. "

"What? Fuck, are you kidding me? They're engaged?" Cole asked.

"Cole. For God's sake, keep it down."

"Oh, come on. There are not many people in here at this time of the night. Maybe, like, five other people, and they don't care about you and Sam." Cole took a sip from his beer and laughed out loud. "Man, she's engaged! I didn't know that."

"Yeah, apparently Jessica saw her trying on wedding dresses at Fatima's," Colin answered.

"So, Jessica was the one who told you Sam was engaged?"

Colin nodded. "She wanted to post it online, but I told her not to. I hope she listened. You know her and her social media accounts. Every detail of her life gets documented."

"That's rough, man, I'm sorry."

"The stupid thing is, I just know that we both felt something. After telling her what happened, and how everything went down with me, it was like the ice began breaking. She started to thaw and I could actually see her loosen up."

"Shit, man, I told you that should've told her all this years ago."

"I know, I know, but I was just a kid and I didn't know how she'd react. I was trying to be the 'big guy.' But I finally had my chance today, and I took it."

"And you told her *everything*? Not just why you left in the first place, but the whole story?"

Colin sat there for a second before answering, "Yeah, pretty much." He didn't want to hear Cole's reaction if he admitted he hadn't told her everything. "I think she was mad that I hadn't said anything before. But, I mean...what could she say? I still love you? I need you? I would have given up everything if I'd known?"

"Fuck man, this is your problem. You did the thinking for her. You never gave her the chance to say what *she* thought," Cole lamented.

"Come on. That's not true and you know it."

"Dude, it *is* true. Anyway, you've been pining for her all these years. You should have just told her you still love her and see what happened."

"I don't know if I still love her," Colin said, knowing he was telling a barefaced lie. He did love her. He'd always loved her. He'd never stopped, and seeing her again just underscored these feelings. Touching her and kissing her was as if he'd found a part of himself that had been lost. And when she responded in the same way, he thought he would burst.

"Well, if you want my advice, you'd better figure it out pretty damned quick because she's leaving in a few days," Cole said, totally frustrated with his brother. For somebody so smart and intuitive, he could be a complete dumbass sometimes.

"What the hell am I supposed to do? Declare my undying love? Break up her engagement? No way I could do that," Colin retorted. "And I've got Jessica to think of. Who knows where that might go?"

"Colin, listen to me. You told me she kissed you back. To me, this is a woman who is not head over heels in love with her fiancé. Say what you want, but come on, I don't think you would want your fiancé kissing her ex-boyfriend?"

Colin shook his head, "No, you're right. I wouldn't, and now I feel like a complete asshole for starting this. I'm not that kind of guy."

"Oh, for Christ's sake, stop with the holier than thou attitude. Everyone *knows* you're not that guy," Cole said. "But, I can tell you, a lot of people are sure as hell wondering what, if anything, will happen now that she is in town for more than two days."

"Look, what other people think couldn't matter less to me. The best thing I can do is stay out of the way, let her go back to New York and marry the zillionaire boyfriend. I can't give her what he can give her. Not even close."

Cole waved to the bartender to bring them another round of beers. What the hell was wrong with his brother? He couldn't believe it. He was perhaps getting a second chance with Sam and he was going to blow it? Colin had given up every relationship he'd had over the last ten years. And why? Because the girl wasn't Sam. He compared every girl to her and nobody ever measured up. How could they? Colin would never admit it, but he had self-sabotaged every relationship he had ever had. He still loved Sam and this bullshit about not thinking he deserved her? What an idiot!

Taking a deep breath, Cole looked his brother in the eyes. "I'm not exactly an expert on long-term relationships, as everyone knows but, fuck, even I know you should let Sam decide for herself. It's not up to you. Look what happened ten years ago. Do you want history to repeat itself?" Cole was working himself up and took a long pull on his beer just to make himself stop talking.

"I'm hearing you, Cole, but ten years ago Sam didn't have a fraction of what she has today. On what planet do you think she would choose a life with me over her current life and the one with Phillip McKnight?" Colin asked, beginning to feel frustrated himself.

"I don't know why you think it's just up to you," Cole shook his head. "You didn't do any explaining ten years ago; you just up and left. Now that she knows *why* you made the decision you made, my advice to you, bro, is don't make the same mistake twice. She has a right to know exactly how you feel. Simple. You love her. If she doesn't feel the same way, then so be it. At least you'll know."

"She had the opportunity to come home all those years ago, too," Colin said.

"I'm calling bullshit!" Cole shouted. A few people in the bar turned around to see what was going on with the Dasher brothers. "Sorry, everyone, my brother's driving me crazy over here."

Cole looked at Colin and felt a little sad for his brother. "Look, I know you did what you thought was best, but, in all reality - you set her up to not come back. Actually, you told her not to come after you. So what the hell was she supposed to do?"

Thankfully, everyone in the bar had gone back to their own conversations, and Colin didn't want to turn this discussion into a spectacle. He knew Cole only wanted the best for him, but what he was talking about was a lot easier said than done. Cole didn't get it. His chick magnet brother had never been in love - not even close. He didn't know anything about sacrificing for the one you truly loved. But Cole was right, he still loved Sam, maybe even more now than ever, and it killed him to know that he hadn't told her. He'd lost his nerve tonight and he knew he wouldn't get another chance.

"I know," Colin sighed heavily. "I totally messed that up ten years ago."

"All I'm saying is, tell her exactly how you feel. Don't miss out this time around. Don't let her leave without telling her what you're feeling. I'm no love counselor, and I know I sound like a freaking crazy person, but I'm right."

"I don't know, Cole, I'll think about it."

"I know you'll do whatever you're going to do, but this is serious. Don't blow it. Don't spend the rest of your life wishing you had taken that second chance."

Colin didn't say a word.

"So," Cole asked, "when you told her that you went back to New York a year later?" He took the last sip of his beer and placed the empty bottle on the bar. "What was her reaction? Did she say anything about it?"

"No, not really," Colin replied, not looking his brother in the eye, afraid he would know the truth.

Colin didn't like lying to his brother, but he didn't know what else to say right now. He hadn't had the nerve to tell Sam that he did go back a year later, having spent the worst year of his life back in Rhode Island. Finally, his family had had enough. They knew he had to work something out with Sam. He got up the nerve, went back to New York to tell her he loved her and hoped she'd take him back when he showed her an engagement ring.

What he hadn't been prepared for was seeing her thrive, without him, and that had rattled him to the core. Hoping to surprise her, he returned to New York, and waited across the street from her building for her to get home. Finally, around dinnertime, he saw her...walking home hand in hand with a guy.

They were laughing and joking as if they'd known each other forever. Colin stood watching from across the street as his big surprise fell to ashes.

With only himself to blame, he flew back to Rhode Island that very night. He didn't try to contact her. He'd gotten the message loud and clear. She had moved on.

It was like being stabbed in the heart, but he'd done it to himself. He'd actually thought that Sam was as miserable as he was, and when he discovered that she wasn't, it shook him. He, himself, had broken this relationship, and it was something that could never be fixed. He finally understood this at that very moment.

That had changed everything for him, and he'd never fully recovered. Thinking back on it now, he probably should have seen a therapist. He was fucked up - he probably still was. He'd dated throughout the years, but never committed, afraid of having his heart hurt or broken again.

"She didn't say anything about it? That seems weird. You didn't ask who the guy was back then, or what she was doing with him? Remember-- we told you--it could've been something innocent..."

Colin had had enough of the inquisition and he interrupted his brother, "No, I didn't ask her, and it doesn't matter at this point."

"I hear you, bro," Cole responded, knowing when to quit.

In an attempt to put the whole discussion to bed, Colin said, "We just got caught up in the moment. I don't think anyone saw us out there in the parking lot—apart from when you showed up."

"Well, I've said my piece. You know what I think. Just don't be an ass this time around."

"Duly noted."

Cole stood up, ready to call it a night. It was well past midnight and he was tired. He and Colin couldn't be more different when it came to women.

Colin was a one-girl type of guy, but he, on the other hand, was different. Despite all the women he had dated, he'd never been in love. He'd been close once or twice, but they had never seemed like *the one*. It could be tough living in a small town where everyone knows everyone, and if you aren't dating the girl next door, you must be looking. And looking was one thing he loved to do, but once he began seeing his friends get married off, he started wishing he could find what they had--someone to make his heart stop. Cole also loved the fact that girls still fawned all over him. He knew he was good looking, and had an air of cockiness about him that girls seemed to love.

"I gotta go, too, but can I ask you something weird?" Colin asked.

"Oh yeah, what's that?" Cole asked as he laid money on the counter.

"Sam never told Phillip about me."

"OK," Cole said. "And what's so weird about that?"

"You don't find it odd?

"I don't know, I don't kiss and tell either," Cole smiled.

"We dated for a long time. I just found it weird that she didn't mention anything about me to him, that's all."

"I think you're overthinking it there," Cole said matter-of-factly. "Sam doesn't need to tell Phillip, or anybody else, *everything* about her past. You didn't tell Jessica about Sam."

Colin nodded and took money out to pay his tab, nodding his head, "I guess you're right."

"Of course I'm right. You're overthinking it. Let it go."

They walked out of the bar and headed to their cars.

"I'll see you bright and early tomorrow, right?" Cole said, as he was about to jump into his jeep.

"Yup, I'll be there around 8am. We've gotta get that Ford transmission pulled out."

"Hey, Colin, one more thing."

"Yeah, what's that?"

"If you do get the balls to tell Sam that you love her, make sure she knows that you mean it. It will mess up everything for you with Jessica, but don't go on not knowing. I, for one, as your brother, can't stand the idea." And with that, he drove out of the parking lot.

Colin watched him drive away and wondered if he would take his brother's advice.

18

S am came downstairs in the wee hours of the morning to find Sasha still passed out on the living room couch. She was definitely sleeping off that bender, and she would probably have a terrible hangover when she woke up. Sam was an early riser and was still programmed to getting up at the crack of dawn. She'd checked on Sasha a few times throughout the night, worried that she'd get sick and not have anyone to help her. She'd never seen Sasha like this before, and she was worried, but, she was sleeping like a baby right now.

Sam didn't want to awaken her just yet, but once their parents came downstairs, Sasha would be answering a lot of uncomfortable questions. She would give her another few minutes and then get her up and out of here. The McKay's were pretty relaxed with their girls, but they had zero tolerance for any of them getting drunk, especially in a local bar. Sam tried to remember who had been in the bar last night, but she hadn't recognized anyone. Hopefully, Sasha's little incident would fly under the radar.

But, right now, she had bigger worries than Sasha's hangover.

She'd lost her mind last night with Colin. She couldn't talk to Sarah; she'd be too stressed with the wedding. She was close with Sasha and Susan, but neither of them had had serious relationships, and they would be ill equipped to listen without judgment and, more importantly, to help her figure out what to do.

She was terrified that Phillip would find out someway, somehow. Not that Phillip knew anyone in town, but the guilt was eating away at her and she was worried he'd find out. The fact that she didn't regret kissing Colin confused her even more. She had no idea what to do at this point.

Should she just tell Phillip?

Should she keep it a secret from him?

Should she tell Colin she was sorry and that it had been a mistake?

Or should she tell Colin how she was feeling?

None of these options were good, and the only one that kept jumping out at her was to keep it a secret from Phillip, for now anyway.

Phillip had not been in bed this morning when she woke up. She figured he had gone out for an early morning run

"Sam?" she heard Sasha whisper. "What time is it? Oh my God, my head."

Jeez, she had almost forgotten about Sasha. Sam looked at her watch. "It's 6. How are you feeling?"

Sasha closed her eyes and put her hands on her hand. It was obvious she was hurting pretty badly. Sam hoped that she'd forgotten all about thinking she'd seen her and Colin kissing. That was the last thing she needed right now.

"Oh my God, Sam. My head is killing me," Sasha

complained. "I need some coffee and a HUGE glass of water."

"Why don't we start with the water first," Sam said. Walking into the kitchen to get a glass of water, she almost jumped when she saw Phillip sitting at the kitchen counter, ear buds in his ears, fully engrossed on his laptop. He looked up, saw Sam, and smiled.

"Hey! You're up! I wasn't sure who was an early riser around here," Phillip said, pulling out his earbuds. "I didn't want to wake anyone," he whispered, "so I figured I'd pop in my earbuds and check my emails and messages."

"What time did you get up?" Sam whispered as she gave him a hug and a kiss.

"Maybe 4:30? I'm not sure. You know me. I'm up before dawn no matter where I am. How about you? You sleep OK? I hope I didn't wake you coming down so early."

"No. Actually, I didn't even know you were down here. When you weren't in bed when I woke up I thought you might have gone for a run."

"How's Sasha doing?" Phillip whispered.

Sam actually laughed. "She's up now, but feeling it big time. I came to get her some water and start the coffee."

"Yeah, I was going to make a pot, but wasn't sure how to use your parent's machine."

Sam laughed, "What you really mean is that you don't know how to make coffee."

"Guilty as charged. Usually, Maggie does all that stuff for me."

Maggie was Phillip's personal assistant and right arm. As much as Phillip was a pro when it came to business, Maggie ran his life. She was 50-ish, single, and had devoted her life to the McKnight family. She didn't have a social life or a family and took great pride in making sure everything for the McKnight family ran like a well-oiled machine. She'd gone to work for Phillip about five years ago and had taken care of him better than anyone had ever done. She usually showed up at his apartment at 5am each morning. She'd have his coffee and breakfast ready for him by 5:30, had his daily schedule printed out and had everything ready for him to begin his day.

Phillip finished reading the message on his laptop and then looked over at Sam, who was in the process of making a pot of coffee.

Phillip laughed, "I didn't even *try* to do it on my own. Thanks for making it, Samantha."

Sam looked over at him and made a funny face, "Well, good thing I still know how to do this!"

In a couple of minutes, she had the coffee brewing and began to set out the mugs and cream and sugar. She might be a successful businesswoman, but she still knew how to do basic tasks. She prided herself on the fact that she really didn't need anyone to do much for her. At this point in her life, help with things like making coffee was purely because her time was better spent on growing her business.

Sasha walked into the kitchen looking disheveled, not the best impression, she knew. Her head was pounding and she could still see stars. She'd let being stood up hit her like a ton of bricks. Why hadn't she just gone home and drowned her sorrows in a pint of ice cream? Instead, she had just kept ordering one drink after another and, before she knew it, she was feeling pretty wasted, but not enough to stop.

"Hey, Sasha," Sam said as she finished filling a glass with water. "You need to drink this immediately, and take these," Sam advised, handing Sasha two Advils.

"Thanks, Sam. I really owe you--big time. I'm so embarrassed right now," Sasha said. "And Phillip, I'm horrified to have you see me like this. I swear I'm not normally like this. I hope you will ignore everything you see at this very minute."

Phillip smiled at Sasha, "Don't even worry about it. I think we've all been there at some point. I'm just glad Sam was there to help you. Sorry I wasn't with her. I think the air here in Barrington is magic. I was out like a light super early last night."

"Oh my God, no apologies necessary. I just feel badly that she was dragged away," Sasha responded and then continued, "thank God Colin was there last night to help me out. I can't thank him enough." She then looked at Sam and said without hesitation, "I hope he wasn't pissed at me."

The sheer mention of Colin's name sent shivers up and down Sam's spine and pure panic at the same time. She tried her best to keep it cool and not look like she was bothered at the mention of his name. "Why would Colin be pissed at you?" she asked.

"I know he was there with Jessica, and I think she got pissed when he walked over to check on me. This was all before you came, but I feel like I totally messed up his date," Sasha answered.

Phillip looked up from his laptop to listen to the sisters, "Whose Colin?" he asked innocently.

"Oh, he's Sam's ex-boyfriend."

Sam wanted to drop off the face of the earth. How could Sasha come right out and say something like that? Phillip looked up from what he was doing and glanced over to Sam, "Your ex-boyfriend? I don't think you've ever mentioned an ex-boyfriend to me before. A guy from home?" He was speaking very innocently, and in a curious tone, almost as if he had somehow managed to pull back a layer from an onion, only to discover another layer.

"You haven't told him about Colin?" Sasha asked, staring directly at Sam.

Could things get any worse? Phillip seemed unperturbed, which, he probably was. He had the self-confidence that came from being born into extreme wealth: never threatened by anyone, for any reason. Sasha might be suffering from the hangover of the century, but she should just zip it up.

Sam shot a look at Sasha, who was completely oblivious. She looked like death warmed over, and it was probably taking all her effort to just stand up.

Sam smiled at Phillip and said, "There's really nothing to tell. Colin was my high school boyfriend. He's a good guy. His parents still live across the street. He thinks of Sasha as a little sister, so I'm glad he was there to help her out."

"I want to thank him myself, and apologize if I messed up his night," answered Sasha.

"I wouldn't worry too much," Sam said to Sasha. "He didn't mention anything to me when I got there. He was just concerned about getting you home safe and sound."

"And thanks to you, I did."

Phillip was back to looking at his messages, and now seemed more interested in that than hearing about Sasha's escapades.

In an attempt to steer the conversation away from Colin, Sam asked, "What exactly happened last night? And where was Susan?"

"Susan was at home. She must have crashed early. I had set up a date with this guy from a dating app. He seemed like a good person. We had a lot in common. We'd talked a couple of times on the phone. I even confirmed with him earlier in the day, but he never showed up. No freaking texts or calls to cancel. Honestly? I'm basically writing off men forever."

"You're trying too hard. You just need to let it happen," Sam replied. "You and Susan have never been good with letting life take its course. Why do you need to push so hard to make it happen?" asked Sam.

"I don't push, Sam," Sasha responded in an annoyed tone. "Since when it is a bad thing to want to be in a relationship. Do you know how hard it is to find anyone in this town? Everyone's either taken, or I've known them since kindergarten."

Suddenly, a knock on the door caused each sister to look at each other in surprise. It was just about 6:30am. Who could be stopping by at this hour? Sam glanced at Sasha, who shrugged her shoulders.

"Maybe it's Colin coming to see how I'm doing?" Sasha suggested.

It was definitely something Colin would do, but not with Phillip here. As much as she'd love to get a look at Colin this morning, she absolutely did not want to deal with both Colin and Phillip together at this time of the day. It would be bad enough seeing them together at the wedding. Sam went to the front door and peeked outside. It wasn't Colin. It was Cole. What was he doing here?

Sam opened the door immediately, "Cole. Hi! Everything ok?" Sam asked nervously, hoping and praying Colin hadn't said anything to him about last night.

"Yeah, everything's fine," he said. "I had to stop by Mom and Dad's before heading into work, and I was just wondering how Sasha was."

Sasha? He came over to check on Sasha? This was so unlike something Cole would normally do.

"You came over to check on Sasha?" Sam asked confused.

"Yeah," Cole smiled, "I'm not *that* insensitive. I actually care about you McKay girls."

"When did that start?" Sam laughed. "What have I missed since I've been gone?"

"Oh, I'm still a royal pain in the ass. Don't you worry!"

Sasha walked into the foyer to see Cole standing there, talking to Sam, "Oh, it's just you," she said. "We didn't know who was knocking this early in the morning."

Cole laughed, "Good to see you, too, Sasha. I came over to pick up dad for work and saw the lights on in the kitchen, so I figured I'd check in on you. You were freaking gone with the wind last night," he said. "I wished I'd gotten videos or photos!"

"Yeah, thanks Cole," Sasha joked back. "Glad you got to see me at my best."

"All kidding aside, just wanted to see how you were feeling. I don't think I've ever seen you drunk in my life!"

"It's something I don't normally do, believe me. But it's actually pretty nice of you to come check on me. You want a cup of coffee?"

"Sure, I'll grab a cup with you ladies," and he walked right in, shutting the door behind him. He knew this house like he knew his parent's house. "If it makes you feel any better, nobody was around last night. The bar was pretty empty for a Wednesday."

"I'm sure you would know," Sasha pushed back. "Most of us normal folks don't hang out at bars on weekday nights."

"Well, most of us don't get stood up either," Cole retorted.

Sasha looked directly at Sam and blurted, "You told him?"

Sam's face turned red as she tried to defend herself, "I didn't tell him anything! Blame it on Colin, he's the one who called me to come get you because you told him your date had stood you up!"

Sasha rolled her eyes and started to walk back to the kitchen.

Cole looked at Sam and smiled, "Always easier to blame it on Colin."

Sam smiled back, knowing that Cole meant more than he was letting on. She knew that Cole probably knew everything about her and Colin. When Colin originally left New York, one of the first people she reached out to was Cole. As kind and sympathetic as Cole had been, she knew he didn't want to cross his brother by saying things he shouldn't.

"Come on down to the kitchen," Sam began to say, "You can meet my boyfriend Phillip, he arrived last night," Sam said.

"Ohhh. The famous Phillip is here! I wouldn't miss meeting him for the world. You think he'd lend me a million dollars?" Cole teased.

Sam slapped Cole on the arm and laughed, "Don't you even joke with him about that, Cole, or I will kill you!"

Cole looked at his phone and said, "I've got about twenty minutes." And with that, he took off towards the McKay kitchen. As Sam followed him, she worried that Colin might have told Cole about last night and their kiss. If he had, surely Cole wouldn't be stupid enough to say anything. Sam's stomach knotted as she walked into the kitchen in time to see Cole walk over to Phillip and shake his hand.

"Hey, Phillip, I'm Cole Dasher," he said.

Phillip smiled and held out his hand. You could tell just by looking at the two of them how different they were. Phillip was sitting at the kitchen counter in a white button down, khaki pants, and brown leather loafers. He had cologne on this early in the morning, even without anywhere to go. His hair was gelled into place. He was always perfectly groomed, something that Sam had just gotten used to. As much as Sam knew that her image impacted her business, she still loved to wake up on a Sunday morning and stay in her pajamas all day with her hair piled on top of her head. Phillip was the complete opposite. He'd always get groomed and dressed first thing, and joke with Sam that she acted like a college student on the weekends.

Phillip smiled and looked over to Sam for some additional information as to who Cole was. She had learned Phillip's mannerisms so well over the last year. At work, he'd usually have someone in his ear, like his assistant, feeding him quick information about someone he'd just met. In this case, he looked to Sam to do the same.

"So, Cole grew up across the street from us. His parents are still there. He happened to be at the bar last night and saw Sasha."

"Oh, wait, is this your ex-boyfriend from high school?"

Cole quickly said, "No, no, no. That's my brother, *Colin*."

"Oh, OK," Phillip said. "So you've known Samantha for a long time then."

"You could say that," Cole said. "We all grew up together, and I've known the McKay's since I was born. When I saw the lights on, I came over to check on the patient, who obviously can't hold liquor to save her life."

"Very funny, Cole," Sasha joked back. "I'm telling you, I didn't think a couple of drinks would hit me that hard. Thank God your brother was there, that's all I have to say."

"You're lucky he happened to have a date," Cole said. "He hardly ever goes out anymore."

"I thought he and Jessica were the hot new couple around town," Sasha joked back.

"Colin and Jessica?" Cole laughed. "Yeah, they're dating, I don't know if I'd call them the hot new couple though. I think she's dating Colin right now to get to Sam!"

"What!?" Sam said. "You're joking."

"I don't know, but according to my brother, Jessica seems thrilled that she's dating Samantha McKay's ex-boyfriend. You seem to be giving him some cred in the girl department, Sam. Who woulda thought that?"

Sam needed to get control of this situation. The last thing she needed was a gabfest about her. Just as she was about to try to turn the conversation to the wedding, Phillip beat her to the punch.

"How long did you two date?" Phillip asked, just seeming genuinely curious.

"Me and his brother?" Sam said, beginning to pull out breakfast things from the fridge, doing her best to sound uninterested.

"Yeah, I don't think I've ever heard you mention any ex-boyfriends. I'm excited to meet this guy that my Samantha dated so many years ago. I feel like I'm going to learn so much about you this weekend."

Sam stopped what she was doing, eyes wide open, then she turned to refill her coffee cup, even though she had barely touched it. She could feel the eyes of Cole and Sasha boring into her back, "We dated in high school, so a few years."

"A few years?" Cole butted in. "You two dated all through high school and a couple years afterwards."

At that moment, Sam wanted to kill Cole right here in the kitchen. She literally wanted to take his head and remove it from his body. This *wasn't* his story to tell. What did it matter who she dated in high school? They weren't dating *now*. She had wanted to start from scratch with Phillip. Clean and neat, with no emotional baggage. Cut and dried, and she loved it that way. It was easy and simple.

"All through high school and after?" Phillip asked, inquisitively looking at Sam.

"Um, yeah. We dated in high school and then he came to New York after high school, too."

"Well, I can't wait to meet him," Philip said. "I didn't know he went to college in New York. I love learning so much about you." Then he turned to Sasha and said, "She never shares too much."

Sam became very quiet as she looked down at her coffee. She hated talking about this, never mind in these circumstances. "He actually didn't go to school while he was in New York," she finally answered. "He waited tables while he was there."

"So he went to New York just to be with you?" Phillip asked, still not seeming to display an inkling of jealousy, just pure curiosity.

"Yup, we all thought he was crazy, but he didn't want to hear it!" Cole laughed. "Can you imagine moving to one of the most expensive cities in the world and just waiting tables? He could've done that here and pocketed so much more money."

Sasha shot Cole such a look that he finally stopped talking long enough to decipher. Cole was definitely not reading the room, and only after Sasha's shut-the-fuck-up glance did he realize that the air in the room had changed and was charged with emotion.

Sam had no option but to carry on, "Yes, he came with me and tried to make it work. We both wanted a change from our small town. We were so young and so naive. After a year or so, it just didn't work out. Colin came back home and I stayed. End of story."

"Will I get a chance to meet him at the wedding?" Philip asked. "Love to shake his hand. If he stole your heart all those years ago, he's got to be a great guy, right?" Phillip smiled at Sam in his special way. This was about as PDA as they usually got in front of people.

"Listen," said Cole, knowing he'd better leave while the leaving was good, "I've got to get going. I actually think I hear your parents coming downstairs. They sound like a herd of elephants," he laughed. "Tell them I said hello. It's almost 7am and Dad's probably wondering where the hell I am right now. Phillip, great to meet you." Cole shook hands with Phillip and said to Sasha, "Glad you're feeling better. Let me know if you want me to take care of that ass who stood you up."

Sasha smiled, "Thanks, Cole."

"I won't even mention how desperate you must be to go on those dating apps," Cole joked, dodging out of Sasha's way before she tried to throw something at him.

As Cole left the room, he quickly returned and looked towards Sam and Phillip, "I forgot to tell you both, CONGRATS!!" And he dashed from their house.

Sam looked at Phillip, and then at Sasha. "What was he talking about?" Sam asked, but before waiting for an answer, Sam knew she needed time alone. Right now. She was about to explode.

19

A fter the craziness of the morning with Phillip, Sasha, and Cole, Sam needed some time to herself. She was beginning to feel overwhelmed and trapped, and she didn't like feeling that way. She knew coming home wouldn't be easy, but this was more than she bargained for. Her emotions were at an all-time high. She hadn't had a moment to catch her breath. She had either been worried about running into Colin, helping with wedding details, or hosting Phillip. She just needed to escape for a couple of hours, so she left Phillip to his emails and agreed to meet him later in town. She then walked to Main Street, the center of town, which was about 1/2 mile away. She wore her big sunglasses and a straw hat in an attempt to be incognito.

Main Street was buzzing that Thursday afternoon. It was a gorgeous day and people were everywhere. As hokey as it may sound, everyone seemed happy to be alive. She loved looking at the shops and boutiques, and seeing the restaurants and cafes all open and busy. Being part of the small town action was so much fun. She could feel her heartbeat slowing down as she looked around.

As she strolled along, looking into the windows, she felt only a little badly for having left Phillip to his work. Sam knew him all too well. He had too many logs in the fire and too many people depending upon him to do 'things,' that he could not take a day off from work during the week. Even his weekends were packed with work and calls and emails. Since she was just like Phillip when she was in the City, which was most of the time, she knew she couldn't be upset. Their commitment to their work was one of the reasons they understood each other so well.

Being away from the City over the last couple of days had been so good. September was Fashion Show season, so she tried to get away to the Hamptons every summer to embrace the quiet and develop new concepts for her line. She worked best when she was busy, but she knew it was important to get away from it all. She needed to be reenergized and rejuvenated, which was why buying her place in the Hamptons had been the best thing for her. It allowed her the peace she needed for a quick getaway here and there.

But the Hamptons in the summer was different than her hometown. She'd forgotten what it was like to walk down the street and feel this sense of home. The same bakery she'd gone to for years was still on Main Street with the same staff behind the counter. The same bagel shop was on Main Street, with the same family running it. The same doctor's office, the same hair salons, the same nail place. It was all still here. There was a sense of belonging, which she hadn't felt in a very long time. She'd spent so much time avoiding the place, that she'd forgotten just how much she'd missed it.

"Is that Samantha McKay?" she heard a woman's voice ask.

Sam turned to see Mrs. Dasher walking along Main Street, carrying a bunch of bakery boxes.

"Oh my God, Mrs. Dasher!" Sam kissed her cheek and immediately grabbed a few of the bakery boxes. "Here, let me take some of those. You're going to drop them all," she laughed.

"You're a gem. Thank you," Poppy Dasher laughed, lightening her load with Sam's help. "I'm parked right over there. I thought I could handle this, but obviously I was wrong. I should have made two trips."

Mrs. Dasher looked exactly the same, maybe an extra grey hair here and there, but still exactly the same. She'd always loved Mrs. Dasher, well before she and Colin had started dating. They'd always had a special connection and it broke Sam's heart, even more, when she and Colin broke up, knowing things would be different between them. She'd always been someone that Sam could turn to when she needed advice or vent about her mom or sisters. Mrs. Dasher had been a safe zone for Sam, and when things with Colin changed, her relationship with Mrs. Dasher inevitably changed, too.

After Colin left New York and made it clear that he was never coming back, Mrs. Dasher had written Sam a note. It wasn't super long, but it let her know, regardless of what the future held for her and Colin, that she loved Sam and would always be there for her. It had touched Sam's heart. Sam didn't have the energy to reply, but she'd kept the note and asked her mother to let Poppy Dasher know that the note meant a lot to her, and that she would save it forever.

"Where are you headed with all of these boxes? Sam asked.

"I like to deliver goodies around town to the local shops and businesses once a month, just to let them know that they're appreciated," Poppy answered with a smile.

"That is so sweet," Sam said. "People must love it when you do that."

"Care to join me? We could catch up!" Mrs. Dasher asked with a big welcoming smile.

Sam didn't have anything going on and spending a little time with Poppy Dasher would be fun. It had been ten years since they'd had a chance to catch up. Phillip was working, so he wouldn't be looking for her. All she'd been able to think about this morning was that kiss with Colin, and the god-awful situation that had unfolded in the kitchen. She needed to get it all out of her head, and walking around with Poppy Dasher for an hour or so was exactly what she needed.

"You know what, Mrs. Dasher? I would love to," Sam said. "It's been too long since we've seen each other."

"Alrighty!" Mrs. Dasher said, lighting up like a Christmas tree. "But I'll only let you join me on one condition."

Sam looked directly at Poppy and was positive she was going to say something about Colin. "You need to stop calling me Mrs. Dasher and start calling me Poppy. You hear me?" she said with a smile.

"If you insist. It just feels so weird, like I'm going to get in trouble from my mom!"

"Tell her I told you to!" Poppy replied. "You're far too old now to be calling me anything other than Poppy. All your sisters do now, so it's time for you, too," smiled Poppy.

The two women put the boxes in the back seat of Poppy's car. "So, I have three stops I need to make. I was planning to head to the Fire Station, the Library and to Fatima's."

"I'm here to help and do whatever you need me to do," Sam said. "It's so nice to be with you. I've missed you." Sam began to tear up. She'd always loved Poppy Dasher and she was recognizing now that not coming home more often had paralyzed a portion of her life. She should have hashed out everything with Colin years and years ago. It took one hour of talking with him to realize that he'd been suffering just as much as she had all these years, but they had both been too proud or too stubborn to admit it to the other.

"Sweet girl, don't you cry," Poppy said. "I missed you, too. I've missed you so much, but I know why you needed to stay away, and I understood. I wish things had turned out differently for you two, but life has a way of working things out on its own. You can't push things."

"I just need you to know that I've missed you so much, and that I've thought about you a lot," Sam said, putting on her sunglasses to hide her tears.

"I know," Poppy said. "I know. And I'm glad that you two finally had the chance to talk. I wish it had been done years ago, but there's no time like the present, right?" Poppy grabbed Sam's hand and rubbed it. "I'm so proud of you and all that you've accomplished. You've had all of us here rooting for you and cheering for you the entire time. Your parents couldn't be prouder of you."

Sam smiled. She'd known her parents were proud of her, but hearing it from Poppy made it even more special. She felt horrible now that she hadn't come home more often. Even when she had come home over the past ten years, she'd never gone out and about in town. She'd always stayed put in her parent's house because she didn't want to run into Colin, or anyone or anything that reminded her of him. She hadn't realized, until this trip, just how much she let herself be swept away in the hurt of him leaving. It had impacted her life dramatically, and the people around her truly did suffer the most.

"Let's wipe away those tears and talk happy thoughts!" Poppy said. "Your sister is getting married this weekend! How exciting is that? Chris is such a nice guy. Cole and Colin have known him forever and they really like him."

"Yeah, I don't know him well, but Sarah is head over heels, and that's all that matters to me," Sam replied.

"He's a nice guy. Always so friendly when I see him, and he's been a real good friend to Colin, even helped put in a good word at the high school when he applied," Poppy said, beaming with pride for her son.

"I'm really happy that Colin found his calling," Sam said. "I'm sure he's a great guidance counselor. He was always so good with kids, and he really seems to get them."

"Yes, he's always had that gift with kids," Poppy agreed. "I always knew he wouldn't stay at the Auto Shop full time. It just wasn't him, as I'm sure you know. I think this is the best of both worlds. He can work with Cole and his dad in the summer and on the weekends. They're all so close, so it's nice to see them together."

"I was surprised when I learned that he had started working with them way back when. He wasn't into cars like Cole and Mr. Dasher," Sam added. She hadn't meant for the conversation to be centered around Colin, but here they were, the two of them talking about him.

"He needed work and knew that it would be the easiest way to make money and support himself, and save for the future, so he went with it," Poppy smiled. She put her key in her ignition and started the car. "I know he wanted to do something bigger with his life, but he got lost and he didn't know which way to turn. It was easier to stay with his dad and brother than it was to break away and find something new."

Sam just stared straight ahead, but she needed to ask the question, "He's happy, right?" asked Sam.

"Oh, yes, dear..." Poppy said while taking a moment to think about what to say. "He really loves being back at the high school, and I hear via the grapevine that he is doing an incredible job, although he would never say that himself. He found a career that he was meant to do. When he decided to go college and get his degree so he could teach and work with kids, I was so happy for him—we all were."

"That's wonderful," Sam said. "I'm so glad it all worked out for him." Sam meant it. She truly felt happiness for him and wanted good things for him. But the one thing she hadn't realized was that he'd been feeling lost, and that it had taken time for him to find his own way. His heart had been broken, too. Two lost souls, unaware of how the other felt, bottling up emotions and afraid to let them out. If she'd only known the truth ten years ago.

"And you, my dear," Poppy smiled as she drove. "Tell me about all the amazing things you've got going on. Your mom keeps me up to date and I look online and read about you, but tell me about some exciting new things that nobody else knows!"

"Oh, gosh," Sam responded. "My life is busy with work, it's really all I do. I've got a new collection coming out in September, but it's nice to be away from it for a few days while I'm here in Barrington. New York is great, but it is always so busy. Work is my baby right now, which is OK. I'm sure Mom would like real grandkids, but she'll have to look to Sarah for those right now."

"And, I'm just going to ask because I'm nosy," Poppy giggled. "What about Phillip McKnight?"

"Yes, he's here in town. Did Mom tell you?"

"She mentioned you were bringing him home for the wedding, yes."

"And...what else did she say?"

"Honestly, that's it. She is excited to get to know him better."

"Yeah, we've been together for a while now, about a year. He's super nice, very good at business, and he's helped me out a ton."

"Oh, nice. Always good to have an extra pair of eyes on things," Poppy said as she turned the corner. "OK, here's our first stop! I love the guys at the Fire Station. They're always so happy to see me walk in with some treats."

Sam helped Poppy carry in two large boxes of cookies and squares for the crew. Everyone cheered, which made Sam smile. She really did love the hometown pride and love that people felt in Barrington. It was a town people loved and a great place to raise their families.

A couple of the firemen were guys she'd known in high school. Once they recognized her, they started joking about Poppy's high-class delivery help. It was fun to see them and they all had a good laugh. They asked for photos and Sam obliged, feeling a sense of hometown pride herself. She knew everyone would most likely post on social media, but Sam was used to that, too. The cat was most likely out of the bag that she was home, and as long as people were respectful of her and her family, she didn't care what was posted. She purposely didn't have personal social media accounts, preferring her personal life to be her own. She didn't want to share all the bits and pieces.

The rest of the hour was spent dropping off boxes at the

library and at Fatima's, and everyone made a big deal about their local celebrity. In New York, Sam was used to people stopping her every now and then, but here it was a different story. Everyone wanted a photo. Everyone wanted to talk. Everyone wanted to share something. Sam loved every single second, and she knew it was important to give time to the people she loved here in Barrington. She could tell Poppy got a kick out of the attention given to her. This generosity of Poppy's gave her the idea to do something like this at her office. People loved a little surprise, and to know they're appreciated and acknowledged.

"Thank you for inviting me today, Poppy," Sam said as they got in the car, ready to drive back to Main Street. "I had such a great time with you. I really needed this today, and thanks doesn't even seem enough."

"Aw, Sweetie, I'm glad you came along. You were a big celebrity today! I felt like a big shot being with you! I can't wait to tell your mom. It was great to spend some time with you. I really have missed you."

"I've missed you, too," Sam smiled.

"Can I say one thing?" Poppy asked with a devious smile.

Sam rolled her eyes and laughed, "Oh, God...what?"

"Colin didn't tell me what you two talked about, but he said you talked and he got everything out. I just want to say that I'm glad you two finally had the chance."

"I'm glad we did, too," Sam said.

"I tried to get more out of him, but you know Colin. He doesn't say much—not like Cole who will never stop talking. I hear too much from one and not enough from the other!"

Sam smiled, "Yes, he's always been the quiet one, huh?"

"Yes, but I'm glad he finally got the opportunity to tell you what happened. He should have done it years ago, but he just never had the nerve. People need to do things on their own timetable and sometimes there's nothing you can do to push them along if they're not ready."

"I know," Sam said, looking down at her hands. "I'm glad that we finally were able to hear each other out. I held so much in and held so much against him for all these years. I didn't know what had happened and now all those questions I had have been answered. It's funny how you can hold onto something for so long, and then... just like that, let it go."

"Matters of the heart aren't always easy," Poppy said. She reached out and put her hand on Sam's, "When he went back a year later, I thought that would be it. But when he came back, he was a different person. I was so worried about him, but Cole kept telling me to let him ride it out, and that he'd eventually be fine. I guess sometimes moms don't always know best."

Sam was confused. She looked over at Poppy, unable to process what she had just heard.

"What?" Sam closed her eyes and shook her head. "Wait. Poppy. Did you just say 'when he came back'?'"

Poppy seemed just as confused. "What do you mean, Honey?"

Sam's heart started to beat faster. She looked directly at Poppy. "He came back? To New York? After he left the first time?" she asked, feeling almost dizzy.

"Oh, no," Poppy stopped suddenly and put her hand over her mouth. "Did I say something I wasn't supposed to say? Did you not know?" she asked, startled.

Sam shook her head and turned to look out the window. He came back. Those three words kept repeating in her head, over and over again. He came back. Why didn't he tell her that? Why didn't she know? This was all news to her, she'd never heard this before, and he certainly hadn't said anything about it to her yesterday.

Sam collected herself and turned to Poppy, "I didn't know he returned to New York a second time. He never told me that."

"He never got in touch with you, a year later?" Poppy asked.

Sam shook her head from side to side and whispered, "No...he didn't."

"Oh, my God, Sam," Poppy whispered, "I feel that I've messed up here. I didn't realize that he hadn't told you."

"Do you know why he came back?" Sam asked, her insides shaking, barely able to process what Poppy was saying.

Poppy reached out and touched Sam's hand, "Yes, Honey, I do know why, but I think you need to talk to him about that. I shouldn't be the one to tell you." Poppy looked like she was going to be sick, "Oh, Sam, I'm so sorry that I even mentioned this. When Colin said he told you everything, I just assumed he actually *did* tell you everything."

20

The moment Poppy dropped Sam off, she picked up her phone and called Colin on his cell. Since she never called during the day, Colin immediately picked up when he saw who it was.

"Hey, Mom," Colin said, feeling a bit uneasy. "Everything OK?"

"Colin, oh my God," Poppy said, clearly flustered. "I just made a huge mistake, and I wanted to get in touch with you immediately. I don't know if she's going to call you or not, but I..."

"Mom, Mom, slow down. I don't know what you're talking about," Colin said, feeling a little worried, as his mom was usually pretty chill.

"I was just with Sam for the last hour and we got to talking," she said quietly.

Colin walked outside of the shop to take the call. His heart was racing a little now, not sure what his mom was going to say next.

"OK, so what happened?" Colin asked impatiently. "What are you talking about? What mistake did you make?"

"I told her you returned to New York."

Colin was silent on the other end. He didn't know what to say at first because, never in a million years, would he have imagined that statement would come out of his mom's mouth.

"How did that even come up, Mom?"

"We were talking about how you two had finally had the chance to talk yesterday, and I was telling her I was so happy about it. Then I said something about how you weren't the same after you came back the second time."

"Mom..." Colin muttered under his breath.

"I'm sorry, Honey. I feel terrible about this."

"Shit," Colin muttered. After a few seconds of silence, he found the words, "I probably should've told her. I just didn't think it really mattered, at least not now."

"I can't believe I said anything. I should know enough to keep quiet about stuff like this. But I just wanted to tell you what happened. We had such a nice time, and it was fun being with her. I simply wanted to her know that I was happy you two had patched things up."

Colin stood outside his auto shop rubbing his greasy hands through his hair.

Walking back toward the shop, he said, "Listen, Mom, I know you didn't mean to say anything, but I really can't talk right now. We're crazy busy here today. I just think that things are okay as they are between us right now. I can't let that part of my life take hold of me anymore. I need to focus on other things."

"I know, Honey. It's just that... " Poppy didn't know if she should say anything else or not, but she knew that if she didn't, she might regret it later.

"What? Mom?" Colin said, impatiently this time. Cole poked his head out of the shop and signaled to Colin.

"What the hell is going on?" Cole mouthed.

"It's Mom," Colin said, gesturing to his phone.

"It's just that Sam seemed very surprised," Poppy said. "Very."

"I'm sure she was, Mom, but what does it matter now? She's engaged to someone else. I let her go a long time ago."

"She's engaged? To Phillip?"

"Yeah, Colin said Jessica saw her trying on wedding gowns at Fatima's with her mom and sister."

"Oh, Colin," Poppy said. "I'm surprised to hear that. She didn't mention anything to me. I don't think she's engaged. I really don't."

"So tell me. What makes you think that?"

"Well, she wasn't wearing a ring. I would've noticed that. And I could tell she was upset to hear that you had gone back to New York."

"Upset?" Colin asked, wishing he could get off this call. "What do you mean, upset? Upset that I didn't tell her?" he asked.

"She seemed upset, Colin. She wanted to know why you came back." Poppy wanted to shake her son at times. Both of her sons were her heart and soul, but they truly didn't "get" women sometimes. Here they were, both thirty years old and single. And not just single, one of her sons was the town playboy and the other had never had the nerve to go after the love of his life.

"Did you tell her why?" Colin asked, walking in circles outside the auto shop. He just needed a minute to process this. He didn't care at the moment how busy they were; let Cole be pissed for a second. All this business about Sam was rattling him to the core.

"No, I didn't. I told her that needed to come from you, not me."

"Thanks, Mom," Colin said with relief in his voice. "I just want to leave things alone right now, the way they are. We ended on good terms. I have to see her tomorrow night at the rehearsal and then at the wedding. She's gone on Sunday morning, and that'll be it. I don't want to worry about crossing paths with her again ever again. Please, let's just leave this alone."

"Is that how you want to leave it, Colin?" Poppy asked, knowing this was her only chance to ask the hard questions.

"It's not how I want to leave it, but it's how I *have* to leave it, Mom. Why would she change anything? Why would she choose me over Phillip McKnight? These are things I will never know," Colin said.

"You won't know until you tell her everything."

"That's not happening. I can't do that, and I don't want to do that."

"And why not, Colin?" Poppy asked with an annoyed tone in her voice. "Why can't you just do this for yourself? For once in your life?"

Colin took a deep breath. He knew the answer to this question. He'd known it for the last ten years. As much as he'd wanted to move on and find the love of his life, he wasn't sure it was possible. He'd come close to finding a few rare diamonds in the rough, but none of them had panned out. It wasn't easy seeing the woman you loved most in this world everywhere you looked. Sam would never be out of his life. Her parents lived across from his parents, she was often in the news and her name was brought up constantly in town. He would never escape Samantha McKay.

"Colin? Are you still there?" Poppy asked after a long silence. "I don't mean to upset you, Honey. I just want to know why you won't do this for yourself. Tell her why you came back."

"I can't do it, Mom. I can handle being the one to walk away, but I can't handle being the one that's walked away from."

"But that's exactly what she thinks you did to her."

"And look how that turned out. She avoided me for ten years. I can't go back."

"Colin, her face drained of color when I told her you went back to New York. That's not the reaction of someone who doesn't care."

"I'm not looking to break up her engagement, Mom. I wish her the best and I want the best for her. Phillip is good for her."

It hurt saying those words out loud. He thought back to their kiss yesterday when every fiber in his body awoke. Her lips, her arms around his neck, her body pressed against his. She was perfect in every way. She was extraordinary in every way. They both knew the kissing was a mistake and they both knew it wouldn't happen again. They'd needed each other in that moment, but it was over now. That's all it could be for them. It was enough to remind them of the past and hold it there.

"Alright, Sweetheart," Poppy said. "You know what my hope is for you?"

"What's that?" he asked.

"I hope you realize that sometimes the only thing a girl wants in life is someone's heart. Because you know what? That heart gives her the world."

21

S am left Poppy Dasher feeling as if the wind had been knocked out of her. She stood in the middle of Main Street, with small town business going on around her, just staring blankly at the people walking past. She silently questioned everything. Colin had come back to New York a year after he first left. Why didn't he tell her? And what made him come back to Rhode Island without contacting her? Did he lose his nerve? Did he change his mind? Why the hell had he come back in the first place? Sam's head was spinning, but she knew the only person who could answer any of these questions was Colin.

She needed to talk to him.

Not knowing if it was right or wrong, she began walking in the direction of the Auto Body shop. It was only 3pm in the afternoon, so he had to be there right now and, if he wasn't, she'd go find him. She needed to see him right now before she lost her nerve. It wouldn't change things, but she needed an answer before she returned to New York on Sunday.

Trying to walk quickly in high-heel espadrilles took some skill, but luckily she didn't have that far to go, less than a mile down the road. As she hustled along, questions started to swirl through her head. How come nobody told her he came to New York a second time? Who else knew besides his mother? Did Cole know? Did her sisters know? Was it top secret?

She was getting close when she heard a familiar male voice calling her name. "SAMANTHA!"

She suddenly froze. She knew that voice. She turned around and saw him. Phillip. It was Phillip calling her name, running down Main Street to catch up with her. He was smiling, holding a gorgeous bouquet of flowers. He was wearing khaki shorts and a polo tee, totally fitting in with the New England vibe here in Barrington. Phillip hardly ever wore shorts, but he did look super cute.

Sam stood waiting for him to catch up. She took a deep breath, needing to calm herself. She didn't want Phillip to see that she was upset or distracted. He'd come all this way to be with her, and she needed to embrace the fact that the past needed to remain in the past. Phillip was her present and her future.

"Oh, wow, you're fast!" Phillip shouted as he caught up to her. "Where the heck were you going so quickly?"

Sam looked at Phillip and wasn't sure how to reply. He loved her in the best way he could, and she'd decided it was enough for her. She knew that he'd never grab her and kiss her like Colin did yesterday, but he would be there for her in a million other ways.

"Samantha, what's the matter? You look like you've seen a ghost. Are you OK?"

Phillip was an understanding man. He'd always been

attentive to Sam, making sure she had everything she needed. Sam looked up into Phillip's eyes and saw true kindness. He really was an amazing friend to her. She knew she'd never doubt his trust, his loyalty or his love for her.

"Are you crying, Samantha?" he asked. "Listen, I know it's your sister's wedding weekend, and that I promised I'd be here for you. You're upset I've been working, aren't you?"

Sam smiled, "No, Phillip, that's not it. I'm fine. Honestly."

He looked down at the large bouquet of wildflowers in his hand and gave them to Sam, "I bought these for you at your sisters' shop. They said they were your favorites."

Sam laughed, "You went shopping for flowers on your own?" She reached out and grabbed them from him and took a whiff of their delightful aroma.

Phillip laughed back, "See, I can do a few things by myself, you know. I'm not *that* dependent on Maggie. And when it comes to you, I'll do anything. I hope you know that by now."

"Well, thank you. These are lovely," Sam responded with a smile. Phillip took her hand as they walked down Main Street. "Want to go to one of my favorite spots around here?" she asked.

Phillip looked down at Sam and smiled. "I'll go anywhere you want right now. I'm all yours, my phone is officially on silent for the rest of the day."

He knew that Sam needed this time, just the two of them. He had arrived early to surprise her, but nothing had gone according to plan. He really did want to be here for her this weekend, knowing she'd been kind of dreading the wedding weekend. It was his job to make sure it was fun, and to make sure she had a good time. He didn't quite understand what Sam's hang-up was about being here. As far as he could tell, Barrington was a gorgeous little New England town, quiet and sweet and quaint. Everyone had smiles on their faces. Everyone waved hello. It was a far cry from their normal New York life.

Sam led Phillip on a twenty-minute walk. She pointed out things along the way, letting him see the different places that had shaped her life. She pointed out her elementary school. She showed him the bike path she rode along as a kid. They walked past lots of little shops, cafes, and restaurants, and she told him stories about each one. They finally ended up at a gorgeous little pond, surrounded by thick, lush green trees.

"And this is my most favorite spot of all. This is where I used to come to sit and dream and plot my future," she said.

What Sam didn't mention was that she was always with Colin when she came here, but now it was time for her to share this spot with someone else - the man who was here with her right now.

"It really is beautiful. I can see why you love it so much. We don't have anything like this back in New York, at least not without hundreds of people sharing it with you."

"Even when the seasons change, it's always been my favorite spot," Sam explained.

As they'd been walking, she knew she needed to tell Phillip the truth about Colin, or at least part of it. She wanted to make sure her past wasn't going to cause any damage to her future.

"What's bothering you, Samantha?"

"I don't know - nothing, everything. I've just had a lot on my mind," she said.

"I can tell you've been a little distracted," answered Phillip.

"Phillip, I'm sorry, I'm so thankful that you came here to be with me. I know taking time away from work isn't easy."

"Oh, don't worry about that. I'm more concerned about you. You're upset that I've been working all morning, aren't you?"

"I'm not upset Phillip, I promise. I know work is important for you. Had this been another time of year, I would be head down somewhere, working like a dog, until just before the wedding. I happened to catch a break between collections on this one."

"So then, what's been on your mind?" he asked.

Sam let go of Phillip's hand and walked a few feet in front of him. She turned around to face him. As she was about to speak, Phillip said something unexpected, "You're so beautiful, Samantha. I don't tell you that enough."

Sam smiled at the unexpected compliment, "Thank you."

"You really are,"

She looked down at her feet and then up at Phillip. "I want to tell you something, Phillip, and I need you to listen and try to understand."

"OK," Phillip said, looking confident and handsome in his own Phillip way. Generally, in his work life, he wasn't used to having people talk to him like this. He usually did the talking. He looked at Samantha amusingly. "What's up?"

"There's a reason I don't like to come home," Sam began.

"I figured there was something because your family is great."

"I don't like to talk about it, but I feel I owe you an explanation," Sam said.

"Sam, you don't owe me anything. If you don't want to talk about it, we don't have to."

"But that's the thing. I *want* to tell you. We don't really share much about our pasts."

"Does this have something to do with another guy?" Phillip asked Sam, now very serious.

Sam glanced away from Phillip and over to the pond in front of her. This pond had always calmed her nerves, and she needed that right now.

"Yes," Sam said. "It has to do with a guy. Actually, the brother of the guy you met this morning."

"The twin of that guy Cole?" Phillip asked. "Your ex-boyfriend from high school?" Phillip sounded a little surprised.

"Yes, Colin. He was my boyfriend throughout high school and, as you now know, he came with me to New York when I first went there for college."

"Yeah, I remember you guys mentioning that this morning."

"What I didn't mention was that he left after being there with me for a year."

"He left?" Phillip asked. "What do you mean? He broke up with you?"

"Yes, he broke up with me and, back then, I was completely devastated. He was the only guy I'd ever been with, and the only guy I'd ever loved. When he left, it destroyed me."

"Destroyed you?" Phillip asked. "I can't believe that any guy would have that kind of power over Samantha McKay."

"Well, believe it, Phillip," Sam said quietly. She looked directly back at Phillip. "I couldn't believe he left me. It really changed everything for me. I was so upset and so hurt that I just put every piece of myself into my craft and my business."

"So it ended up being a good thing?" Phillip still looked confused.

"It was a good thing, Phillip...for my work, but my heart was shattered. Colin was everything to me back then and it really hurt my ego and my heart. After that, I just couldn't come home because I didn't want to see him. I *couldn't* see him."

"So, when he left, he moved back here and he's been here ever since?" Phillip asked.

"Yes. He's a guidance counselor and runs the auto shop with his family."

"He's a teacher and a mechanic?" Phillip asked in a judgmental tone.

"Phillip, that's not nice. Don't be so judgmental," Sam said quickly.

Phillip caught himself and walked over to Sam. "I'm sorry, I didn't mean that. It came out the wrong way. I just meant, I just can't imagine you with a mechanic, that's all."

Sam knew that Phillip hadn't meant it the way it sounded. As much as Phillip grew up with a silver spoon in his mouth, he wasn't an ass. He was kind to everyone, and she did always appreciate that about him. He treated the parking lot attendant like a CEO, so this comment was uncharacteristic.

"Colin was an incredible athlete, but instead of pursuing anything after high school, he followed me to New York so we could be together," Sam explained.

"And you two haven't kept in touch in all these years?" Phillip asked.

Sam shook her head, "No. I've always been too upset to see him."

"Why's that? Even after all these years?" Philip asked.

Sam didn't know the best way to answer this question, so

she just went with her heart. "I was upset because he left me. It impacted my trust in men for years. I felt like he didn't believe in me or us, and that always hurt me to the core. Coming home was always hard. I didn't want to see him or talk to him. So I stayed in New York. I worked hard, and part of what drove me was to make him suffer."

Phillip let out a laugh, "Suffer? You wanted to make the guy suffer? Remind me not to break up with you."

"OK. Maybe not suffer, but I wanted him to regret what he did," Sam explained.

"So, in some odd way, you owe him thanks for your success."

Sam rolled her eyes at Phillip, "You're missing my point here!"

Phillip laughed, "I'm not missing anything. I get it. He was here, and you didn't want to come home. It makes perfect sense to me. But listen, it's been ten years. Don't you think it's time to let it go? You're successful and happy, and that's all that matters."

He *was* missing the point, and Sam knew it. She wanted to tell him that she still felt something for Colin, but she just didn't know how to tell him. Phillip wasn't concerned about her feelings for Colin. He was just not the type to let something like this bother him. For him, it was old business—move on, find somebody else.

"I guess so, Phillip. I just - I don't know - I felt like I needed to tell you," Sam explained.

Phillip took both of Sam's hands in his own and looked into her eyes, "I'm glad you did. I hope you know, Samantha, that your past doesn't matter to me, just the future. We're a perfect match, you and me, a great partnership, and there's nothing I want more than to be with you. And now, meeting your family and seeing your hometown, it was the last piece of the puzzle for us."

Sam didn't know what to say, so she smiled and looked down at their hands.

"I've been thinking about us lately, a lot," Phillip continued. "I feel like we're two people going in the same direction, and we want the same things. I actually thought the reason you didn't want to come home was that your sister was engaged and you weren't."

Sam looked up at him surprised, "Really? You thought that was why?"

"Yes, I thought that maybe you saw her engaged and getting married, and wondered why it wasn't you."

"Honestly, I never thought that, I swear," Sam said.

Phillip smiled and put his arms around Sam, "I know, Samantha, I know that now, but I did think about it. It made me look at us and what we have, and wonder why we haven't taken the next steps yet."

Sam began to realize where this talk was going.

"And so I came early yesterday to talk to your parents and ask their permission about something very important. Something that I probably should've asked you a couple of months ago, especially when I realized how compatible we are with each other."

Sam just stood there, holding the flowers, knowing what was coming next, but completely unable to fully process the next part.

Phillip took one step back, reached into his pocket for a velvet box, then got down on one knee.

"Samantha McKay," Phillip began without a twinge of nervousness. "I will give you everything you need in life. You won't want for a thing, ever. I will be your partner and support you in every way possible. I will be here for you for everything. Will you marry me?"

Sam couldn't believe this was happening. She wasn't prepared for a marriage proposal. Not any of it. It suddenly made perfect sense why Phillip had arrived yesterday. He'd wanted to ask her parents for her hand in marriage.

"Oh, Phillip...." Sam said, and bent down to help him up. Sam had tears well up in her eyes. Phillip was standing in front of her, asking her to marry him. She'd wanted this. She did. She knew he would be the perfect partner for her. She knew he'd take care of her. She knew her life would be set with Phillip.

Phillip seemed a little confused as to why Sam hadn't said anything, looking at her with a hint of confusion in his voice, "Sam?"

"Phillip..." Sam said.

"Is something wrong? I thought this was something you wanted," Phillip asked.

Sam smiled and looked at Phillip. It was the first glimpse she got of the ring he was holding. It had to be the size of a penny. It was HUGE and gorgeous and square cut. It was big enough to use as a paperweight, not that that mattered to her.

"Nothing is wrong, Phillip. I'm just surprised. You caught me off guard," and she leaned forward to kiss him.

"Your parents seemed surprised, too, but I assured them that even though it's only been a year that we've been serious, my intentions are honorable."

That sounded exactly like something Phillip would say. At that moment she stood there, knowing the only answer she could give. She was going back to New York, and she was letting this quick little trip home get into her head. She needed to remember that her life was in New York. She couldn't stay here. She had her entire life and business elsewhere. Nothing about the past could be changed, but she could make sure her future was set. Phillip *was* her future and here he was, standing before her, asking for her hand, asking to be with her forever. She needed to finally let everything else go; this was her sign from the universe.

Sam closed her eyes, not knowing if what she was about to say was the right answer, but she knew it was the only answer. She opened her eyes, looked up at Phillip, and said, "Yes, Phillip. I will marry you."

22

Ann McKay had outdone herself planning for Sarah and Chris's rehearsal dinner. Sarah wanted the dinner hosted at her childhood home, in the backyard, and it was spectacular. Ann had created a masterpiece for her daughter. White fairy lights were hung in all of the trees, making it look like stars in the sky. Tables were set up all around the McKay's backyard, adorned in gorgeous white tablecloths and white dinnerware. Vases were placed on every table, overflowing with beautiful blue hydrangeas. It looked like a fairy tale in the McKay backyard, and that was the exact look Ann wanted for Sarah. Her daughter's fairy tale was coming true, and she wanted the perfect beginning for her.

The rehearsal at the church had gone very smoothly. It was a relatively small wedding party, and the rehearsal had gone by in a flash. Sarah had just her three sisters in the wedding party, and Chris had chosen three close friends to stand up with him, so the planning had been pretty simple. Once the rehearsal was over, everyone was looking forward to heading back to the McKay house to enjoy the festivities.

Sam had purposely not worn her engagement ring to the rehearsal dinner. She didn't want to take any attention away from Sarah. She knew in her heart that Sarah would be happy for her, but she also knew that Sarah would worry about her, too. Sam didn't want to convince Sarah on her own wedding weekend that she was making the right decision. She wanted it to be all about Sarah and nobody else. As much as Phillip was surprised that she didn't want to share the news with her sisters immediately, he agreed that it would be their secret - and her parents - until after the wedding.

The last twenty-four hours had helped Sam to think clearly again. After Phillip's proposal, they headed back to the McKay house to pack their things and check into the hotel they had reserved for the next two nights. Sam felt that being alone with Phillip for the next two nights was what she needed. They needed to be in bed together and alone, solely focused on each other. They didn't leave their hotel room on Thursday night and had spent all Friday morning together in bed. They had ordered room service and just relaxed and talked, something they never did. Sam sensed that Phillip knew something was off a bit because every time his phone rang, he either ignored it or told whoever was on the line that he'd get back to them later. Sam knew he was trying. She saw the effort, and she knew that being with him and making love to him was exactly what she needed. She needed to feel whole again and he made her feel that way.

As much as Sam had felt torn when Poppy Dasher told her about Colin's second trip to New York, she realized that she was allowing past scenarios to impact her present. She didn't want that. As much as her kiss with Colin was hot and passionate, and had sent shivers up and down her body, she had to end that chapter of her life. She felt guilty about kissing Colin, but was too nervous to tell Phillip because she didn't want it to impact their relationship. The way Sam thought about it now, the truth was that Colin *hadn't* come back after her, even if he did come to New York a second time. She had to accept that this was how things were and that nothing could change the past. He hadn't told her about it, so why should she hold onto any hope or desire that things could have been different? She didn't want to lose what she had for something that might never be. Colin had made his choice all those years ago, and that choice truly impacted the decisions she made for her future.

And Phillip was her future.

For the dinner, Sam was dressed in a black sheath dress with a sexy lace overlay. It was one of her own designs and it hugged her body in all the right ways. Before the rehearsal at the church, Sam had arranged for a team of hair and makeup artists to come to the family home and work their magic on herself and her sisters and mother. The four sisters looked like supermodels, each of them dressed beautifully with their hair down in gorgeous waves. With the summer in full swing, each of them had a glistening glow that made them standouts. All their close family and friends would be at the rehearsal dinner and at the wedding tomorrow where they were expecting around 250 people. Sam felt that tonight's party would be better than tomorrow's because there would be only about 75 people, or so.

"If I haven't told you already," Phillip said as they were driving back to the McKay house for the rehearsal dinner, "You look sensational tonight."

Sam smiled, "Thank you, Sweetie. You look pretty handsome yourself, too." Sam knew that Phillip loved to stand out in a crowd. He was a social butterfly and worked a room like no one else, meeting as many people as possible. He was used to the fact that people would introduce themselves to him just because he was a McKnight. He wasn't arrogant about it at all, but he did enjoy the extra attention. She also knew that Phillip enjoyed having her on his arm, and together, they made an incredible couple. Again, nothing arrogant, just that he loved having an equal match on his arm. She knew that was important to his family, too.

Colin wasn't at the rehearsal because he wasn't in the wedding party, but she knew he'd be at the house for the dinner. Poppy had actually helped her mother with many of the details and, since they were like family, it was never a question that the Dasher family would be invited. Sam had taken a peek at the rehearsal seating chart and was relieved to see that she wasn't sitting near Colin. He was clear across the yard, and either her mom or Sarah had made that master move on her behalf.

"How long do you think dinner will be tonight?" Phillip asked with a sly smile as they parked the car and walked into her parent's home. "Love to pick up where we left off this afternoon."

Sam laughed and reached down to hold his hand. "I don't know, but I do know that after dinner, a lot of people are heading to Bluewater Bar."

"Do you think Sasha will be joining the group?" Phillip laughed.

"Phillip!" Sam giggled, "Whatever you do, please don't bring that up in front of her! We're all just going to pretend it never happened."

As they walked into the McKay backyard, Sam's breath was taken away. It looked absolutely gorgeous. The wedding party was a little late getting back from the church and the backyard was already filled with people. Her mom had completely outdone herself, truly transforming her childhood backyard into an enchanting summer wonderland.

"It looks beautiful back here," Sam said to Phillip, "Doesn't it?"

"I hardly recognize it from when I arrived!" Phillip agreed. "I spy the bar in the back. I'm going to go grab us some drinks."

Sam nodded as Phillip took off into the crowd of people, smiling as he walked away. She never had to worry about Phillip feeling at loose ends. He always had a confidence about him that she loved. She often thought it was one of the most attractive things about him. He could walk into any situation and adapt, and not many people could do that so effortlessly.

"Hi, Sam." Sam turned quickly to her right and saw Cole standing there. He looked very handsome, just as he normally did when he was cleaned up. He was wearing a Vineyard Vines blue polo with khaki pants and loafers. He looked as if he'd just come off his yacht in Newport.

"Hi, Cole! Wow, you're looking handsome tonight," Sam reached over and gave him a hug, his faux pas of the other day forgotten.

"A shower can do wonders, huh?" Cole laughed. "I heard there were going to be a lot of single ladies here tonight and tomorrow, so it's game on for me."

"Oh, my God, you're insane!" Sam joked back. "I feel that all the single girls who'll be here tonight and tomorrow, are people you've already met, hooked up with or know pretty well. So, looks like your game might be off a bit for this one."

Cole smiled and put his hand through his hair. Both he and Colin instinctively made that gesture when they weren't sure what to say next. It always used to make Sam smile because she knew she had Colin stumped on something when he did that.

"Maybe I'll get lucky and meet someone new. You never know," Cole smiled back. "Phillip here?" he asked.

"Yeah, he's just grabbing some drinks for us." Sam looked at Cole and suddenly remembered something that he had said to her the other day that had puzzled her, "Hey Cole, the other day when you were leaving the house, you came back and congratulated me. What was that for? I meant to ask you. I just couldn't figure it out."

Cole looked confused for a second, trying to jog his memory, but then he remembered, "On your engagement. Colin told me you were engaged, so I didn't want to be the last one to congratulate you."

"On my engagement?" Sam asked, confused. "The other day you were congratulating me on my engagement? But I wasn't engaged yet." Sam caught her mistake and tried to correct herself, "I mean, I'm not engaged. Why would Colin think that?"

"He said Jessica saw you trying on wedding dresses at Fatima's," Cole responded. "So, wait. You're not engaged?"

Sam didn't want to lie, but she didn't want the cat out of the bag yet. She knew telling Cole would mean the entire room would know about it in less than thirty minutes. The only thing she could do was lie. She needed to make sure Sarah's wedding day remained the only big McKay news for the time being.

"Oh, my God! She saw that? That was just me playing dress up. I'm not engaged to Phillip. Not yet, anyway." Sam felt annoyed with herself just then, and also with Jessica for spreading that rumor. Thank God it didn't make it online.

Cole nodded his head and looked out at the crowd in the backyard. "But you will be, at some point, right?"

Sam didn't want to make eye contact with Cole for fear that he would read her like a book. "Yes, at some point, I will be."

As if on cue, Phillip arrived by her side with a glass of champagne. "Phillip, you remember Cole from the other day, right?" Sam asked.

"Of course. Hi, Cole, good to see you again," Phillip said, reaching out to shake hands with Cole.

"Hi, Phillip. Good seeing you. If you'll excuse me, I'm going to go try to find my mother in this crowd, and hopefully a single girl or two. I'll see you both later," Cole said, and off he went.

Sam took a sip of the champagne and let it glide slowly down her throat. Engaged? Jessica saw her trying on dresses and went right to Colin with the news? Colin must have thought that was it, and that he had nothing to lose by kissing her the night before. Sam shook her head and tried to forget any thoughts of Colin. That door was closed, and all she wanted to do was look ahead and start planning her wedding with Phillip. She needed to ignore the tugging at her heart and just put a lock and key on it. It didn't matter anymore. She had to stop thinking about Colin and what would've been.

"Let's go find our seats," Sam said to Phillip. "It looks like dinner is about to be served. I see my mother trying to herd everyone to their tables. Let's make it easy on her."

As they walked to their table, so many relatives grabbed Sam's arm to say hello and give a quick hug. There were quite a few people from out of town, and she hadn't seen many of them in ages, but it was so nice to see them now and for them to be so excited about her career.

"Here we are," Phillip announced and pulled out Sam's chair for her.

Sam froze. Seated directly across from her at the table was Colin. He looked just as uncomfortable as she felt. He was trying to play it cool with his arm draped over the chair next to him, but nobody was sitting there yet. Jessica must be running late. Sam was trying her hardest to stay calm and look relaxed, but it was not easy. When she'd scoured the seating chart, he was definitely not at her table. He was supposed to be clear across the room at his parent's table. How did this happen?

"OMG! Yay - we're all at the same table. This is great!" Sasha shouted from a couple of feet away. "I was hoping Mom wouldn't move everything again after I changed it this morning. Can you imagine all of us *not* sitting together?"

Leave it to Sasha to meddle and make something like this happen. Sam could kill her right now. Did she have no thought about how Colin and Phillip and her might feel about being placed at the same table?

"You did this?" Cole asked, sounding less than enthused. "I thought I'd be at the singles' table, not with all of you guys."

"Don't be a drag, Cole!" Sasha said, annoyed, "We are not at a club. I thought it would be fun to sit together rather than with some randoms or relatives. I hardly know Chris's groomsmen, and they're all married anyway, so I told Mom to put the McKay girls and the Dasher boys at the same table. She didn't, so I did."

Everyone sat down and Sam looked directly at Sasha, who was sitting next to her, and whispered in her ear, "I am going to kill you. I can't believe you put us all together at the same table."

Sasha rolled her eyes and whispered back, "Get over it, Sam. It's been a decade!"

Sam sat up in her chair and reached over to rub Phillip's arm. He was typing away on his phone, barely aware of what was going on. Something was occupying his attention and she could tell he was trying to get it dealt with as quickly as possible. Sam looked up, trying not to make eye contact with Colin, but he was directly across from her. She couldn't help it. They locked eyes for a quick second and Sam literally felt her insides go to mush. He looked incredible. When he was tanned, he always looked good in a white button down. He was wearing a blue striped tie and looked like a model right off the pages of Vineyard Vines. Both he and Cole had been incredibly blessed in the looks department. They were - in a word - gorgeous.

Colin smiled across the table at Sam, trying not to feel affected by Phillip sitting next to her. Thankfully, Susan came over at that moment with her date for the night, and then, before too long, Jessica was back at the table.

Sam looked over at Phillip and whispered, "Are you almost done?"

He looked up quickly and then back down. "Sorry, Samantha. Big issue with a deal that I've been working on. I'm trying to smooth something over, quickly."

"On a Friday night?" Sam asked a little impatiently.

"You know how it is. People don't care what day or time it is," he answered quietly.

Sam took another sip of champagne and looked up to see Jessica with her hands wrapped around Colin's arm. She was whispering something to him and he was smiling. She'd never seen Colin with someone else, and it hurt to see them snuggling and being so close. She didn't want to look, but for some reason, she couldn't tear her eyes away. She didn't like how it made her feel. She didn't like how she felt seeing Jessica touch Colin in a possessive way. Her Colin. But he wasn't her Colin. He wasn't hers at all.

Colin happened to catch Sam looking over at them and slowly tried to reposition himself so Jessica wasn't hanging on his arm. He liked Jessica, but she was getting a little too close and a little too clingy for his liking.

Phillip finally placed his phone on the table and looked over at Sam, "All done."

"Thank God," Sam responded.

"I mean, for now. I will probably be going back and forth on this all night. I'm so sorry, Samantha. This deal *has* to go through, nothing can hold it up, so I need to make sure I'm on it," he explained.

Sam nodded and took in a deep breath, wanting to grab a bottle of champagne and chug it down in one gulp. She understood Phillip, and she knew she'd be doing the same thing if the roles were reversed. Phillip grabbed his drink and took a sip. He looked around the table and noticed that it was full, so he started saying hello to everyone and introducing himself to people he didn't know. Sam sat waiting for the Colin ticking time bomb to go off. She wasn't sure if Phillip would say anything, but she knew he'd at least connect the dots. She was watching him go around the table, finally getting to Colin in what felt like slow motion. Sam knew that it was just a matter of time.

"Hi, I'm Phillip McKnight," he said looking across the table at Colin.

"Nice to meet you, I'm Colin Dasher."

Phillip paused for a moment and looked over at Sam and smiled. "Is this 'the' Colin?" he asked, looking at Sam without a trace of threat or jealousy in his voice. "I should've known immediately," referencing Cole and the fact that they were identical twins.

Colin looked a little confused and slightly amused by the introduction and answered, "I think that's the first time I've ever been referred to as 'the Colin.'"

23

Colin couldn't believe he was sitting directly across from Sam. Of all the tables in this backyard, they had to be placed together? Did her family hate him? Did they hate her? Why would they place them at the same table, both of them with other people? It was like a sick joke. To make matters worse, Sam looked incredible. She always looked good in black and with her tan and her hair down and wavy, she looked stunning. He had to make himself look the other way, which was tough to do.

Jessica had promised to be cool with Sam. He had prepped her ahead of time saying that this was an important family occasion, and she shouldn't bother with photos or anything of that nature. She promised that she wouldn't post anything on social media about Sam. Thus far, she'd held up to her end of the promise by not posting anything prior to this evening, which was tough for someone like Jessica. Tonight, Jess had taken his request to heart and was practically ignoring Sam. He actually felt a little badly for Jess and hoped she was enjoying herself all the same.

Colin had spent the last twenty-four hours trying to

decide what to do now that Sam knew he'd returned to New York a second time. But he also knew that she'd never say a thing about it to him. His mother had driven him crazy trying to convince him to tell her. Not to mention Cole, who would not shut up about it. He'd done an okay job over the last ten years gliding through life, making a relationship work here and there. He knew he might never find that head-over-heels kind of love, but he also realized that he didn't actually need it. He had a full life. He was happy.

Cole kept giving Colin looks from across the table, but he ignored him. He wasn't sure what Cole wanted, but he didn't want to know. It was bad enough having to sit at the same table with Sam and Phillip without his own brother giving him weird looks. He was sick and tired of feeling on edge, and almost suffocated with Sam being here. It was as if he wouldn't be able to breathe properly until she returned to New York. He just wanted to be left alone. That shouldn't be too much to ask.

"I'm going to go get another drink," Jessica whispered in Colin's ear. "Do you want to come with me?"

Colin knew this was a perfect diversion and a great excuse to get away from the table for a little bit. Watching Phillip rub Sam's back was more than he could handle. She seemed distracted. He knew her like a book, and she definitely seemed as uncomfortable as he was. He was pretty certain that she probably had no idea that they would be seated at the same table. Sam could probably thank one of her sisters for that sly move.

"Yeah, let's head over and grab something," Colin said to Jessica. He tried his best to look relaxed as he looked around the table and asked, "Can I grab anyone a drink while we're up?"

"I'd love a gin and tonic while you're over there," Phillip responded.

Sam shot Phillip a glance that Colin knew meant trouble. She obviously didn't like the idea that Phillip had asked for something. She tried to act as if it was no big deal, but then she turned to Phillip and said, "It's OK, Phillip. We'll head over there in a little bit."

Phillip, completely thrown by Sam's interruption, looked at her and said, "He asked, Sam."

Colin, still standing with Jessica, looked at Phillip and said, "Honestly--it's no big deal. I'll grab you one. Anyone else?" Colin looked around the table, but there were no takers.

As they walked away from the table, Jessica grabbed his hand. He felt bad, but being here tonight was the last place he wanted to be. For the first time, in a long time, he felt like going home and getting drunk. Fate was messing with him, right here, in front of everyone. And fate was doing a good job, too, reminding him of what he'd given up. He wasn't going to make a scene and leave, but he also knew he wouldn't be staying long. Sitting across from the woman he loved, while she was sitting with the man she loved, was not his idea of a good time.

"Are you OK?" Jessica asked. "Are you upset? You don't seem like yourself."

Colin looked at Jessica and knew he couldn't take his feelings out on her. She was beautiful, smart, kind, and bubbly, and he'd be crazy not to feel happy. She was - for all intents and purposes - any guy's dream girl. She just wasn't *his* dream girl. He didn't want her to have a bad night, so he swallowed his feelings and knew he had to make it through the next two days as best he could. Sam would be leaving on

Sunday, and that would be the end of it. He could get back to normal, the way he'd done for the last ten years.

"I'm fine," Colin smiled at her. "Sorry, I guess I'm just tired, and sitting with Phillip McKnight is a little weird. I mean, it's crazy, right?"

"I know! I can't believe everyone else at the table is so calm. I'm going crazy inside. I know you said to make sure I toned it down with Sam, but holy crap!"

Colin grabbed their drinks and they headed back to the table. He just needed to get through dinner.

As Colin was about to hand Phillip his drink, Phillip got up and said, "Thanks so much." Adding, "So Colin," he began, "Samantha told me that the two of you dated some years ago."

Colin and Sam both froze. They didn't know where this conversation was going, but they were aware that you could hear a pin drop at their table at that moment. Everyone here knew their history except Phillip, Jessica, and Susan's date, but it was obvious that everyone else felt a moment of unease. Colin knew the only thing he could do was respond.

"Yeah, that's right. We dated back in high school."

"And how was my Samantha all those years ago?" Phillip asked, thinking he was making a light comment.

'*My Samantha*'? The words cut through him. Every eye at the table was on Colin. Nobody knew what he was going to say, and even Colin didn't know himself. He knew he could fluff over the question, or answer it directly and honestly. Colin looked at Sam as he answered Phillip truthfully, "She was amazing. Smart, kind, determined. Beautiful. She knew what she wanted out of life. And, to be honest with you, it doesn't look like much has changed. You're a lucky guy."

Colin wasn't sure how she'd react, but he hoped she'd hear it and know that he meant it, every single word. Sam felt his glance and looked over at Colin and smiled. She didn't say it, but it was her way of saying "thank you" to him.

"She really is a go-getter, isn't she? I love that about her," Phillip said.

"Yeah, she has always been that way. She's the biggest celebrity our little town has ever had," Colin smiled and looked down to grab his drink.

"Sam said you and your family own the auto body shop in town?" Phillip asked, seemingly interested.

Colin looked up, wishing this little conversation would end, but instead he smiled and carried on, "Yeah. When I came back to Rhode Island after leaving New York, I went into the family business with my dad and brother. Thanks to Cole over here," Colin pointed at him, "we run a pretty successful local business."

"Something to be proud of," Phillip cheered them both with his drink. "Not always easy trying to keep small businesses afloat these days, especially in small towns."

Sam exclaimed, "Phillip!"

"WHAT? I meant it as a compliment. Running a business in any small town today isn't easy, and if you can make it work, that's incredible." He looked at Cole and Colin, "I hope you didn't take offense to my comment. I truly meant it as a compliment."

Cole was the first to speak up, "No offense taken. You're right, it's not easy to run a business, and we've been lucky enough to have great people rely on us for years. We have our dad to thank for that."

"That's great. My hat is off to you guys, truly."

"Thanks, Phillip," Colin answered. "It's not always easy,

but we get along and we have fun working together, right Cole?"

Phillip smiled at the two brothers. He genuinely didn't mean any harm by his comment. He wasn't threatened by Colin one bit, even though the guy seemed to be every girl's fantasy in the looks department. Phillip was so secure in himself that it never occurred to him to feel jealous. He also wasn't the type of guy to read too much into an old romance and didn't give Colin and Sam a second thought about their years together. He had plenty of old romances himself, and he never thought about any of them. In his mind, he knew Sam was far better off in New York than she would be here in Rhode Island.

Just as Colin thought that their conversation had come to an end, Phillip asked, "So, Colin, why did you end up staying in Rhode Island?"

The question surprised Colin so much so that his eyes immediately darted towards Sam, trying to discern if she'd put him up to the question. But by the look on Sam's face, it was obvious she hadn't.

"Uh, well, it was so long ago, but I just never felt like I fit in, in New York." As much as he wanted to look at Phillip, his eyes stayed with Sam. It was almost like he was getting one more opportunity to explain it to her, too. "It always seemed so big and busy to me. I just never found my true place there."

"I can't imagine it's easy for anyone from a small town to move to a place like New York, never mind from a small New England town. It's the complete opposite," Phillip said. "I give you credit for trying. Most people wouldn't even get that far!"

"Yeah. It was, well, an adventure for me."

Colin looked around the table and was relieved to see

everyone had gone back to their own conversations. Cole and Sasha were talking animatedly about something. Susan and her date were chatting quietly. It was good to see that the spotlight was off them for the moment, although they had the undivided attention of Sam and Jessica.

Colin took a sip of his drink and then looked at Phillip. He could tell he wasn't a bad guy. Sam would never date an asshole. Phillip had been thrown into a crazy situation, likely not one he knew much about and he was making the best of it. "Have you ever lived anywhere else?" Colin asked, trying to make small talk with Phillip and move the conversation away from himself.

"Yeah, actually I went to Yale, so I lived in Connecticut for four years. Then I lived abroad in London for two years after college." Phillip reached for his drink. "I traveled Europe for a year after that, just going place to place, knowing I wouldn't have the opportunity to do that once I started working."

"Wow, so you've really seen a lot of the world," Colin responded. He knew that Sam probably loved this about Phillip. He was a world traveler. He'd been all over, not confined to a small town in Rhode Island. "New York called you back, huh?"

"Oh, yeah," Phillip said excitedly. "It's the best city in the world. Of all the places I've been, it's the one place that still excites my soul. You can be anything you want to be in New York and there's something special about that, and the business opportunities are endless."

Colin nodded his head, "Must feel good to have New York as your home. You seem to belong there." Colin didn't know if he was talking to Phillip or Sam, knowing New York was home for Sam, as well. He didn't really understand her deep love for the city. Maybe if he had given it a real chance, he might feel the same way.

"Ever regret leaving?" Phillip asked.

That was the million-dollar question. Colin took a deep breath and exhaled, looking straight at Sam and not at Phillip. This time everyone at the table was listening again. Sam's eyes locked with his and he knew what he needed to say, here, in front of everyone, so that nobody could say he didn't try. He didn't want to hurt Jessica, but he knew she had to know, on some level, how he felt. If he didn't say it or get it off his chest, he knew he'd regret this moment for years to come. He was done with regret. He loved being the good guy and the nice guy, but right now he needed to be the honest-to-God guy. Colin closed his eyes for a second and then opened them, still looking straight at Sam, "Yes, I've regretted leaving New York, not once, but twice. I've regretted it every single day of my life for the last ten years. Every single day."

And with that, Colin excused himself, turned, and walked away. He knew that Phillip wouldn't be happy with that answer, but Phillip had Sam, and he didn't.

Phillip turned to look at Sam and saw that her cheeks were flushed. She looked like she was going to cry, but no tears had fallen. Her sister Sasha was holding Sam's arm and Cole looked up to see where his brother was going and then followed him. Jessica left and went toward the house. Nobody said a word. Everyone at the table looked uncomfortable and Phillip was watching it all unfold in front of him. Slowly, he began to connect the dots. Colin regretted leaving Samantha because he was still in love with her. But was Samantha still in love with him? From the look on her face, he thought he knew the answer.

24

"What the fuck was that?" Cole asked Colin as he caught up with him at the bar where nobody else was around.

"What the fuck was what?" Colin asked again, knowing full well what his brother meant.

"I've been telling you to come clean with her for the past few days and you decide, in front of everyone at the table, to make it freaking awkward," Cole said, his voice full of exasperation.

Colin shrugged and ordered a Sam Adams. He knew he had made it awkward. He hadn't intended to, but after dealing with Phillip and seeing the two of them right there in front of him, he couldn't help himself. In fact, right now, he felt like pounding the shit out of Phillip, and Cole, and anyone else who felt compelled to share their opinions with him. He finally looked over at his brother and said, "To be honest, right now, I don't give a shit. I really don't care what you or anybody else thinks. She's in my freaking head, and I can't get her out of it."

Cole huffed, knowing he was on thin ice, "And Dude,

you just walked away? What the hell is going on with you? This isn't like you."

"Jesus, Cole. Just give me a second, OK?" Colin said, sounding frustrated and upset. "I mean, I'm sitting there making meaningless small talk with Phillip FREAKING McKnight, listening to an account of his exceptional stellar life, all while watching Sam. Not easy, believe me. I tried my best to keep the conversation light, but when he asked me if I regretted leaving, what was I supposed to say?"

"I don't know, Bro," Cole said. "Lie to him, maybe. But, Jesus, our whole table didn't know what to do, Jessica included."

At the mention of her name, Colin looked around to see where Jessica was. The last thing he wanted to do was hurt her or put her in a weird position. "Shit, do you know where she went?"

"It looked like she walked towards the house, so maybe she went to the bathroom or something," answered Cole.

"I didn't mean to put Jessica in an awkward position, but I'd had enough. Shit."

"Listen, Colin, you've got to be straight with yourself. You have to stop doing this to yourself. You've got a great girl in Jessica. She really likes you. If you don't like her, you can't string her along."

"Geez, spoken like a true dating expert," Colin answered.

Cole laughed, "I may not have found the one to settle down with, but Jessica's a nice girl, and I honestly felt bad for her. Sasha gave me a look, so she may have gone after Jessica."

Colin looked at Cole, "What about Sam?"

"What about her, Colin? What do you expect her to do? You haven't been totally honest with her, so she's probably confused, too. I love you bro, but man, you're an ass when it comes to your love life. It's almost like you enjoy the heartbreak."

Colin shook his head and turned around to look towards their table. Phillip was still sitting there with Sam, but Sasha and Jessica were missing. He didn't know what to do. Now it felt weird to go back over to the table. They hadn't even eaten dinner yet, so he wasn't sure what he should do. He knew he couldn't return and pretend nothing had happened, but he didn't feel like explaining anything either. Why did he always put himself in these situations with Sam? It could never just be easy with the two of them.

"I'm going to go find Jessica and try to smooth things over," Colin told Cole.

"Are you going to head back to the table?" Cole said.

"How can I at this point?" Colin responded. "I can't sit there with the two of them. He probably wants to punch me in the face, too."

Cole shook his head from side to side, "I don't know what goes through your head sometimes. You love hard, my brother, that's for sure," Cole put his arm around Colin's shoulder, "Listen, go find Jessica and explain things to her. Just be honest and let her know the deal with you and Sam. She's probably confused as hell right now."

"You're right," Colin responded, then headed off to find Jessica. The last thing he wanted to do was hurt her, or embarrass her, and, truthfully, he felt like he'd done both at the moment. If Sam had never come home, or if their paths hadn't crossed, or their lips hadn't touched, he probably would be able to move forward with Jessica. He would have gone into autopilot and known that this was a good relationship and tried to make it work. It was crazy to think that even after all of these years, Sam still held that kind of power over his heart. He always thought deep down inside that she did too, but he was able to hide it and not have to deal with it. The hardest part was knowing how he felt and knowing that she wouldn't be his again.

Colin walked into the McKay house and saw Jessica standing against the bathroom door next to Sasha. She didn't look like she was crying, so that was good, but she did seem upset. When she looked up and saw Colin coming towards her, she whispered something to Sasha. Colin wasn't sure what she'd said, but Sasha nodded, politely smiled at Colin, and then walked away.

"Hey," Colin said with a smile. "Listen, I think we need to talk."

Jessica nodded her head, "Yeah, seems like we do." He grabbed her hand and led her towards the front of the McKay house. Colin didn't want to talk inside with people everywhere, so he led Jessica across the street, directly in front of his parent's house.

Jessica looked up at Colin, directly in his eyes, with hurt in her voice, "You're still in love with her, aren't you?"

Colin didn't know what to say. He didn't like being put on the spot, but he also knew he owed Jessica the truth. Unfortunately, he was at a loss for words.

"You don't have to answer me, Colin. I can tell," she looked down at her feet and then back up at Colin. "Please don't lie to me. I had a feeling you still felt something for her."

"You did?" Colin asked.

"I never knew who was responsible for creating the fence around your heart, but now I know."

Colin laughed a little, "Fence around my heart? What do you mean by that?"

"Colin, I'm not a fool. I was hoping this," she pointed to him and then to herself, "would pan into something. You're a great guy. You're smart and sweet and well-liked throughout town. I've always wondered why you were still single, and then when we started dating I could tell right away you had a guard up around you when it came to your heart. You have a tough time letting someone in. I was willing to stick around and see if there was a way to get over that fence, but tonight I realized it's an impossible thing to do. I can't compete with someone who still controls your heart. She has already won. I haven't, and I won't."

Colin blushed as she talked, not wanting to look into her eyes, but knowing he owed her at least that much. He felt badly that he didn't feel for Jessica what she felt for him.

"Jessica... I'm so sorry."

"Are you? I mean, were you ever going to tell me? Or were you just waiting for her to leave town so that everything between us would be fine again? Was any of this real?"

Colin felt horrible. He hadn't wanted to hurt Jessica, but realized now that it had already been done. "Yes, of course, all of it was real between us. I really like being with you, Jessica. It's just that Sam and I have a complicated past," Colin said.

"But she's engaged, so why are you doing this to yourself?" Jessica spoke loudly, clearly exasperated. "You know, I feel so stupid. When I think back, you had a look in your eye the first night we saw her, when we were out to dinner together. You were completely distracted after you chatted with her, and I remember thinking that maybe you were just star-struck," she said.

"You mean, like you were?" Colin asked, trying to joke and make the situation a little lighter.

That seemed to break the ice a little. A smile spread across Jessica's face as she thought back. "Yes, like me. I probably made a fool of myself this week."

"Don't worry about that. But, in all honesty, Jess, I didn't know my feelings for Sam were still so strong. You might not believe me, but I always had good intentions with you, with us. I always knew that she held a piece of my heart, but we ended on such bad terms a long time ago that I tried to lock things away and not think about her. When I saw her this week, for the first time in ten years, it was like a lightning bolt for me. I didn't expect it, I swear. I need you to know that."

"I believe you, Colin. As much as it sucks for me, I do believe you," Jessica said in a whisper, feeling slightly badly for him, knowing that he didn't have a chance with Sam again. "She seems like a great girl from a great family. And honestly, I was hoping this would go somewhere," pointing at the two of them again, "but I'm glad I know now. Both of us deserve to be happy, and not waste our time on things that will never be."

"For what it's worth, you're a great girl. Anyone will be lucky to have you," Colin said to Jessica.

"Just not you," Jessica replied, staring up at the night sky. "You know, like I said, I always knew something was blocking us, but now everything connects for me. I hope that someday your heart opens up and you are able to love someone else, Colin. You're a good man, and you deserve happiness and love. She may still have your heart right now, but don't let her keep it forever. You'll miss out on what could be. That would be a sad way to live your life."

Colin stood there absorbing Jessica's words, and feeling bad for having hurt her. She was upset, but at least she wasn't acting crazy. They might not have been dating for long, but Jess knew exactly what was going on.

"Listen, I don't think it's right for me to go to the

wedding, Colin. I would feel uncomfortable and I don't want to feel like that."

"I understand. I want you to do whatever you think best. I don't want to cause you any more grief."

"I'm going to head out. Please apologize to everyone. I'll make sure to connect with them after the wedding."

Colin nodded, feeling relieved that he and Jessica had talked, but feeling deflated that she was leaving feeling hurt and embarrassed. She had been looking forward to this wedding since he'd asked her to come with him. He couldn't have done a better job of ruining it for her.

"I'm really sorry, Jess," Colin said, genuinely meaning it. "I hope that we can still be friends."

"Just give me some time," Jess said, smiling politely but with tears in her eyes. "And for what it's worth, if she's not willing to fight for you, I don't know why you're fighting so hard for her."

25

S am was stunned by what had just happened and felt sick to her stomach. She could tell Phillip was confused, and he hadn't said a word after Colin left the table. He was actually giving her the silent treatment, which was not like him. They'd never really had a fight or a disagreement before, so having it right here at her parent's house, during her sister's wedding rehearsal dinner, was absolutely awful. She had to do something.

Leaning over to Phillip, she whispered to him, "Can we go inside and talk for a second?"

"What. Right now? Isn't dinner supposed to be coming out any second?"

"Phillip, please. I want to talk to you about what just happened. I don't want it to be weird like this between us."

"I didn't make it weird, Sam. That happened all on its own," he said as he glanced over to where Colin had been sitting.

"Please, can we talk about this inside?" said Sam, desperate to get away from the table.

Phillip sighed a bit, but nodded his head. He did love

Sam and he didn't want to be fighting with her, but she had clearly left out a few details as to how serious she and Colin had been - and maybe still were. "Sure, let's go somewhere quiet."

"We can go up to my room. Nobody will be up there," Sam said, and with that, they left

the table and headed into the house.

Sam didn't know where Colin and Jessica had gone and she was hoping they wouldn't be in the house. Running into them was the last thing any of them needed, and she didn't want to deal with that added headache right now. She just wanted to get upstairs and talk to Phillip.

As they walked into her bedroom, she suddenly felt her heart start to sink. She didn't want to do this right now, but she knew she had to. She owed it to Phillip to be 100% honest this time, to explain to him just how important Colin had been in her life, and that he *had* been more than a high school boyfriend, much more than that.

As soon as Sam shut the door, she looked over at Phillip who was sitting on her bed, his phone buzzing like crazy, but he wasn't reaching for it. He was just looking at her, wanting to know what was going on.

"Do you want to get those texts?" Sam asked.

"Honestly? Right now all I can think about is you. What the hell just happened down there with Colin?"

Sitting next to Phillip on the bed, she slowly began to explain, "Colin and I began dating in 8th grade and we continued until I was a sophomore at Parsons. He was my person."

"Your person?" Phillip asked, turning sideways to face her. "What does that mean?"

"He was my everything, Phillip. *Everything*."

The word hit Phillip slowly, but with the power of a

sucker punch. He understood exactly what she had just said.

"So, what happened?" Phillip asked. "What *really* happened?"

"In all honestly, I didn't know until a couple of days ago," Sam answered. "I thought we were fine in New York and then one day he just up and left."

"Just like that?" Phillip asked.

Sam nodded, "Just like that." She started fidgeting with the blanket on her bed. "Naturally, I was devastated and tried my best to get him to come back. I was even prepared to come back to Rhode Island, but he wouldn't take my calls or anything. He literally just ended things and I never knew why."

"And now you do?"

"For the first time in ten years, I've seen Colin. He finally told me that he had been miserable in New York and just felt he was happier here in Rhode Island. I was going to school and having the time of my life with friends and my classes, and feeling like I had finally found my place. All the while, he was there waiting tables and waiting for me to graduate. Thinking back now, it had to have been horrible for him. I was at the beginning of my new life, and he wasn't sure where he fit in. He saw me having a great time and meeting new people and creating a world for myself. He felt lost."

"So he left and never returned?"

"Yes, that's what I thought, but this week I found out that he had come back a year later, but I never saw him."

"And this made you never want to come back home?" Phillip asked, sounding uncertain.

"Phillip, he broke my heart into a million pieces and never stopped to think that it would affect me the way it did.

I was never able to forgive him. Coming home after that meant I risked seeing him, and I just didn't even want to look at him at that point. I can't explain it anymore than that. My heart was truly shattered."

"But you're OK with him now?" Phillip asked, obviously still confused.

"I'm OK because now I understand. He left for me. He knew I'd quit school and come back with him if he didn't end things badly. He needed me to be mad and hurt so I wouldn't follow him. He ignited a fire in me that I just refused to put out. I threw myself into my studies and work, and I kept going to prove that I would make it. I didn't need him there to help me do it."

"I love that about you, Samantha. You're a go-getter and you focus on what needs to be done. It's one of the many reasons I love you."

"I want you to know that I love you, Phillip. I do. This week shook me. I'm not going to lie. It brought up feelings that I didn't know I still had. I think avoiding Colin for so long, and trying to bury what happened, really did a number on me."

"So let me ask the big question, where do you and Colin stand now?"

"I don't really know, Phillip." She looked at him and smiled with a caring eye. "I know that's not the answer you want to hear. I've felt lost this week but, at the same time..." she walked across the room and looked out at the Dasher house, "I've also felt whole for the first time in a long time."

Phillip stood up and walked over to where Sam was standing. "I love you, Samantha, but you need to figure out what it is that you want. I thought it was me, and our future together. But now, I'm unsure. I saw your face when Colin said he regretted leaving. You went white. I actually thought for a second that you might chase after him."

"Oh, Phillip," Sam said, taking a moment to reassure him. "I'm here with you. I would never have left you sitting there. I love you, Phillip, I do. I'm sorry I've been off this week. I just wasn't prepared for everything that has happened."

During their conversation, Phillip's phone kept buzzing nonstop. Sam had never seen Phillip blatantly ignore it like this. She was floored and shocked at the same time.

"Honestly, Phillip. You can get your phone. I'm not going anywhere. I'll wait right here," Sam said.

He grabbed his phone and looked down, visibly agitated by something. "I gotta make a quick call, Samantha. This whole deal is going to fold if I don't get on and smooth things over. It's just a freaking mess."

"You stay here and make your calls. I'm going to head back to the party," Sam said, kissing Phillip on the cheek and giving his arm a squeeze.

"I'm all in, Samantha," Phillip said. "I just want you to know that. I believe in us and I know we will make a beautiful life together. When we get back to New York, things will be different. We're leaving in two days and you won't have to worry about any of this anymore. I promise. I just need to make sure you're still in this, too."

26

Sam returned to the rehearsal dinner and smiled when she saw Sarah and Chris across the room, holding hands and whispering to each other. True love. It was a beautiful sight to see. They were head-over-heels. That was the best way to describe them. They were each other's best friends and confidants, each other's everything. Sam was so happy for her sister and Chris. They deserved this kind of love.

David McKay walked over and put his arm around her. He'd heard what had happened at their table, but didn't want to pry. Raising four daughters had taught him one thing in life - there were no such things as secrets. His girls were gossip hounds, especially Sasha and Susan, so he knew something was amiss when he noticed that Phillip, Colin, and Jessica were nowhere to be seen. As a dad, he knew the best thing he could do for his daughter was to just let her know he was there for her.

"How's my girl?" he asked, giving her a kiss on the cheek.

"I'm fine, Dad, just taking it all in. Sarah looks really

happy, huh?" They both looked in her direction and smiled simultaneously.

"She sure does, Honey."

"I know you know that Phillip proposed to me," Sam said, looking up at him.

He smiled, "I was wondering when he was going to pop the question. I'm keeping things quiet, but your mother? She's another story!"

"I wanted to wait until after the wedding to say anything. I didn't want to take anything away from Sarah and Chris and their big weekend."

"And that's the older sister in you, always there, and always will be. We just want you to be happy, Sam. That's my only wish for all of my girls - happiness. Be with someone who makes you happy. Be with someone who lights you up. Be with someone who will love you no matter what."

"Thanks, Dad. That's just I want," and she pointed at Mom waving to him across the room with a big smile. "It's beautiful what you and Mom have."

"Thirty-five years and she still puts up with me. I'm a lucky guy!" And with that, he walked over to join his wife.

Sam smiled as she watched him walk across the yard. The love they shared for each other had always been something she admired, and seeing them so in love after all this time was an inspiration.

Sam wasn't sure how long Phillip would be on the phone, perhaps the rest of the night, but she didn't want to sit by herself making unnecessary small talk with people. She just wanted to head back to the hotel, put on her pajamas, and go to bed. She knew she couldn't leave yet, and decided to walk to the side of the house and sit for a little bit. Her mother had a secret garden along one side of the house that had always been her pride and joy. There was a small bench there and was the perfect place to retreat. She'd head over there for a few minutes to collect herself and take a deep breath without someone breathing down her neck.

As Sam rounded the corner, she felt the tension in her body start to subside. She could still hear guests around the corner of the house, but she was just far enough removed that it felt peaceful and quiet. Her mother had done an exceptional job with the flowers in this garden, everything was gorgeous and the vibrant colors were spectacular. She sat down, taking it all in, sitting there in the moonlight with the stars above.

"I did come back for you."

Sam knew that voice. She didn't even need to look. It was Colin.

She turned to see him walk out from the shadows of the garden. He looked so handsome in the glow of the moonlight.

"So I heard," was all she could say. She looked at him, wanting to know more, but not knowing if he was going to share or not.

Colin nodded his head and walked closer to her, but he was still at least five feet away. "I wasn't sure if you ever knew that I came back."

"No, nobody ever told me."

"I didn't want you to know," Colin said. "I actually went to surprise you."

"Surprise me? I never saw you. And then you left? Again?" Sam was very confused as to why he'd even come back to New York that second time.

Colin took a deep breath and walked a little closer to Sam. He looked directly into her eyes, "I came back to ask you to marry me."

Sam froze. Her eyes didn't leave Colin's. She was trying to process what he was saying, but she couldn't quite grasp the words. She blinked, trying to break the trance between them.

"You came back to propose?" Sam finally asked.

Colin nodded. "When I moved back home the first time, I was miserable. I mean, immediately miserable. Funny thing was that I moved back because I was miserable in New York, so I thought being home would be easier. But it was hell on earth. I was here *without you*. Everything reminded me of you. Everyone reminded me of you. I couldn't walk down the street without feeling like a part of me was missing."

Sam just continued to stare, completely speechless.

"I didn't know what to do," Colin continued. I was just dying here. I realized pretty quickly that as much as New York didn't feel like home to me, home was only where you were. I knew I had been wrong, leaving you there, but in my mind, I loved you enough to let you go. I didn't know if you'd come back with me, but I didn't want to put you in the position to have to choose. Like I told you, I knew you were destined for great things and those things weren't here in Rhode Island."

"So what happened?" Sam asked.

"Well, I knew I needed to see you. But I also knew that you probably weren't going to just take me back that easily. I mean, I had broken your heart, so why would you believe that I wouldn't do it again."

Colin was now less than a foot away.

"I knew I needed to go back with guns blazing. I worked my ass off for six months, saving up for a ring. That was my only goal, I wanted to buy you a ring that was worthy of you."

Sam was still frozen, and she could hear herself breathing heavily, not sure if he could tell that she had tears starting to form in her eyes.

"I went back to New York, *exactly* one year later. The only people who knew were my parents and Cole. I didn't even ask your parents for your hand, as I was afraid they'd say no. The only thing I knew was that I needed you, and I prayed you felt the same way."

"But why didn't you ever ask me?" Sam asked, as a single tear trickled down her cheek.

"Oh, Sam, I wanted to ask you." Colin's voice started to crack. He looked down at his feet and then swallowed hard. He needed a second to collect himself. "I knew you were still living in the same apartment, so I waited across the street, hoping to surprise you—in a good way."

Colin turned around and walked a couple of feet away, trying to figure out how to get the next part out. He wasn't looking at her. He was looking out into the darkness in front of him.

"Colin?"

He slowly turned around and she saw his eyes were filled with tears, "I saw you walking down the sidewalk with another guy, holding his hand."

"What? Who?" Sam asked, horrified and confused.

Colin shook his head, "I don't know, but I saw you and him together, and you looked so happy and so lit up. I watched the two of you walk into your building together, and it was in that moment that I knew I had lost you. It was my own fault. I had waited too long."

Sam looked up and tried to think of who she could have been walking with that day. That was a long time ago, and she certainly hadn't been dating anyone seriously for a very long time after Colin left. She had been so upset, she had sworn off men. Who could it have been? Then, just like a balloon popping, she suddenly remembered.

"Wait a second," Sam whispered. "Oh, my God, I think you're talking about Adam."

"Adam?" Colin asked.

"Yes, Colin. Adam. My neighbor. Oh, Colin. Nothing was ever going on with Adam. He and his boyfriend lived across the hallway from me. We were just good friends. We took a class together at Parsons and would always walk home together after. That must have been Adam you saw. Not a boyfriend."

That vision of Sam walking home with her hand in another guy's hand had haunted him for years. Even now, thinking about that day, his stomach was in knots. That moment had defined his future. Hearing her say it was a misunderstanding was crushing, heart and soul-crushing.

"So all these years of being here and miserable without you were just a twist-of-fate misunderstanding?"

"I'm so sorry, Colin," was all Sam could say. "I think so. I never dated anyone for years after you left. I couldn't."

"Fate," Colin said. "It's a funny thing, huh?"

"I don't know what to say, Colin," Sam said. "I had no idea, I wish I had known."

Colin turned his back to her again and walked away a bit. He was trying to comprehend what he had just found out. All these years. All these days. All these moments. If he'd just gone to her and told her, none of this would have happened. If he had just fought for her, it would be different now. He let her go without a fight all those years ago.

"I would have said yes," Sam said from behind him, her voice almost a whisper. "I would've absolutely said yes to you."

Colin turned back around. "You would have?"

Sam was crying now. All she could do was slowly nod her head up and down.

"And now?" Colin asked, gasping for air and not knowing what would happen, but knowing that if he didn't fight some way, somehow, he wouldn't be able to move on with his life.

Sam just stood there. Tears streaming down her cheeks.

"Now?" she wiped the tears from her cheeks. "Colin, I'm engaged to Phillip."

He just nodded. He knew. He couldn't compete with that. She had found a way to move on, and he needed to do the same. He knew that he shouldn't touch her, but he didn't know what else to do. He walked over and hugged Sam. It wasn't a hug to ignite the passion within them; it was a hug to say good-bye. This was the closure he needed. He knew this story needed an ending. He needed the potential to find and start another love story with someone else.

Their hug lasted a couple of minutes, both of them feeling it and knowing the power of it. Colin looked down at her and pulled away. He breathed in and started to walk away, knowing that their absence from the party would most likely be noticed by now. As Sam turned to walk off, Colin had a feeling in his heart. Something within him felt like fighting, and he knew he had nothing to lose.

"Sam," Colin said.

She turned and looked at Colin, her eyes puffy and red.

"If I don't tell you this, I will regret it for the rest of my life." Colin was nervous, his voice was shaking, but he knew he needed to tell her. "I love you with all of my heart and soul. I've loved you since I was a kid. I've never stopped loving you, and I know this because of how I feel right now, miserable and lost in love with you." Colin looked up at the darkness of the sky, looking for strength to keep going. "I loved you enough all those years ago to let you go because I thought that was best. I was wrong. I should've had more faith in you, and in us. I was young and stupid. I knew I messed up, which is why I returned to try to fix things. I've lived the last ten years without the love of my life, hoping and praying someone else would come along. But it just never happened.

"I know that you're engaged and that you're going to marry Phillip McKnight. He can give more than I can in terms of things, this I know. I can't give you the kind of stuff he can, but I'm telling you, I can give you love. I love all of you, every part of you. I will always love you." Colin took a deep breath and exhaled it out loudly, "You're my person."

With that, Colin turned and walked into the darkness toward his parent's house, knowing that he wouldn't be returning to the party and most likely would not going to the wedding tomorrow.

Sam just stood there, watching him walk off into the darkness, unable to say a word.

27

W hen Sam woke up the next morning, she felt as if she had a terrible hangover, but it wasn't from drinking. The heaviness and pounding in her head had made her not want to open her eyes or get out of bed. She just lay there, staring at the ceiling, wondering how she'd even fallen asleep. She was surprised she'd slept at all. She couldn't get that conversation with Colin out of her head. He loved her. He wanted to be with her. He had chosen her and had always chosen her. There was nobody else. She almost couldn't comprehend what he had told her. She hadn't expected it - not at all. She'd felt the sparks and the passion and the heart flutters all week when she'd been around Colin, but she hadn't known how he felt. Their kiss was hot, but she didn't know if it was just old flames burning or true passion heating up again. Listening to him pour his heart out to her, she realized the depth of his feelings. She wished he'd said all those things to her years ago.

"You awake?" Phillip asked as he turned over in bed to face her. He reached over and planted a kiss on her cheek.

Sam turned to look at him and smiled, "Yeah, I'm awake. I feel like hell, but I'm awake."

"You hardly slept last night. You were tossing and turning all night."

"Yeah, sorry for the restlessness. I slept badly."

"Well, you still look beautiful in the morning, even when you don't sleep," Phillip assured her.

"You're lying, or you need glasses, but thank you," Sam smiled and gave him a kiss.

"Listen, if your sleeplessness had anything to do with our talk last night, I'm sorry Samantha. I didn't mean to upset you. I just wanted to make sure we were on the same page. I thought proposing here, this week, would have gone a little differently."

"I'm sorry, Phillip, I really am. I know this week has not gone the way you planned. I wanted to keep our engagement a secret until after the wedding. I just didn't want to take anything away from Sarah."

"I know Samantha, I'm not mad about that, I understand. I just want you to know that I'm here for you. I know everything got a little messy with Colin and I'm sorry about that. My only concern is to make sure you're OK."

'Messy' didn't even begin to cover it. Phillip had no idea what had happened after she'd left him working in her bedroom last night. She would never tell him what Colin had told her. She couldn't. She needed to make sure that Phillip knew, despite everything, that she still intended to keep her promise to be with him.

"Everything is fine, Phillip," she said again as she started to get herself up and out of bed, trying to ignore her splitting headache. "Colin and I were a couple a long time ago. Being home definitely brought up stuff that has been brewing for a long time, but heading back home will be the best thing for me. I know that I just need to get back to the City, back to work, and back to our normal lives."

Phillip smiled and started to get out of bed, too. "That's what I figured. I mean, being here with your family, it's been great getting to know them a little better, but it's so different here from our normal lives. Once we're home and back into our regular routines, I know things will settle down and we'll be back to normal."

Sam knew that heading home to New York wouldn't be the easy "Band-Aid" that Phillip was thinking it would be, but she didn't want to talk about this anymore. She had so much going on in her head about Colin, that she just needed time to sort everything out. Last night, as she lay awake, she kept thinking about what her life would have been like here in Rhode Island. What would she have done? Where would she have lived? Would she have been happy? Would she have taken over at Fatima's? The questions raced through her head, but she didn't know the answers to any of them. That life was worlds away from her life now. She'd established herself, money wasn't an issue and status wasn't something that concerned her. She had accomplished everything she had set out to accomplish, and was now at the point where she had an incredible team in place to help her keep reaching and growing. She knew now that she would keep in better touch with her parents and sisters, Mrs. Dasher and also Fatima, too. These were the silver linings of being home.

Running the shower, she did a mental checklist of the busy day ahead. Despite thinking about her 'job-to-do' list, she thought about seeing him today. She wasn't sure how she'd face Colin. He had walked off last night and left her with a loss of words.

As she was about to get into the shower, she thought she

heard Phillip talking to her. She quickly popped her head out of the bathroom to tell him that she couldn't hear him, but she realized he was on the phone again. He was visibly upset, so she decided to leave him to it and into the shower and let the hot water do its magic.

After ten minutes or so of pure bliss, Sam toweled off and just then Phillip opened the bathroom door. "You're not going to believe this, but I've got to head back to the City," he said. "This damn deal needs me there or it's not going to happen."

Sam looked at him, "But it's my sister's wedding! You can't go home yet. Can't you just head home tonight?"

Phillip rubbed his eyes and looked agitated, "I don't know, Samantha. This is a really big deal worth hundreds of millions. A lot of people are involved and I can't afford to lose this. I've been working on it for months."

"Well, this is Sarah's wedding and it's a big deal to me, too," Sam answered, now irritated.

"I know, Sam. How about this? I'll stay for the ceremony, but I'll leave right after that. I'm going to have my father send the private plane for me tonight. Do you want to come home with me then?"

"Phillip!" Sam shouted, "I can't come home with you tonight. It's the reception and I want to be there. I was planning on heading home with you tomorrow afternoon."

Phillip walked over to Sam. "I wish I could stay here 'til tomorrow, Samantha. Unfortunately, I can't. I need to head back to recover this deal. I'll stay through dinner tonight and then head out. I'll make sure to give Sarah and Chris a really wonderful gift for leaving early," he said.

Sam smiled a little, "Don't worry about that. They really don't care about that kind of stuff."

Phillip didn't look as upset as he had when he first

walked into the bathroom. Seeing Sam naked had taken his anxiety down a few levels, and now all he wanted to do was join her. But Sam wasn't feeling it. Her mind was mush at the moment. Trying to deter him, she quickly asked him to grab her a fresh towel and made an excuse about how she was running late and had to get going.

"I've got to head out, Phillip! I booked the hair and makeup for everyone today and if I'm not there to greet them, all hell will break loose," she explained.

"Fine. GO!!" Phillip pronounced. "I'll meet you at the church. Are you set for tomorrow? Do you need me to have Maggie book you anything?"

"Oh, crap! Yes! I need her to book me a flight home. I can fly from the Providence Airport to New York. I'll take any flight she can book for me, as long as it's after 5pm."

"I'll call Maggie right now," Phillip said as he grabbed his phone.

Flying home alone to New York actually seemed like the best thing. It would give her time alone after this insane week. She just needed time to think. That's all she needed. She knew that she loved Phillip, but she needed to know if she was *crazy* in love with Phillip.

Or was she still crazy in love with Colin?

28

S arah's wedding ceremony was spectacular. Sarah had been deliriously happy just before they all walked down the aisle, the crazy love kind of happy. This was confirmed when Sam saw her sister lock eyes with Chris. She loved him with all of her heart and soul. They were different, sure, but they had a love that she knew would last. There wasn't a second of doubt about that. As Sarah exchanged vows with Chris before of all of their family and friends, Sam looked out at the congregation and saw Phillip smiling at her. She knew that he was thinking about the two of them and how they'd be next.

Sam didn't see Colin anywhere in the church. She didn't want to look obvious, but every time she had the chance to look out at the hundreds of people in the church, she thought she would see him and lock eyes. She spotted Mr. and Mrs. Dasher, along with Cole, but no Colin. As far as she could see, he wasn't sitting with them or near them. She knew she'd see him at the reception. That was inevitable. But she wasn't sure what she would say, or how she would react. It made her jittery just thinking about it.

As Sarah and Chris exchanged vows and kissed in front of everyone, all Sam could do was wonder about her own future. A wedding ceremony was taking place directly in front of her, with all of its beauty, elegance, and love, and Sam was having an out-of-body experience. It was like she was watching from above. She was there, but she wasn't there. Her mind was cluttered with what would happen next. She did not want to face Colin today.

Standing in front of the church, after the ceremony, with all the guests milling around, Sam tried to find Phillip. She didn't feel like talking to many people and, thankfully, everyone wanted a piece of Sarah and Chris, which was perfect.

"Samantha!" Sam heard someone call from behind her. She turned to see Phillip walking toward her with Maggie, his assistant. Sam did a double-take because she couldn't believe Maggie was at her sister's wedding, here at the church.

"Maggie?" Sam asked, looking at her and then at Phillip.

"Hi Samantha," Maggie went in to give Sam a hug and a kiss on the cheek. "You look beautiful, as always," Maggie smiled.

"Thank you, but what are you doing here?" Sam laughed.

"You probably haven't had a chance to talk to Phillip since this morning. As soon as Phillip said he needed the private plane sent here for tonight, he suggested I hop on so we could go over everything on the way home tonight."

Phillip smiled at Maggie and then looked at Sam. "Honestly—I've got the best assistant in the world," Phillip beamed. "I had her meet me here to give me some things that needed my signature. She's going to email them to the office and then get back to the plane while we're at the reception. As soon as dinner is over, I'm going to head to the airport."

"Sounds good, I'm glad you can come for a little bit," Sam responded. She knew when Phillip was crazy busy with work, there wasn't much she could do but let him get on with it. The fact that he was even staying through dinner was surprising. Normally, she would have just told him to leave, but she was nervous about having to face Colin and she knew Phillip would be a good distraction for her at the reception.

"And Maggie, before Phillip leaves the reception, I'll make sure he brings you a plate from dinner," Sam smiled. "I can't imagine you've eaten much if you just got off the plane and came right here."

"That's sweet of you Sam. Thank you."

Phillip and Sam joined the wedding party and headed off to the reception with everyone. Sam loved being with her sisters. They had been so close when they were younger, and it was evident to Sam that the four of them were still very tight. She felt badly that she'd allowed her life to derail her relationships with her sisters and her parents. She should have done a better job of managing that, and, as of this moment, she committed herself to putting things right. She felt a little twinge of guilt and jealousy watching them laugh with one another. Even though she'd been out of the sister loop for a long time, they brought her right back in. It made her smile to be part of the incredible McKay foursome.

As they walked into the reception, Phillip grabbed Sam's hand and led her to their table. They were seated at the head table, along with the rest of her family and Chris's family. Thankfully, there were no Dasher place names at the table. It was going to be a fun evening and she was sorry that Phillip was going to miss it.

"Penny for your thoughts," Phillip asked as he grabbed two glasses of champagne from a waiter.

"My thoughts?" Sam smiled.

"You've looked a little distant, like you've been thinking about something. The only other time I see you like this is when you're in design mode and need to be head down without anyone distracting you."

"Oh," Sam smiled. "Nothing's wrong. I'm just thinking about my sister and Chris, and I'm so happy for them. It was a beautiful ceremony."

"AND IT'S neat to think that we'll be next, huh?" Phillip smiled.

Sam looked up at Phillip and didn't know what to say, so she just smiled.

"I hope you're not angry that I'm taking off. I know you want me to stay, but I just can't, Samantha."

"I know, Phillip," Sam said. "I'm not upset about it, I swear. It would be nice to have you here, but I'm heading back home tomorrow, so I will see you tomorrow night. Nothing's going to happen after you leave, but I just can't take off tonight. It wouldn't go over well with my family."

As they sat down to dinner, Sam quickly looked around the room to see if she could spot Colin, but it almost seemed as if he wasn't there. She looked around to see where Cole was sitting and she spotted him at a large table full of people, including his parents and two empty seats next to him.

Sam turned toward her sister Sasha and whispered into her ear, "Have you seen Colin at all?"

Sasha looked at Sam and shook her head, "No. Why? You don't see him?"

"No, I haven't seen him anywhere, not at the ceremony, nor here at the reception."

Sasha looked around the room for a few seconds, "That's odd. I'm sure he's here somewhere. I don't think anyone canceled. Besides, you know that we would have heard about it by now!"

Sam laughed, "Very true."

Sasha looked over at Phillip and then whispered back to Sam, "Did you need to talk to him?"

Sam shook her head, "Oh, no, nothing like that. I just wanted to see if he was here."

Sasha looked at her sister and then scanned the room one more time. She did see the empty seats at the Dasher table. She knew that something had happened between Sam and Colin this week, but Sam hadn't opened up yet about it. She seemed very different tonight, very quiet. She wasn't sure if it was because Phillip was here, or that she would be leaving tomorrow. Her sister had seemed like her old self this entire week, and for the first time since she'd arrived, she'd kind of retreated into a shell.

"Let me know if you need anything, OK?" Sasha said, and then she reached over and touched Sam's hand. "And, Sam? I'm sorry about last night. I'm such an idiot. I didn't even think about Phillip and Colin. I shouldn't have messed around with the seating plan. I know now it must have been awkward for the guys, and for Jessica."

"Thanks, Sash," Sam smiled back. "I swear you just can't help yourself sometimes, huh?"

"I felt horrible all night. I was just trying to avoid sitting with the married groomsmen," she smiled. "But I didn't stop to think about the situation I was creating for you and everyone else. I really am sorry, Sam. I embarrassed every-one, including myself. I love you, and I hope you can forgive me. I've learned my lesson."

"I love you too, Sis, and I do forgive you—just don't do it again, you crazy girl."

As dinner came to an end, Phillip looked at his watch and let Sam know that he had to take off. It was getting late, and he needed to get going and fly back home.

"I'll walk you out," Sam said as he got up and said his good-byes to Sarah and Chris and the rest of the family. Everyone seemed to like Phillip. He was gracious, kind, and sweet. He was well mannered and very generous. Sam knew that he was the kind of man she could walk into any function or event with, and she'd be fine. Colin had always been a little on the shy side, so whenever they went anywhere, she knew that she'd need to be the one to make the first move. Phillip was the polar opposite.

Phillip's car was waiting outside the reception venue. A waiter followed them out with two doggie bags of food for Phillip to take along with him for Maggie. Phillip leaned down and kissed Sam. "I love you Samantha, I'll see you tomorrow night."

"I love you, too, Phillip. Have a safe flight and let me know when you get in tonight," answered Sam.

"Don't dance with too many guys while I'm gone," Phillip teased. "I can just imagine the long line waiting for you once you head back in."

"Oh, stop!" Sam laughed.

"And let me know how your family reacts to the news."

Sam looked confused, "What news?"

Phillip looked surprised for a second and then said, "*Our engagement.*"

Sam closed her eyes and smiled, "Of course, Phillip! I will let you know."

Sam stood watching drive Phillip's car drive off until she couldn't see the taillights anymore. It was a beautiful night, so she knew his flight home would be seamless. She didn't feel like heading back into the reception and putting on a happy face, but she knew she needed to do exactly that for her sister. The place was packed inside and it spoke to how much everyone loved Sarah and Chris. Friends and family all wanted to be there to see them begin their life together. Sarah's last-minute ideas of creating a homegrown wedding did come together beautifully. Sam had to give it to her.

With the evening being so warm, Sam decided to walk outside for a few minutes. She needed some air. It had been such a busy week and a walk seemed like a good idea. As she passed by the windows of the ballroom, she scanned the room again for Colin, not having to worry about people wondering who she was looking for. She could be a little bit invisible. She stood silently, looking everywhere, but nothing. He wasn't here. She couldn't see him anywhere.

"He's not here tonight," said a voice from behind her.

Sam turned to see Cole standing on the path. He looked so handsome in a suit, just like Colin would have, too.

"What do you mean?" Sam asked, trying to stay cool.

"I watched you looking around the church. I saw you looking around at the reception, and I know you weren't looking for me," Cole smiled.

"So Colin didn't come to Sarah's wedding?" Sam asked, looking serious for a moment, needing Cole to tell her where he was and hoping he wouldn't do his normal joking around thing.

"He called Sarah this morning and told her he wasn't

feeling well and that he and Jessica would not be attending the wedding," Cole said.

"So he suddenly got sick after last night?" Sam asked.

Cole walked over to Sam. "You know, I always thought you two would find your way back to each other, somehow, someway. I don't know everything that's gone down between the two of you in all this time, but I know enough."

"And what's that?"

"I know that he still loves you."

Sam looked at Cole and shook her head, "It doesn't matter anymore, Cole. I'm engaged to be married. He's here. I'm there. We're on different paths, and neither one of us is willing to change anything."

"Neither one of you has ever asked the other to give anything up?" asked Cole.

"How can we possibly be together?" asked Sam. "He's here, I'm there."

"How do you know he's not willing to move?" answered Cole.

Sam stood still, looking at Cole, then turned back to the window to look at everyone dancing and laughing.

"I don't know, Cole," Sam whispered. "Maybe we just missed our moment all those years ago. Maybe true love does happen, but there is no guarantee that it will last forever. You know you had it, and you're happy you experienced it when you did. But not everyone can be as lucky as Sarah and Chris."

"Well, if that's what you believe, Sam, I'm not here to convince you otherwise," Cole replied. "I just want you to know that he does love you."

"I know he does," Sam whispered. Tears formed in her eyes as she continued, "He told me last night. He told me everything. He told me about coming back to New York to propose."

"He did?" Colin asked, a little bit shocked to hear it. "I didn't think he would ever tell you."

Sam nodded, "Well, he did. I had no idea he had done that. Nobody told me. But, Cole... you can't just tell me, or anyone else, something like that ten years later and expect them to change their life."

Cole walked over to Sam and hugged her. He knew that she was hurting and confused. He didn't want to make anything worse. He'd always loved Sam. She was like a sister to him, and he felt badly seeing her in pain, just as he had seen his brother in the same kind of pain.

"I will tell you this, Sam," Cole said as he hugged her, "Colin doesn't expect you to change anything about your life. He just needed you to know how he felt. I've been telling him to tell you about this for ten years. He needed to get it off of his chest so he can move on. That's all he wants, and that's all I want for him, too. He deserves love, just like you do. He knows he can't compete with Phillip, and he doesn't want to try, but he needed you to know that he loves you."

Sam pulled back from Cole's hug and looked up into his eyes, "Will you do me a favor?"

"What's that?" asked Cole.

"Tell him that he will always and forever have a piece of my heart."

Sam walked back into the reception, knowing that Colin wasn't there and Phillip wasn't there, either. She wiped her tears in the bathroom, feeling like she'd cried more this week than she had in ten years. She took a deep breath and thought about her sister Sarah. She knew she needed to put everything out of her mind for the rest of the night and be there with her family. She'd missed out on so much already, and she knew she needed to start fresh now. And as hard as it was to pretend that everything was OK, Sam tried her best all night long. She visited, she danced, and she was the image of a happy guest.

And as the night was ending and the DJ played the final song, "We Are Family," Sam stood in a huddle with her three sisters and swayed the final minutes of the night away, this time shedding happy tears, not sad ones. She'd needed to let loose and dance out the stress, the pain and the utter craziness of the week. She was so happy just to be with her sisters and to forget about Colin and Phillip. She needed this moment to be the start of her next chapter.

29

Flying private was a heck of a lot different than flying commercial. As much as Sam had tried to remain the same Sam McKay as she built and grew her business, there were just some things in life that she loved, and flying private was one of them. Since Phillip had switched things up by flying home the night before, Maggie had been kind enough to get her on a flight out of Providence the next day at 5pm, first-class, but still not private.

As she sat down in her seat, Sam saw an older woman get on board with the help of the flight attendant. She was a tiny woman, dressed immaculately. She had short, dyed blonde hair and looked to be in her 80's. Without missing a beat, Sam jumped up to help the flight attendant help the woman to her seat.

"What seat are you, ma'am?" Sam asked.

"2A," the woman responded, a little out of breath.

"Oh!" Sam smiled. "You're right next to me."

With that news, the woman smiled and Sam helped her into her seat and made sure she was buckled in.

"I'm not a big flyer," the woman confessed.

"It's going to be fine," Sam smiled. "Are you heading back home, or are you going somewhere else?" Sam asked, trying to distract the woman from her flying fear.

"I'm heading home," the woman smiled. "I was visiting my daughter here in Rhode Island for the week, but it's time to head home to my husband. He's lost without me."

Sam smiled, "Awe...that's beautiful."

As the plane filled with people, the lady shared with Sam everything she had done while in Rhode Island visiting her daughter. Sam could tell that the woman was beginning to relax more and more as she talked about her visit.

"Are you heading home to your love, too?" the woman asked as she realized they were about to take off.

Sam looked straight ahead and then back at the woman, "I think so."

"You think so?" the woman asked. "My dear - you either are or you aren't. There's no in-between when it comes to matters of the heart."

"Then...yes, I'm heading home to my love," Sam smiled, and then looked down at her hands, trying to sound convincing, but not sure she was making a good job of it.

The lady sensed something, "Oh, dear, love shouldn't be a confusing thing, Sweetie. Tell me, what's weighing on your mind. Or in your heart? I can tell if someone is confused about love from a mile away. I've lived a lot of life. You can't fool an old lady."

"Oh, I don't want to bore you. It's nothing," answered Sam.

"Bore me?" she laughed. "You should ask my husband. Nothing makes me happier than hearing a good love story."

"Oh, is that so?" Sam laughed. "Well, then you must have a really good one with your husband."

The woman smiled and looked at her hands, folded in

her lap. "Our love story had a lot of bumps in the road at the beginning, but I've always said, when it's meant to be, there's not much else that can happen in life. It's meant to be."

This lady had her attention, and Sam looked at the woman. She used to believe in happily-ever-afters. She used to believe her happily-ever-after would be with Colin. When she was in high school, she was convinced that their love could and would survive anything because it was meant to be. The foolishness of a teenager. But now? With the realities of life, she wasn't so sure. The universe hadn't exactly made things easy.

"What do you mean by that?" Sam asked.

"Well, there were two men that I loved while growing up."

"Two men?" Sam laughed.

The woman chuckled, "It sounds bad when I say it like that, but the truth is that there were two men who had my heart in some way, way back then."

As Sam looked away, the woman suddenly realized that her story would somehow make an impact on this lovely young woman. She didn't know who Sam was, or know the story behind Sam's sad eyes, but she knew that by telling her story, maybe it would help this poor girl who looked lost in love.

"I met Charlie when I was sixteen years old. Oh, we were in love and inseparable. We did everything together. He was the kindest and smartest man I had ever met. There wasn't a second I wasn't thinking about him, or writing him some kind of love note," she said, smiling at the memories.

"Young love, huh?" Sam smiled, thinking of Colin. "I had that, too, when I was in high school."

The woman looked at Sam and smiled, "Yes, we were lucky when we were young. Not many people have that when they're that age. But - you see - my parents didn't like Charlie. Charlie wasn't from a good family. His family had a lot of financial issues and they were worried that my life would be one of constant struggle."

"Oh...," Sam said, "So what happened?"

"Well, there was a boy that they kept wanting me to meet, and I kept saying 'NO' over and over. I just wanted to be with Charlie. I knew he'd make something of himself someday, but my parents just didn't believe it. Finally, one day they invited this young man named George to our house to meet me. My parents had met his parents at church and they all thought it would be a good match. You see, back then if we didn't go to college, we got married and started families. It was a different time."

Sam nodded, wanting to hear more.

"I met George and I instantly liked him. He was a fine man, and sweet and kind and very good to me. My parents were thrilled that we had hit it off so well."

"But what about Charlie?"

"Ahhh...yes, Charlie. Well, you see, I was a little rebel back then and whenever I could sneak out to see him, I did. My parents never knew, but I also had to be honest with Charlie about George. I was afraid that Charlie would see me out with George and not know what was going on."

"What did Charlie say when you told him about George?" Sam asked, now very curious.

"He was very hurt, but he wanted the best for me and told me that if George would give me a better life, then he would understand. But it was a decision I needed to make. Charlie also vowed that he would make something of his life, if I just gave him the chance."

"Oh my God, that's so amazing and mature," Sam said. "He didn't want to lose you."

The old woman shook her head, "No, he didn't. He was willing to fight for me, but I was sixteen years old. I didn't know what he could do or give at that age. I dated George for two years, all while still loving Charlie. I did love George, not in the way that I loved Charlie, but George was a wonderful man. The only difference between Charlie and George was that George came from an established family and Charlie didn't. Not to mention, I had given my full heart to Charlie."

Sam stared at the old woman, "So what did you do?"

"I did what I knew I had to do. I had to go with my parents' choice. I knew it was the right thing to do, and what everyone expected of me. When I told Charlie, I thought his heart had actually broken. He was so upset and so sad, but he kissed me on the cheek and wished me the best in life. He told me he would always love me, always, forever, and ever. And I believed him. I knew he would."

"That must have been a very difficult decision for you."

"It was, but I did love George, just in a different way, and I knew that it was easier this way. I told my parents that I would live in a tent with Charlie in the woods! I didn't care about money or anything like that; I just wanted to be with him. They didn't listen. They wanted the best for me, and I was afraid to lose my family."

Sam sat with a tear tracing a path down her cheek.

"Oh, sweet girl. I didn't mean to make you cry," the old woman said, grabbing Sam's arm.

"It's nothing. It's just that, in a small way, I understand your story," Sam said, "And so, you chose George?"

"As our wedding day neared," the woman continued, "I just kept telling myself that I had made the right decision. George knew that something was wrong, but he didn't dare ask. I had accepted his proposal and he knew that he would give me a good life, and I knew that too."

"So what did Charlie do?" Sam asked.

"Oh, I don't know what he did the day of the wedding. I know that the last time I saw him, maybe two weeks before George and I were to be married, he begged me one last time. And I just kept praying to God to give me the answer I needed, to guide me."

"And...." Sam asked, "Did he?"

"Yes, yes, he did. I'll never forget being so nervous, hoping and praying that I had made the right choice with George. You see, I didn't want to hurt him either, so I was left in a conundrum. But the day of our wedding, when I started walking down the aisle toward George, our eyes locked, and you know what? In that very moment, when I was in this gorgeous white dress and him looking so handsome in a black tuxedo, a peaceful feeling came over me, and I just knew."

Sam smiled and reached over and grabbed her hand. "Thank you for this story, I believe the universe sent you to me today."

Sam sat back in her seat and took a deep breath. This beautiful little old lady next to her was her gift from God. She had married her George, who was her Phillip, and life turned out to be the way it was supposed to be. She may not have been crazy in love with him, but she had had a good life with him and she'd been happy. She needed this message from the universe to let her know that although her heart ached deep down for Colin, she had made the right choice. That ache would go away. She would marry Phillip and not look back.

Sam chatted with the old woman for the rest of the hour-long flight. She learned that her name was Lily Rose and that she had three children, two daughters and one son. She lived in Queens and had lived there her entire life. She talked about her life, and her husband, and all the things they had done. Her kids were scattered throughout the country and she loved to visit for a week or two when she knew they could get time off from work.

Sam had intended to catch up on some work on the way home, but knew her time with Lily Rose was so much more important. They literally talked from takeoff 'til touchdown.

As the plane landed and the passengers were given the green light to exit, Sam asked Lily Rose if she could help her. She'd been given such a huge gift from her, that helping her get to the baggage area was a small thank you.

"Please, let me help you, it's the least I can do," Sam smiled.

"Oh, you are so kind. I would love that. These old legs need some help and I feel bad saying this, but the airport staff always tends to rush me off!"

Sam grabbed Lily Rose's bag and hooked her arm to escort her off the plane. As they walked down the ramp to head to the baggage area, Sam asked Lily Rose if anyone was coming to pick her up, or if she needed a ride home. Sam was more than willing to drive her wherever she needed to go. Sam's town car was already at the airport, her driver at the baggage area waiting for her.

"Oh, no..." Lily Rose smiled. "My husband is here to get me. I'm sure he's been here for an hour waiting for me!"

Sam smiled, knowing that she would meet the infamous George. She thought it was so sweet that he was here waiting for her. She hoped and wished that someday when she was eighty, she'd have that same kind of partner waiting for her.

As they walked to the baggage area, Sam saw the cutest

little old man jump up when he saw the two of them come down the escalator. He was holding a beautiful bouquet of flowers and his face lit up when he saw Lily Rose. This adorable old man was what love stories were inspired by, this kind of undying and unending love. It actually brought tears to Sam's eyes to see them so happy to see each other.

As Sam helped Lily Rose off the escalator, she saw Lily Rose reach out to her husband, "I missed you so much. Next time you're coming with me. Allison would've loved to have seen you, and you should see how big the grandkids are getting!"

He smiled and embraced her, "I missed you, too."

Lily Rose turned and looked at Sam. "I want to introduce you to my new friend. This is Sam. She chatted with me the entire time and took my mind right off the flight. Sam, this is my husband.'

Sam reached out her hand, "So nice to meet you, George. I feel like I know you and your whole story."

"George?" he asked, then turned to Lily Rose. "You love telling people our love story, don't you?"

He looked at Sam and then she heard Lily Rose chuckle a little.

Sam stood still, looking back and forth between them. She knew she was missing something, but couldn't put her finger on it. "I'm a little bit confused!" she smiled. "What's going on? Am I missing something?"

The old gentleman reached out his hand, "Nice to meet you Sam, I'm Charlie."

Sam's heart stopped. Charlie? It couldn't be. Charlie? How was this possible? Didn't she say she'd married George? This wonderful gentleman in front of her was Charlie? He was the one who Lily Rose married and had three children with? She couldn't process it at the moment. She was supposed to marry George.

Sam looked at Lily Rose, "But you told me, on your wedding day, you locked eyes with George as you were walking down the aisle and just knew…"

Lily Rose took Sam's hands into hers, "I did know, sweet girl. The second I locked eyes with George I knew what I needed to do…" and she looked at Charlie and smiled, "I needed to be with the one that I truly loved. I needed to marry Charlie."

Sam let out a gasp, almost like a cry, loud enough for people around them to stop to see what was going on.

"Are you OK, honey?" Lily Rose asked, concerned.

Sam looked at the two of them standing in front of her. They were adorable. They still had their happily ever after decades together. Lily Rose had chosen Charlie. She'd chosen that special love over everything else.

"And so you ran… " Sam whispered.

Lily Rose nodded, "And so I ran…" Lily Rose looked over at Charlie and smiled, "I ran as fast as I possibly could, until I found him that very same day. And we have built the most beautiful and perfect life together ever since."

Lily Rose took Sam's hands and placed them on Sam's heart. "Follow your heart, sweet girl. I don't know what is stopping you, and I don't know all the reasons, but I will tell you this; you look confused and lost. Just follow your heart and everything else will fall into place."

Sam McKay smiled at Lily Rose and kissed her on the cheek. She felt lighter than she had felt in years. She knew exactly what she needed to do, without doubt, and without hesitation. For the first time in ten years, she was going to listen to her heart.

30

Colin arrived at work around 5am on Monday morning. He'd been working hard for a few hours, listening to the radio, trying to stay focused on each job. He hadn't slept much since Friday night and knew the only thing he could do now was throw himself into work. The shop was always busy with tune-ups, oil changes and random tweaks here and there on Mondays, so getting in super early just meant more work would get done. He needed to work. He needed to concentrate on something other than Sam. She was all he had thought about since Friday night. Actually, she'd been all he had been thinking about since she had arrived in town last week. He still couldn't believe that he'd finally had the courage to pour out his heart to her. He had played that scene over and over in his head, never thinking he'd actually have the chance to say what was on his mind, but was so relieved he had. The problem was, he thought he'd feel better. And so far? Nothing was different.

He knew Sam had traveled back to New York the day before, and wasn't worried about running into her. He had hardly left his house over the weekend because he didn't want to face her. All he could think about was how she had just stood there, Friday night, staring at him, saying nothing other than that she was with Phillip. He'd lost his chance. He'd lost it years ago and it was time to face facts and move on. Her decision had been made, and although Colin felt a twinge of embarrassment about what he said to her, he was relieved that he had spoken with his heart.

At 8am, he checked his texts to see if Cole had messaged him. Usually, Cole was in by now. His father rolled in around 9 or 10am, which always gave Colin and Cole plenty of time to get the schedule set for the day. Colin knew Cole would be strolling in soon enough. They had a big week ahead of them and he was ready to bang through it. He needed a good distraction. The summer heat had been unbearable lately, so working in the morning was better than the afternoon when the place felt like a blast furnace.

Colin heard the door swing open and figured it was Cole, finally making his way into work. Mondays were always lazy days for his brother, especially after his crazy weekends. He hadn't had the nerve to show up to Sarah's wedding, something that he did regret, but hoped that Sarah would understand. He knew Cole had been there and had stayed late. Cole didn't call him yesterday, but he did get a text from him saying that it had been a great wedding and that he was kicking it back at home all day. Since he knew his brother would be sporting a residual Monday morning hangover, he didn't bother pulling himself up from under the hood of the car to say hello. He waited a few minutes to see if Cole was going to say anything, but he heard nothing. Finally, he called out, "You OK? What the hell took you so long to get in this morning?"

Again, silence. Colin figured maybe Cole didn't hear

him, but the shop wasn't that large, and the radio wasn't on too loud. Colin rolled his eyes and pulled himself from under the hood. He had oil covering his hands, wiped them on jeans and used his sweaty white tee to wipe his brow.

He turned around and said, "Cole? What are you doing? Didn't you hear me?" It was then that he saw her. Sam. She was right here, in his shop, standing before him.

"Hi," she smiled.

Colin couldn't believe his eyes, "Sam? What are you doing here? I thought you went back to New York yesterday."

"I did," Sam answered. "I left, but I came back last night."

Colin couldn't get over how beautiful she looked, standing there in his shop. She had her hair pulled back in a ponytail, no makeup, wearing a yellow sundress. Her tanned skin gave her an extra glow, making her look like a blonde summer goddess. She was beautiful.

"You came back?" Colin answered. Colin looked down at his hands and again wiped them on his pants. He was sure he looked like a sweaty mess, but he didn't know what to do. He wasn't prepared, in his wildest imaginings, to see her here today.

"I came back to see you, Colin," Sam said and walked toward him to close the gap between them. "I needed to see you."

Colin looked down at his hands again, and felt his heart start to pick up a beat. He didn't quite know what to make of this visit. As steady as he could make his voice, he looked at her and said, "Are you going to tell me why?"

"Because of everything you said," Sam answered quickly. "I didn't know what to say the other night. It all surprised me, and I wasn't prepared to hear you say that you still loved me."

Colin nervously laughed, looked away, and then back at Sam, "Listen, Sam, you didn't need to come back to make sure I'm OK. I just needed to tell you, that's all."

Sam smiled. She knew Colin was nervous and she didn't want to make it any worse for him. "I didn't come back to see if you were OK, Colin."

"You didn't?"

"No, I didn't." Sam smiled and moved even closer to Colin. "I came back to tell you that I'm sorry."

"You're sorry?"

"Yes, I'm sorry that I didn't just come after you all those years ago. I'm sorry that I didn't just go with my heart and my gut and chase you, even though you told me not to, and tell you to stay. I'm sorry that I let all those years go by without telling you the one thing that I've always known deep in my heart."

Colin began to realize where this might be going, and his heart started to thump wildly. He looked at Sam, directly into her eyes, "And what's that?"

Sam looked back at Colin, "To tell you that I love you. That I've always loved you. My heart has always been yours. After all of those years, and seeing you this week, I realized just how deeply in love with you I am."

Colin's face lit up and he grabbed Sam. As their lips touched, it was as if all the years melted away. The aching and the longing and the passion were all right there in that kiss. They were intertwined with each other and didn't let go. That kiss was everything each of them had dreamt about for years, but neither had had the courage to tell the other.

As their lips parted, and each came up for air, Colin looked at Sam and asked, "What made you come back?"

Sam smiled at him, "A little old lady and a little old man."

Colin looked confused and then just laughed, "OK... well, I need to thank this little old lady and little old man!" Then he squeezed Sam as tightly as he could. She was his, she had chosen him. "And what about Phillip?"

"He's going to be OK, believe me. With Phillip, our relationship was more of a partnership than a deep love, and he always knew that, too. And there was something I realized this week with Phillip."

"What's that?"

"I know you said that Phillip could give me the world, right?"

Colin nodded. "Hmm."

"He could give me every material thing in the world," Sam said. "But the one thing he couldn't give me was true love. True, crazy, over the top, crazy love."

Colin looked at the love of his life, "I will love you every single day of my life, Sam."

Sam looked at Colin, "I know you will. And as I was flying home, I realized that I couldn't let another day go by without telling you how much I love you, and how much I want to be with you, and how much I've missed you. We lost ten years, Colin. And I didn't want to lose one more minute. I know it's going to be hard to figure everything out, but I don't care. I just want to be with you."

"And I just want to be with you," Colin answered. "I'm willing to do whatever needs to be done to make this work. I'll move to New York. I'll move to Timbuktu, I'll do whatever it takes, Sam. I just want to be with you, too. That's all that matters to me. I wasn't sure what you were thinking the other night. I thought I blown it with you, that I had lost you forever."

Sam smiled, "You didn't lose me, you could never lose me. I think I always knew deep down that we would find our way back to each other."

Colin kissed Sam again. "I love you, Sam."

"I love you, Colin. What can I say? I'm in love with my hometown boy!"

EPILOGUE

One year later, Sam stood arm in arm with her father, ready to walk down the aisle to the man of her dreams, Colin Dasher. They had chosen to be married in Barrington at the church they both attended growing up. Sam and Colin had come a long way since 8th grade, but their love story had endured and had led them back to one another.

As the doors to the church opened, the congregation stood and all eyes turned to look at Sam. She was breathtaking, and the guests gave a collective gasp as Sam made her entrance. There were smiles and joyful tears among her family and friends. Everyone in the church, on this beautiful summer day, knew theirs was a special love that had not just happened overnight. It was a love that had developed and grown, a love so powerful that it had triumphed over the years of heartbreak and challenge. Everyone here knew Sam and Colin's love story, and everyone was thrilled to witness the beginning of a new chapter for both of them.

Sam proceeded down the aisle in the custom gown she had designed herself. She looked like a fairy princess in a strapless ball gown with a sweetheart neckline and yards and yards of tulle. Gorgeous crystals covered the bodice and the sweetheart neckline was the perfect mix of sweet and sexy. Fatima had done the final alterations for her and the dress fit perfectly.

Just as Sarah had done, her three sisters stood up for her. She couldn't possibly pick just one to be her maid of honor, so the three of them shared the duties. They each looked beautiful, dressed in elegant off-the-shoulder tea-length dresses in various shades of blue.

Colin looked handsome as ever in a classic black tuxedo with a notched lapel. Colin could make a brown bag look incredible, but seeing him a tuxedo made Sam's heart race. He chose Cole to be his best man, which was fitting because there was no one he was closer to than his twin brother.

They had chosen to have a small wedding, and there were 75 people here to see them tie the knot. Keeping it to family and close friends, they hoped to avoid the paparazzi as much as possible. A small-town wedding was what they wanted, and that's exactly what they got.

All eyes were on Sam, but her eyes were focused on just one person - the handsome man standing at the altar. He was the most gorgeous man she'd ever seen and he was beaming at her as she made her way down the aisle. As they looked at one another, she knew that this was the man she loved with all her heart and soul. She had always been meant to be with Colin. Nobody else. Sam had found her man, her person, and she thanked God every day that they were finally going to be together for the rest of their lives. She thought of Lily Rose who had found her one true love and now, she was doing the same.

The next half hour was almost a blur, but when the priest smiled at the two of them and proudly declared them husband and wife, Colin and Sam couldn't stop smiling, both of them happier than they had ever been, feeling overwhelmed with love and joy for each other. They'd believed in each other and fought for each other, and they knew that their love story was just beginning. As they kissed, they heard the church go wild with applause. They looked at each other and laughed, knowing there was only one thing to say, "I love you."

READY TO SEE which McKay sister is next to fall in love? Click here for information on my next book, At Last.

PREVIEW OF AT LAST

Sasha heard the mail drop through her door slot and walked over to the mess of envelopes and magazines scattered over her floor. She immediately noticed the massive white envelope with gold lettering addressed to her. She had been expecting it. The invitation had officially arrived.

Sasha hated to admit it, but it looked beautiful, gorgeous, special, and all the things a wedding invitation should be. But that was only part of the story. She loved her friend Lauren and wished her the best with Michael, but she just wasn't looking forward to this wedding, and she wished that someway, somehow, they'd change their minds and just run off and elope.

But her selfish wish had no chance of coming true. Looking at the envelope, it was clear that whomever had been hired to script the names on the envelopes was very talented. Sasha's name had never looked so fancy. She picked up the envelope, ignoring everything else on the carpet, and ran her finger over 'Ms. Sasha McKay and Guest', written in the most beautiful cursive. It was as if the universe was mocking her single life status.

A bang coming from the kitchen startled her and she quickly looked in that direction, coming off her pity party trance.

"It's just me," yelled a familiar voice from the kitchen. "I can't find my phone. Have you seen it?"

Walking into the kitchen, she saw her sister Susan rummaging through the contents of her handbag. Everything was scattered on the counter . Susan wasn't known for being the most organized person, so this mess was no surprise.

Susan looked up as Sasha walked in and immediately knew something was wrong. You couldn't fool a McKay sister.

"Oh, my God. What's wrong?" she asked. "You look as if you've seen a ghost."

Sasha held up the invitation and waved it in front of Susan's face. "It just arrived."

Susan stuck out her tongue at the envelope, attempting to make Sasha laugh. She knew her sister had been dreading this invitation.

Susan walked over and grabbed the envelope from Sasha's hand. "Well, here's what to do," she said with authority. "You knew it was coming, so just tear it open, decide if you're going, and just get it over with." With that, Susan threw it on the counter.

Sasha rolled her eyes at Susan and then looked over at the envelope. "Easy for you to say. You're not invited to this one, and there's no stopping this wedding. It's happening alright."

Sasha and Susan had attended six weddings in the last six months. It felt like all their childhood friends from their hometown of Barrington had suddenly chosen this particular summer to tie the knot. As crazy as the summer had gotten with wedding after wedding to go to, it had always been nice to have each other there, too. Not to mention, weddings in Rhode Island were beautiful in the summer because most of their friends had gotten married in Newport or Narragansett, right along the water.

Susan gently handed the white envelope to her sister. "I still think you should decline," she said, "it's a perfectly reasonable thing to do."

"How can I decline? Lauren has become one of my best friends. She's been talking about this forever. If I don't go I'll look like a pathetic crybaby who is just trying to be miserable."

"Well, aren't you?" Susan laughed, knowing right away that she had blurted out the wrong thing.

"You're terrible," Sasha snapped back. "Why is it, in my time of need you decide to make fun of me? Some sister you are. Where are Sarah and Sam when I need them?"

Susan continued to laugh as she began to collect all her stuff from the counter and shove it back into her handbag, "Listen. Nobody is going to love or support you like a sister. And, ahem," clearing her throat dramatically, "Nobody's going to tell it to you straighter then your sister."

"Believe me, I know!" Sasha shot back. "And I do appreciate what you are saying, but I can't take a pass on this wedding. Yes, it's going to suck to have to see him again. And it's probably going to hurt like hell to see him, especially since he'll have a date. But if I don't go, it's like he wins, and I don't want him to have that kind of power over me."

"Do you think he even expects you to show up?" Susan asked.

"Who the hell knows? We haven't spoken in more than three or four months, and I never ask Lauren about him."

Susan thought for a few seconds and then offered a

suggestion, "Maybe Lauren could give you some intel on whether he's bringing a date or not. I know she would understand. I can't imagine her not knowing you would be curious about it. I'm actually surprised she hasn't said anything to you already."

Sasha took a seat on one of the stools at their kitchen counter.

"The thing is... I really love Lauren. I'm happy for her, and I know how much she's been dreaming about this wedding...like forever. Not to mention how much she's been there for me over the last six months. We still talk at least once a week."

"Well - I guess it's not her fault that her fiancé's brother is an asshole," Susan blurted out, looking very self-righteous.

Now it was Sasha's turn to start laughing at her sister. She loved that her three sisters always had her back. They also never backed down from telling her how they felt about things, too. The irony was that among the four McKay sisters, Sasha was normally the one whom was never tongue-tied when it came to delivering the truth. She always give it to her sisters straight on. She had no problem telling them exactly what she was thinking without messing around.

"I just thought Greg was 'the one', that's all," Sasha said dreamily to Susan.

"You always think you've met 'the one', Sash," Susan responded.

"Oh? And like you don't?" Sasha zinged back.

"I'm not as bad as you. Besides, you know I just started dating Mark and, for the first time in my life, I'm taking it date by date. And honestly? We've had three dates...and I'm already kind of over him. I mean, he wears turtlenecks!"

Sasha couldn't help but let out a belly laugh, which was just what she needed.

"But, let's face it Sasha, you've always been more boy crazy than the rest of us put together. Besides, now that Sarah and Sam are both happily married, we are the only eligible McKay girls left. We have a reputation to live up to —we can't goof up."

Sasha did admit that of all of the McKay sisters, she was always the one "in love." She had been the boy crazy, *in-love-with-a-new-guy-every-week* type of girl in high school. College was much the same for her, too. She had always hoped for "the one" to come along, but she had never found him.

The thing about Sasha - and really all of the McKay sisters - was that they never had trouble attracting guys. The McKay sisters were blessed with brains *and* beauty. The four sisters, all born a year apart, were carbon copies of each other. They all had blonde hair, green eyes and a dimple on their right cheeks. They were natural beauties and the older they got, the more beautiful they became. Men couldn't stay away from them. But the trouble was finding a good one.

"I just want what Mom and Dad, and what Sarah and Sam have. Is that too much to ask? I actually thought Greg and I were a great match, and then everything was perfect until it wasn't."

Susan glanced down at the envelope again, looked at the clock on the microwave, and then turned to grab two wine glasses from the cabinet. It wasn't quite 5, but she knew that wine would be needed. "So, are you going to open that envelope, or not?"

Sasha slowly began to rip the seal and then she pulled out the invitation. She took a good long look at it. The wedding was five weeks away, on New Year's Eve, at one of the most sought after venues in Boston--the Union Club. She had known Lauren wanted a New Year's Eve wedding, which would make seeing Greg suck even more. What a waste of a perfectly good evening.

Sasha put the invitation down on the counter and Susan reached over to take a good look at it.

Giving it the once over, Susan suddenly froze. "Oh, my God, you didn't tell me it was a *New Year's Eve wedding*!" she said, waving the invitation in the air. "Why am I just finding out about this now? Who the hell does that?" she asked.

Sasha rolled her eyes, "So can you see why I was hoping they'd just decide to elope? Not only will I have to see Greg, but New Year's Eve will be a complete bust this year."

"If you're going to go--and I don't think you should," her sister said seriously, "and you're going to go against my advice, which I know you will do, but you have to bring a date."

"Oh, believe me, I know," Sasha answered, as Susan watched the wheels in her head already spinning. "I guess the only question is--who can I bring who will drive Greg crazy?"

Susan laughed as she handed Sasha her wine, "That's my girl!"

DID YOU LIKE THE BOOK?

Reviews are important for authors (especially new ones). If you liked this book, I would be grateful if you left a short review.

JOIN MY HAPPILY-EVER-AFTER

There's nothing like a good romance, am I right? There's just something about a happily-ever-after that always gives me goosebumps!

Love for you to join my newsletter to stay in the loop as to what I have coming up. I will also be sharing book giveaways, interviews, special releases, behind the scenes, bonus chapters and so much more.

~

Join my NEWSLETTER:
www.subscribepage.com/Audrey

ACKNOWLEDGMENTS

Hometown Boy couldn't have been written without the inspiration of my own personal love story. I met my husband in college back in 1998 and fell head over heels. He's been my constant muse and inspiration over the last 23 years. I love you, Matthew.

Thank you to my kids William, Alex, Ben, Henry and Victoria for putting up with all my Hallmark movie watching to get extra inspiration. They know I love a good happily-ever-after. I hope they see that it's never too late in life to go after a new dream.

Thank you to my mom and dad for being my sounding boards, proofreaders, researchers, helpers and constant supporters. Your love and guidance means the world to me.

Thank you to my editor Valerie Gray, for whom I will be forever grateful for taking a chance on me. The second we started working together, I knew it was a perfect fit.

Thank you to Cecelia Mecca. Your friendship, knowledge, expertise, support, and guidance to help me start this new journey will never be forgotten.

Thank you to my sister Jane and my best friend Vera for

encouraging me to keep writing. You both know how much I love a happily-ever-after.

And thank you to Marshall and Josh. The first words written for *Hometown Boy* were on the flight to your wedding.

ABOUT THE AUTHOR

Audrey McClelland, is a digital influencer and the founder of MomGenerations.com, an online destination for mothers. Mom Generations is in its 13th year and is a lifestyle destination for mothers. Audrey is the mother of 5 children.

Audrey was named to "The Power Pack" Moms in Nielson's Online Power Moms list, naming her one of the most influential moms online. Audrey's naturally honest and positive approach to sharing parenting advice has led to features in numerous parenting and lifestyle magazines, TV shows, news segments, radio shows, and popular websites.

Audrey has a B.A. in Theatre Arts from Brown University and lives in Providence, RI with her husband and children.

Find me online:
    MomGenerations.com
    Instagram: @AudreyMcClellan

facebook.com/AuthorAudreyMcClelland

twitter.com/AudreyMcClellan

instagram.com/AudreyMcClellan

Made in the USA
Monee, IL
15 February 2022

91297231R10159